Bolan triggered a burst just as the grenade exploded

A volley of hot lead ripped holes in the gunman's body, shredding vital organs. The Executioner turned to the sniper, who had taken off in a different direction following the explosion.

The sudden screech of tires demanded Bolan's attention. Coming up the road at a roaring clip were three squad cars. The soldier scanned the area for the sniper, finally catching sight of the man as he slipped into the brush.

Not that it mattered; it was obvious that the cops were headed right toward Bolan, who took off for his sedan even though he knew the effort was wasted. The three squads ground to a halt, and a half-dozen armed officers emerged, the muzzles of their weapons pointed at Bolan.

The soldier considered his options, then did the only thing he could—he let his weapon fall to the ground and raised his hands.

DON PENDLETON'S MACK BOLAN®

WAR EVERLASTING

A GOLD EAGLE BOOK FROM

WORLDWIDE®

TORONTO • NEW YORK • LONDON
AMSTERDAM • PARIS • SYDNEY • HAMBURG
STOCKHOLM • ATHENS • TOKYO • MILAN
MADRID • WARSAW • BUDAPEST • AUCKLAND

Recycling programs
for this product may
not exist in your area.

First edition December 2015

ISBN-13: 978-0-373-61581-0

Special thanks and acknowledgment to
Jon Guenther for his contribution to this work.

War Everlasting

Printed in U.S.A.

To plunder, to slaughter, to steal, these things they misname empire; and where they make a wilderness, they call it peace.

> —Cornelius Tacitus,
> 56 AD–117 AD

The empires of some men are built on the wholesale slaughter and exploitation of the innocent. By force and fire, I will prevail over them. I am judgment.

> —Mack Bolan

CHAPTER ONE

Bering Sea, 166° N, 58° W

As the Cessna UC-35A out of Anchorage, Alaska, banked in a turn bound for Unalaska Island, something went wrong. Warning alarms erupted in the cockpit. Cabin air pressure plummeted, and oxygen masks dropped. The sudden loss in pressure and gross shift in altitude signaled that the plane had just lost an engine, and yet there didn't seem to be any less power. The lone flight attendant aboard remained in her seat with belt fastened, ass did all the passengers by the captain's orders.

In the cockpit, First Officer Donna Wickersham glanced at the pilot and waited for orders while trying not to let the panic show in her eyes.

Sweat beaded Captain Leon Garza's lip as he pulled on the stick with all his might. "I don't understand!"

"What is it, sir?" Wickersham asked. "We're *still* losing altitude."

"I'm doing my best over here! No matter how far I pull back we continue to drop!"

Garza cursed. "Get on the stick with me!" he ordered.

As Wickersham moved to comply, Garza reached above his head and flipped the switches that would put the entire aircraft on manual control. He also activated the underwater beacon and the automated distress call. The emergency procedures completed, Garza put his attention back to correcting their course by mechanical means.

"There's still no response, sir!" Wickersham said through gritted teeth.

"I shut off the autopilot!" he replied, even as he began to watch the numbers fall on the altimeter.

Alarms sounded once more, and a voice-over warned that the plane was rapidly continuing to lose altitude and had now descended below safe parameters. Wickersham called off numbers from the various gauges as her job required, but it sounded a bit futile even in her own ears. Garza undoubtedly knew just as Wickersham did that they were losing the battle, and it seemed as if she was counting down to the inevitable finale.

Finally, Garza cut her off. "Okay, we can't gain altitude, and we can't pull out of it. Our next best bet will be to cut our airspeed as much as possible."

"How?"

"Kill the engines."

"What? But, sir—"

"Don't argue, just kill them! Hurry!"

Wickersham flipped the switches that disengaged the ignition lock, which prevented any accidental shutdown procedure. Garza could have done it without her assistance, but Wickersham realized he'd wanted to keep her in the loop on exactly what he was doing. Even as he reached for the switch that would power down the engines, Wickersham had engaged the intercom and warned their passengers.

"Attention! Please ensure your seat belts are firmly fastened and brace for impact!"

Neither noise nor panic arose from the cabin, and Wickersham felt a degree of relief. These were military personnel and courageous to a fault. They wouldn't cry or whine or demand—they would sit calmly and extend every confidence to their crew in spirit. Besides, it was more likely at this point they were all in prayer mode.

Garza kept checking the instrumentation, kept the stick pulled back so tight the knuckles on his right hand were now white, and was flipping every switch possible to attempt to regain some control of his aircraft.

Finally, he looked Wickersham in the eye. "I've tried everything I know to pull us out of this. It's no use. Even with the engines dead, we still can't get control of the flaps. Suggestions?"

Wickersham shook her head, thinking furiously but sure of the answer. "Nothing you haven't already tried, sir."

"Well," Garza said, turning to look through the cockpit that was now a solid wall of blue-green water. "It's been a pleasure serving with you, Donna."

"Yes, sir, Captain," Wickersham said, extending her free left hand to grip his shoulder. "The privilege has been all mine."

WITHIN TWO HOURS of the captain's Mayday call to the tower at the mainland out of Marine Safety Unit Valdez, the US Coast Guard had dispatched a search-and-rescue vessel and low-alt observation aircraft per standard operating procedures for a rescue effort. Nobody at MSU Valdez wanted to speculate on the plane's fate. Since there had been no contact after the Mayday call and nothing on the radar, it was a foregone conclusion flight 195B had gone down somewhere in the icy ocean north of the Aleutian Islands.

Petty Officer Second Class Sarah Helmut scanned the screens in front of her. The first vessel to respond to the Mayday call from the flight was the USCGC *Llewellyn*, a Hamilton-class cutter on training maneuvers in Bristol Bay. The ship set course for the last-known position of the aircraft, its HH-65C helicopter traversing the rescue area in advance of the vessel. The ship arrived within three hours of the call, and operations got immediately underway.

"This is USCGC *Llewellyn*, on scene of the target's last-known coordinates. No wreckage has been observed yet. I am taking command of the incident," was the captain's report.

Helmut smiled. "MSU Valdez receives and acknowledges, *Llewellyn*. Begin standard search patterns and reporting protocols. Good hunting, sir."

As soon as he'd received the last communication from MSU Valdez, Commander Louis Ducati peered out the bridge of the cutter and raised binoculars to his eyes.

The sun gleamed off the whitecaps of the Bering Sea. It troubled Ducati that the crew of the military flight was unable to respond to one of the *Llewellyn*'s repeated hails. To not respond when capable of doing so violated protocol, and it could mean that something had knocked out their communications. They also weren't transmitting an underwater beacon, which could mean that the plane was still airborne. Only a full, midair explosion could cause significant damage so that the UWB might not sound.

Which brought Ducati to wonder if the sudden disappearance of flight 195B was an act of terrorism. His worst fears seemed realized in the sentiments of his first officer, as the reports started coming in from the SAR team aboard the HH-65C helicopter.

"Sir," Lieutenant Commander Gareth Keller informed him, "Halo Two is reporting no findings at or immediately below the surface. They're not picking up any signals from the UWB, either."

"What about ultrasonic?"

"Not even a burp, sir."

"Okay, engage in standard search patterns." Ducati thought a moment and then added, "Let's also get a couple of finders in the water, see if we can run across some sort of debris."

"Aye-aye, sir!" As Keller turned to relay the orders, Ducati turned and stepped outside the bridge to view the search area once more with his binoculars.

It didn't make a damn bit of sense. If the plane had crashed, why didn't the UWB sound off? If they'd exploded in midair, wouldn't there be wreckage spread across a mile or so of water? Wouldn't they see some indication of the plane's destruction, *something* to shed light on what had happened? No, this didn't make one damn bit of sense, and Ducati wasn't going to leave until he had some answers.

One way or another, he would find out what the hell happened.

"Lieutenant Commander Keller, recall the chopper," Ducati called into the bridge through the open door.

"She's got to be starting to run low on fuel, and I want her ready for phase two ops once we find something."

Keller tossed a salute of acknowledgment and went about the business of passing on Ducati's orders.

CHAPTER TWO

Stony Man Farm, Virginia

Mack Bolan watched as Barbara Price reached out and traced the scar on his chest with her finger, just one of the many scars that were the spoils of his War Everlasting. Her face was pressed against his shoulder, and her honey-blonde hair cascaded across his upper body. He stroked the small of her back with surprising gentleness, although there wasn't anything weak about that hand. The power and strength that flowed from him seemed almost electric. The buzz of the house phone intercom intruded on the moment, and Bolan had to hold back a groan of frustration as Brognola's voice came on the line. "Striker, are you there?"

"Yes, I am, Hal," Bolan replied.

"I need to see you in the War Room, pronto. And I need Barb here, too, if she's there with you or wherever."

The immediate clearing of the throat by his longtime friend and ally brought a smile to Bolan's face. "I'm sure I can find her. Give me time to get cleaned up and I'll be down."

Brognola muttered something that passed for a goodbye and then signed off.

Bolan sighed, and Price patted his chest before lifting her head. She left him with a gentle kiss, slid from the bed and padded toward the door to the hall. She would shower in her own quarters and leave Bolan to his own ablutions.

BY THE TIME the Executioner had arrived in the War Room, Price and Brognola awaited him with expectant glances.

The big Fed sat with an impassive expression and an unlit cigar jammed between his teeth. "Okay, now that you're both here, let's get right to business."

The soldier took a seat. He and Brognola had known each other for what seemed to be several lifetimes. Their relationship had begun as one of lawman against fugitive, but as time and fate would have it, the very nature of that relationship would turn them into close allies.

"So, what's up?" Bolan asked.

"In short, there have been some incidents in the Aleutian Islands over the past twenty-four hours that have the White House highly concerned."

"What kind of incidents?"

"The kind that involve the disappearances of American service personnel," Brognola replied.

"Talk to me."

The big Fed laid it out for him in no uncertain terms, beginning with the distress call and subsequent disappearance of flight 195B followed by the immediate response of the USCGC *Llewellyn*. "They reported their response and arrival at the SAR site to Marine Safety Unit Valdez, but at their next scheduled check-in, Valdez received no response. All radar transmissions stopped just fifteen minutes before that. They sent two fighters and a land-based Chinook, and diverted an AWACS. Nothing. It's as if both vessels simply disappeared."

"Air national guard planes and US Coast Guard cutters don't just disappear without a trace," Bolan said. "Something's definitely wrong."

"We thought so, as well," Brognola said. "Unfortunately, the US Navy acted immediately and sent an Office of Naval Intelligence investigation team immediately. They also put the Elmendorf-Richardson AFB on full alert."

"Not good," Bolan said. "It's going to make it much more difficult to operate inconspicuously in a place crawling with military investigators."

"Understood, and I can't tell you how sincerely sorry I am about that," Brognola said. "But I didn't have any choice in the matter.

"We thought you'd be able to work best under your military cover of Brandon Stone," Brognola suggested. "That was until we figured that would draw even more attention."

"Good thinking, but you were right to dismiss the idea," Bolan said. "I can get a lot further if I go in as a local looking for work. That will draw much less attention. The military thinks like military, and they won't be looking at the common folks for the answers. They'll want to engage members of their own kind. If I mix with the local crowd, it'll make my inquiries easier and make avoiding them easier, too."

"Aaron dredged up one of your old cover names. Mike Blansky—that's with a *y*, not an *i*. He did a complete rework on the ID and wiped all previous references. You have brand-new credentials, including an employment history and clean social security number, the works. I even had him add a little questionable material, a couple previous arrests for public brawling, but nothing serious. Just what you'd expect to see for a guy with the kind of cover we thought you'd need."

"You went the extra mile," Bolan remarked.

"Correct," Brognola said.

"We knew it would be important that your cover seem as inconspicuous as possible," Price said. "This way the military investigators up there probably won't give you a second glance. They've frozen all transportation to and from the Aleutians and are permitting only major commercial air and rail traffic on the mainland. But just before you joined us, I managed to squeak you in under a hardship."

"What's my final destination?" Bolan asked.

"You'll ultimately be headed to the port city of Adak," Price replied. "You'll fly into Unalaska, and you can arrange your own transportation from there. You're slated with experience as a dockworker, so that ought to put you in pretty good with the locals."

"If anyone will have heard about any strange goings-on in the area, those guys will. It's a closed society there."

"There's one other thing, Striker," Brognola added. "We don't know what's happened to either the flight with a few military personnel onboard or the crew of the *Llewellyn*. We're sending you the vitals of the commanding officers who were assigned to those assets, respectively. If this *is* a terrorist attack of some kind, then there's no question we're up against some type of new technology that has the ability to make whole planes and ships disappear."

"In other words, I won't just have terrorists to worry about, but anyone else who might want to get their hands on said technology."

"Correct."

"As usual, I have my work cut out for me."

"Right," Price replied. "Jack's on his way and should be here within the hour. You'll take the helicopter to Reagan and then a direct flight to Unalaska with a refuel in Seattle."

"As soon as I get my equipment together, we'll be off."

"Godspeed, Striker," Brognola said. "And good luck."

Unalaska

MACK BOLAN LOOKED out the port side window of the Gulfstream C-35 jet as Jack Grimaldi banked the plane for its final approach into Alaska. The city of Unalaska covered all of Amaknak Island and was spread across more than one hundred miles of terrain.

"Wheels down in a few a minutes, Sarge," Grimaldi announced over the headset.

Bolan gave him a thumbs-up, took the headset from his ears and hung the unit on the wall before fastening his seat belt. He then gave the computer terminal in front of him his full attention. He'd reviewed carefully the files of all four officers in the missing plane and Coast Guard cutter. All boasted impeccable service records, and Bolan had no reason to think they were involved in whatever had transpired in the Bering Sea.

Bolan had considered having Grimaldi make one pass, but the area crawled with boats and planes and he didn't feel like getting into a hassle. To have appeared in that area would have flown directly in the face of what he hoped to accomplish, and that was to draw as little attention as possible. There wouldn't be an easy way to explain how they were that far off course when he was supposed to be heading into Unalaska in the hopes of signing on with one of the local shipping companies that operated out of the port city of Adak.

First things, first, however—he had to make his way through the red tape and find a job as a stevedore. It wouldn't be easy to stay under the radar, even posing as a civilian. The net population in Adak was about four hundred people, and that was a liberal estimate. It was probably less than that. At one time the city had thrived when there was a military station there, but since the closing of the naval air station in the late '90s the population had dropped dramatically from more than fifteen thousand to just a few hundred. Many businesses had left the area or simply folded, no longer supported by the military community.

Still, Adak had a lot to offer those who chose to live there, with the entirety of the city's facilities belonging to The Aleut Corp, aka TAC. Bolan would have to visit their affiliate on Unalaska, the Onalash Corporation, if he hoped to get work on the island. Typically they only offered jobs to Alaskan natives, and it was something they stuck to since it was part of their claims settlement with the United States government. They were hard core about their treaties and with very good reason.

Within a few minutes Grimaldi had received clearance to land and touched down without a problem. Bolan managed to bypass any flak with customs since the area was part of the United States, and thus they weren't overly concerned, despite the heightened sense of security. The events in the Bering Sea had the military on high alert, but the civilian population seemed woefully ignorant of the situation. Somehow they'd managed to keep the incidents about the flight and Coast Guard ship under wraps. Bolan knew it wouldn't last long.

"You want me to tag along?" Grimaldi asked hopefully.

Bolan shook his head as he slid into shoulder leather. "Not this time, Jack. I need you to stand by here in case we have to get wheels up fast. If I manage to get on the inside of this thing, I'll need fast transport to Adak."

"Sure thing," Grimaldi said. "I'll be right here waiting, then."

"Thanks."

Bolan checked the action on the Beretta 93-R, secured it in the holster and then shrugged into a heavy navy peacoat. If he was going to be a stevedore, he would have to look the part. He didn't know if he could get work, not being a native, but he was hoping that Stony Man could pull some strings on that score. Bolan descended the stairwell of the plane and climbed behind the wheel of the rented sedan Stony Man had arranged. He cranked the engine, gave it a minute to warm up, then powered out of the terminal and followed the vehicle routing arrows until he reached a gate. He showed a guard the paperwork for the rental. The security man seemed only half interested, apparently more worried about getting back to the ball game that was being piped into the small guard shack via a satellite relay dish.

Within minutes, Mack Bolan had left the airport and was headed toward the Dutch Harbor Development Company in downtown Unalaska. As he drove along Airport Beach Road and headed southwest toward his destination, he considered his angle of approach. The DHDC didn't necessarily offer employment, but they had the information and connections that would get Bolan on the inside. Something had convinced Stony Man the answers to what had happened in the mysterious disappearances of military resources *had* to be somewhere in the Aleutian Islands, and Bolan was equally convinced Stony Man's intelligence was correct. It only followed: if the military transport and Coast Guard cutter had run afoul of terrorists, then whoever was behind the disappearances was somewhere in the Aleutians. And if there was some sort of new satellite technology or weapons that had actually destroyed the vessels, then whoever had pulled the trigger had been close enough to target them, and the only proximal landmass for a base of operations to operate such advanced equipment was the Aleutians.

Regardless of how Bolan looked at it, the answers he sought were in the Aleutians. His premonition became hard reality when sunlight on metal flashed in his peripheral vision. The late model SUV convertible roared down the road perpendicular to the one Bolan traversed on a course that looked as if its driver intended to intercept him. He eased his foot on to the brake—enough to slow but not so much to alert the newcomers to the fact he'd spotted them—while simultaneously reaching into the side pocket of the oversize backpack in the passenger seat. Bolan snatched the binoculars and put them to his eyes, checking the road periodically as he did.

Beside the driver, four men occupied the open-air Jeep Wrangler Rubicon. The passenger had one leg cocked to the side, foot resting on the step-up bar, and cradled a high-powered rifle with scope between his legs. Three men in back all toted what looked like full-sized assault rifles.

Bolan dropped the binoculars on to the seat and eased his foot on to the gas pedal, speeding up so he could reach the area up ahead where the roads intersected. He beat the other vehicle by about a quarter-mile and did exactly what they wouldn't have expected. Instead of going past, he slammed on the brakes, timed the turn so the rear followed smoothly in a slide, and pointed the nose so it faced the road. He stomped on the accelerator and powered on a direct collision course with the Rubicon.

The occupants were taken by surprise, but they reacted with speed and resolve. Unfortunately for them, they were no match for the mettle of the Executioner. Years of combat had honed Bolan's skills, and some thugs with guns, even assault rifles, weren't going to be any match.

He waited until he was nearly on top of them before maneuvering the sedan out of their path. The driver of the Jeep blinked first, however, and the soldier waited until he knew for certain which direction the driver would choose before heading in the opposite one. The Jeep rushed past him, and the driver kept his speed, powering down only a little as he swerved off the road and slowed so that he could turn. Bolan had a different plan, bringing his vehicle to a skidding halt and then going EVA.

From the arsenal in his pack he withdrew a Diehl DM-51 grenade and an FN-FNC assault rifle that was chambered for 5.56 mm ammo. With an effective firing range of nearly 400 meters and a muzzle velocity just shy of a thousand meters per second, it was a lethal tool in Mack Bolan's hands.

Bolan lined up the sights on the careening Jeep as the driver tried to slow enough to make a turn without flipping the vehicle or tossing out its occupants. He figured the first, best option would be to disable the driver. The gamble paid off as he sighted on the windshield just as the nose of the Jeep swerved in his direction. Bolan stroked the trigger twice, delivering a 3-round burst in each instance. The first three rounds spider-webbed the windshield at the base, effectively blocking the view of the passenger, and the second burst made contact with the driver.

A red smear splashed across the windshield, and the vehicle immediately began to falter and shimmy. The passenger was undoubtedly leaning over the console attempting to keep the vehicle under control, but he had no idea where he was going, thanks to Bolan's handiwork on the windshield. It had the desired effect, and the three men in back decided it was better to take their chances on foot than stay inside the Jeep bound for whatever crazy and unpredictable path the passenger managed to navigate.

Bolan swung the muzzle of the FNC into target acquisition before the trio had barely gotten boots on the ground. The first guy managed to stand, but that was

all he had time for as the Executioner delivered a volley
from his weapon that caused the man to stagger back,
his body flailing under the impact of the high-velocity
rounds. Another hardman managed to find cover, but
not before Bolan winged him with a shot that tore a
fleshy chunk from his arm.

The third guy reached cover behind a rock, but that
position didn't give him any advantage over Bolan. The
gunner didn't think his enemy could defend himself
against three armed men, and he'd remained ignorant
of the fact that Bolan had reduced their numbers by
better than half. The gunner broke from the protection
of the large outcropping and tore for higher ground that
would give him the best advantage against Bolan. The
Executioner sighted in on his enemy, leading him just
enough to account for wind and speed before he triggered a 3-round burst. All three rounds connected. The
impact drove him to the ground where he twitched a
few times before going still.

Bolan swung the assault rifle toward the target he'd
winged before, and noticed the Jeep was now stopped
and the passenger had gone EVA. The guy was definitely toting some kind of high-powered rifle with a
scope, probably a hunting piece. Be it 7 mm or .30-06,
it didn't make much difference—if he'd brought that
kind of weapon to this game, then odds were good he
knew how to use it with proficiency.

The Executioner intended to make sure he never
got that chance.

Bolan broke from the cover of the sedan, concerned
they might try to take out his transportation if they
couldn't get him directly. If the sniper decided to take

out a tire or two, Bolan would be pinned down with no place to go. He had to get in close enough to make some noise and shake up his enemy, and he thought he knew exactly how to do that. The DM-51 grenades would come in handy for this play. He primed the first one as he charged toward the sniper on an intercept course.

The Executioner tossed the grenade at the large rock the sniper had rushed toward, then threw his body prone in the dust just as the wounded gunner shot at him. The soldier rolled to avoid the angry rounds that burned the air just inches above his head or slapped into the dirt where he'd lain a moment before. He got to one knee, steadied the FNC and triggered a sustained burst in the direction of the enemy gunner just as the grenade exploded. A volley of hot lead ripped holes in the gunman's body, shredding vital organs. Bolan turned his attention to the sniper who had done exactly as predicted and headed in a different direction following the explosion. Unfortunately for the sniper, there wasn't decent cover to be had nearby. He apparently felt the Jeep was his next best option.

The sudden screech of tires demanded Bolan's full attention. Coming up the road at a roaring clip were three squad cars. Unalaska police. Bolan looked for the sniper, watching as the man managed to get to some brush—he would be invisible from that angle.

Not that it mattered; it was obvious that the cops were headed right toward Bolan.

The Executioner took off for his sedan even though he knew the effort was wasted. His chances of escape were grim, at best, a prediction that became fact as Bolan reached his car. The three squads ground to a halt with a squeal of tires, and a half-dozen armed officers emerged, the muzzles of their weapons pointed at him.

The soldier considered his options, then did the only thing he could—he let his weapon fall to the ground and raised his hands.

CHAPTER THREE

The woman who pushed through the plate-glass door had neither height nor size on her side. Despite that, she somehow managed to carry an aura of authority.

Bolan sat in the chair of her office—he'd found it interesting that the officers brought him straight into this office instead of depositing him in a lockup—his hands cuffed behind him. The steel bracelets were tight, and they bit into his wrists. He'd thought about asking one of the officers to loosen them, then thought better of it. If he didn't make any trouble for them, he might get cooperation. He would definitely need it if he planned to talk his way out of this one. The arrival of this woman with brass on her collar and a glint in her eye told Bolan immediately that she might give him the chance he sought.

She stopped just inside her office door, looked him in the eye, and grabbed his shoulder. She nudged him forward in the chair and reached behind him. A moment later, the cuffs eased off his wrists, and she loosened one while using the other, now no longer on his left wrist, to manacle him to the arm of the chair. Since the chair wasn't bolted to the ground, it wouldn't do her much good, but he decided not to point that out.

She took the keys and reattached them to the keeper on her police belt, then unbuckled the gun belt and slung it over a nearby coatrack before taking a seat behind her desk. She sighed, glanced over a few papers that the officers had left there with Bolan, then looked at him. Bolan pegged her in her mid-forties. She was an attractive woman, with long dark hair that she wore in a ponytail, and dark brown eyes that looked misty under the bright lights of the office.

"Your ID says your name is Mike Blansky," she said.

"That's right," Bolan replied easily.

"Is that your real name or a cover?"

"Excuse me?"

"You heard me," she said. "Let's try this. My real name is Brenda Shaffernik. I'm the deputy chief of the Unalaska DPS. Now it's your turn."

"The name's Blansky," Bolan replied. "Just like my ID says."

"Okay, we'll go with that, then. So why not tell me exactly what you were doing on Airport Beach Road shooting at a bunch of people?"

"Because they were shooting at me first."

"Really? That's all you've got?" Shaffernik shook her head and sat back, folding her arms. "You know, when they called me out of a conference with the mayor and director to tell me about this, I told them to bring you straight here. I thought *maybe* this might have something to do with what happened out in the Bering Sea yesterday."

"What happened?"

"Oh, come off it!" Shaffernik slapped her hand on the desk. "If you're not military, then you're a government agent of some kind here to investigate the disappearance of a military aircraft."

Bolan took a moment to consider her statement and then said, "All right, Shaffernik, I'll give you the no-bull version. If you're privy to what's happened already, then there's little chance the military will be able to keep this secret. I'm going to trust my instincts over how Wonderland would prefer this be handled. I'm here in a rather unofficial capacity."

"Special military black ops or something?"

"I'm the 'or something.'" Bolan pinned her with a cool gaze. "Frankly, I'm a freelancer here by special request of those who would prefer to remain anonymous."

"Politicos?"

"Let's just say they're well above your pay grade."

Shaffernik nodded with a knowing smile, and that cast a wicked aspect to her dark eyes. "Okay, sounds like you're leveling with me now. That's all I want. So how much *can* I know?"

"Well, maybe if you tell me what's been happening around here, I can tell you something to help you maintain order."

"Don't need much help there," Shaffernik said. "Keeping order here has never been a problem for me. The director and chief let me run the show. They're more...politicians. And as such, they handle the politicking and leave the policing to me, although Chief Meltrieger is an experienced and decorated policeman with more than twenty-five years of experience and a hell of a fine cop. I respect him, and I'm honored to be working under him."

"And I'm sure you can police this island with one arm tied behind your back under normal conditions," Bolan stated. "Unfortunately, what happened to me today doesn't qualify as normal. Now, what do you know about the men who attacked me?"

"Nothing, so far."

"Locals?"

"No, not a single one of them. And before you ask, we had no luck finding your mystery guy with the rifle. This isn't necessarily a big island, but a guy like that could ditch that thing in the bay and blend in with the locals in no time at all."

"Maybe," Bolan said.

"Were they professionals?"

"Depends on your definition of the word," Bolan said. "They didn't react like I would expect professional combatants to do. There were also other places they could have chosen to mount an assault like that."

"Or certainly *easier* places."

Bolan nodded at her, suddenly finding a bit more respect when he considered Shaffernik's observations. He wasn't dealing with an amateur here by any means.

"So let's say a professional did send them," Shaffernik replied. "How would they have known about you or your affiliation with the government? Especially if you're the freelancer you claim to be."

"I don't know," Bolan said. "But I'm guessing if someone's smart enough and has the proper resources to bring down military assets, they're smart enough to figure out I'm not one of the crowd. Which is where I'm going to need your help."

"My help?"

"Yeah," Bolan said. He reached into his shirt pocket and withdrew a small card with a phone number emblazoned on it. He set it on her desk with a nod. "That's an encrypted number. It invokes a secure line, no matter where you call from. Talk to whoever answers at the other end and ask whatever questions you want. I guarantee they'll corroborate what I've told you."

Shaffernik frowned. "I'll get to it. But for now I've decided to take what you say at face value."

"Because?"

"Because, for one, a common thug wouldn't be armed with assault weapons and military-grade explosives, let alone get them on to the island successfully with the entire region on high alert. That suggests some sort of strings got pulled. We're in the aftermath of what our military liaisons have only told us could be a full-blown terrorist action."

"You see, it's that kind of information that can help me," Bolan said. "Exactly the kind of intelligence that might take me hours or even days to get from the US military, even with backing direct from the Pentagon."

"It would also expose any cover you might hope to operate under."

"And that's another reason I think you'd be invaluable," Bolan said. "You're a quick study."

His remark produced an amused expression. "I'm a sucker for short explanations."

"Me, too," Bolan said. "So maybe you can give me one regarding the plane that was headed here."

"Shoot."

"There were four passengers aboard that military hop, along with two crew."

"Right."

"According to their flight plan, they were coming here."

"Also correct."

"Why?"

"I'm sorry?"

"Why?" Bolan splayed his hands. "There's no military installation here on Unalaska to speak of, and all the military bases on the other Aleutians are closed except for a couple of remote airspace monitoring stations. Yet there were six military personnel bound for Unalaska, then they disappear."

"You think something here provoked this? What the hell could it be? There's nothing of any significant value on Unalaska that I know of."

"Then how does a rescue ship, also filled with military personnel, fail its check in? A nearly four-hundred-foot cutter vanished without a trace."

"What?" Shaffernik shook her head emphatically. "All I knew about was the plane. I didn't know anything about any ships disappearing!"

Bolan wanted to bite his lip and curse, but he refrained. It wouldn't do any good at this point, and she'd know immediately from his reaction that he'd blundered into saying something he shouldn't have. He'd just assumed she knew about the ship, too. It wasn't a mistake he'd make again. The best he could do now was cover his tracks and hope she still wanted to work with him.

"What makes you think they'd announce something like that publicly?" Bolan said. "Especially when they don't know what they're dealing with. They're not just going to come right out and tell you about it."

"Of course," Shaffernik said, her complexion darkened by anger. "So…why did you tell me?"

"We were going to be straight with each other. Now you know the full story and why it's more important than ever that I maintain my cover."

"So, what could I possibly do to help you? You sure as hell know more than I do about what's going on."

"Yes, but you know this island like the back of your hand," Bolan said. "I have a lead. Now I need to make a connection with someone *inside* the Onalash Corporation. Know anybody?"

"I might," Shaffernik said. "I just might. But we have one problem."

"What's that?"

"It's going to look strange if I release you." She waved at the congregation of officers that were bustling about the central area just outside. "Everyone in my command just observed you brought in on a half-dozen beefs, including violating federal weapons laws and attempted murder."

"Self-defense," Bolan reminded her.

"Maybe so, but word gets around quickly. Even if I release you, as I'm not really inclined to do, your cover won't last long once you're back on the streets."

"I'm open to suggestions."

Shaffernik didn't reply immediately. Then she said, "Look, maybe if I have two officers follow you. I'll give them a story, that you're represented by an attorney and I got a phone call from the magistrate advising I had nothing solid to hold you on."

"You think they'll believe it?"

"What choice do they have?" she asked with a quirk of her lips. "I'm the deputy chief."

For the next five minutes she stood up and launched into a tirade, putting on a show and yelling loud enough she could be heard. She even included some nice obscenities just to make the frosting taste all that much better for all of the officers observing her. Then she came around her desk, behind which she'd paced during her angry production, reached down and uncuffed Bolan's wrist.

"Nice job," he whispered.

"Thanks." She pressed her lips together and added quickly, "Let's just hope I didn't oversell it."

BOLAN USED THE pay phone to call a cab, then placed a second call to Jack Grimaldi.

"So, what's the gig?" the Stony Man pilot asked.

"I'll call again once I reach my destination. I'm going to need a resupply."

"You want it supersized?"

"Better keep it to the minimum, this time."

"What happened to the other stuff?"

"Don't ask. Just be ready when I call."

"Your wish is my command."

"Thanks."

Bolan hung up and took a quick glance at the central booking and processing area, but everyone appeared to be busy. Two men stood in a corner conversing with Shaffernik. Bolan knew she could sell the plan if she wanted to. That didn't concern him as much as the fact he'd decided to trust her implicitly. It wasn't something he could put his finger on—it just…*was*. The Executioner had learned to trust his gut over the years. Shaffernik was different. He'd meant his remark about her being a quick study.

Only time would tell if his instinct to trust her proved correct.

Bolan's cab awaited him when he stepped into the

street. The light was fading fast, and the temperature had dropped dramatically. The lack of light would last only a couple of hours, so Bolan figured now would be the best time to make the acquaintance of the locals. He found them just where Shaffernik had told him they would be—an old tavern down by the docks short on modern facilities and long on personality—many just off work and still dressed in clothing styles that ranged from uniforms to run-of-the-mill dock wear.

The music in the place had reached a volume that nearly deafened the soldier. It seemed intolerable when combined with the boisterous laughter and shouting of its more inebriated patrons, which Bolan noted most of them were. This was the crowd he'd have to infiltrate, and for a moment he began to wonder if Shaffernik's words had been a little on the prophetic side. Nothing but a tight-knit crew here, a fact that became obvious when no less than a dozen pair of eyes settled on him as soon as he entered the place.

Bolan kept an impassive, almost tired expression as he sidled up to the bar and ordered a beer on tap. The bartender passed it along to him and shouted to be heard over the noise. "Cash or you want a marker?"

The soldier thought about it for a moment, shook his head, dipped into his pocket and withdrew a wad of bills. Careful to keep the stash covered with his hand, he peeled off a five dollar bill and slapped it on the bar while mouthing "keep it," before turning to search for an open seat. A dollar tip on a four-buck beer; not miserly but not overt. He figured that ought to solidify his cover some.

There were a decent number of tables crammed into

the place, an assortment filling every nook and cranny, and the patrons had every seat filled. Mostly women occupied the chairs and men either sat next to them or hovered close by on their feet. Bolan watched a minute or two, but he didn't recognize a single face in the crowd, save for the two cops who came through the door a moment later, now dressed in civilian clothes. Bolan watched, noticing that they got the same attention as everybody had given him. The sense of a presence on his right commanded his attention.

Bolan turned and found himself looking into a pair of the darkest brown eyes he could recall seeing. They belonged to a woman who couldn't have been a day over forty. She had a strong build but how shapely seemed more difficult to determine behind the bulky clothing and reefer jacket. She smiled at him as the song that had been blasting over the speakers came to a close.

"Hi," she said in a husky voice.

"Hello," Bolan replied with a nod.

They didn't say much more to each other, which suited Bolan fine since the music started blaring, and he didn't really feel like shouting. After a little bit of time, the woman tugged on his shirtsleeve.

"Are you new here?"

Bolan thought about a moment. She was attractive, and as he looked in her eyes he thought he saw just a glimmer of mischief there. He wasn't sure now would be the best time to let a local latch on to him, but the more he thought about it, the more the idea seemed like a good one. If he could bring her around, a woman the rest of the bar patrons knew, it might be easier to get the crowd to accept him. He could blend in with them—become one of them, really, and that was the whole idea.

"Just got in."

She nodded in the direction of the two undercover cops who weren't looking nearly as inconspicuous as they thought they were. "I see you got friends."

Bolan's eyes flicked toward the two, then quickly away. He didn't want to spook them; he needed them distracted for when he made his exit. He decided to play out some line and see who took the bait. "What makes you think they're here to watch me?"

"Because they haven't stopped watching *you* since they came in," the woman replied.

"You're pretty sharp," Bolan said, genuinely impressed.

She laughed. "You look a little out of place."

"Is that right?"

"I think you're trying to look like you fit in, but it ain't working."

"What would you suggest?"

"You'd have to agree to leave with me," she said. She waved at his attire, looking him up and down, then said, "Step out of your little comfort zone or whatever it is you've got going on here."

"I'm not really looking for that kind of company."

"And neither am I. But if you want to fit in, or even if you don't but you'd like to draw less attention to yourself, there's another way to do it."

"Okay," Bolan said, turning to set his half-finished beer on the bar. "Lead the way."

As they were walking out, Bolan leaned over and shouted, "You didn't tell me your name."

"It's Maddie Corsack. And yours?"

"Mike Blansky."

She reached up to her shoulder and Bolan took her hand reflexively, resting it on her shoulder as if they were just a couple leaving. "Well, I'm pleased to meet you, Mike Blansky."

CHAPTER FOUR

They were a half mile from the bar when it all went to hell.

The vehicle came out of nowhere and nearly smashed into the front of Corsack's SUV, but Bolan was quicker on the draw and managed to grab the wheel in time to steer them off course. The enemy's vehicle blasted by in a flash of headlights on metal in a bare miss. Corsack stepped on the brakes, and Bolan released the wheel. He'd have to leave the driving to her because the men who bailed from the enemy vehicle looked too anxious to do their jobs.

Bolan went EVA from the passenger seat before the vehicle had fully stopped, Beretta 93-R in hand. It was the only weapon Shaffernik had been able to return to him without drawing attention. The soldier aligned his sights on the first target and took him with a double-tap to the head. The 9 mm Parabellum rounds punched through the guy's face and blew out the better part of his skull.

The Executioner had already acquired a second target when the roar of a big engine filled his ears—a two-ton pickup truck ground to a halt between him and his attackers. Bolan looked through the side window as it lowered and found himself staring at the grinning face of Jack Grimaldi.

"It's about time," Bolan said with a smile.

"Need a lift?"

"Some bigger firepower would help."

"Got you covered," Grimaldi replied before sticking his arm out the window, an Uzi in his left hand.

The Stony Man pilot fired a swarm of 9 mm slugs on full-auto burn as he swept the battle zone. The attackers suddenly realized they were no longer up against a lone gunman. They scattered for cover, but Grimaldi didn't let up, taking two more of them out of the action without ever having to leave the pickup.

Bolan used the distraction to open the passenger door and reached into the long bag he found on the floor. He came clear with an M16A2E2, the stock retracted, and grinned when he spotted the blued finish of an M203 grenade launcher. Bolan dipped his hand into the bag once more and wrapped it around the smooth, oblong shape of a 40 mm grenade. He loaded it, braced the weapon across the hood of the truck, flipped the leaf sight into acquisition on the enemy vehicle and took aim. They never knew what hit them. The high-explosive grenade blew on contact with enough force to shatter the engine into dozens of pieces and lift the front end off the ground. Bolan and Grimaldi ducked as deadly, superheated missiles of shrapnel whistled through the air. The acrid sting of spent explosives assailed their nostrils.

As the remnants of the blast died down, Bolan risked a look around the front of the truck. No more enemy gunners remained to shoot at him. "Thanks, Jack," Bolan said simply.

"Don't mention it."

Maddie Corsack finally climbed from the relative safety of her SUV and stared at the Executioner with interest.

Her reaction surprised Bolan. He would have expected to see shock on her face, perhaps even horror at watching him eliminate their attackers in such a violent manner. Yet she only appeared to watch him with an expression of mixed surprise and mild interest.

"I knew there was more to you than met the eye," Corsack finally said.

"Looks like you were right," Bolan replied. He gestured toward Grimaldi, who'd joined them near the hood of the pickup. "That's Jack."

"Pleased to meet you," she said with a nod in his direction.

She turned her full attention to Bolan. "Are you with the government?"

"Sort of."

"You're here about the plane that went down," she said matter-of-factly.

"Guess there'd be little point in denying that now."

"You're right. And before you try to deny it, I know about the—"

"I hate to interrupt," Grimaldi told them, "but shouldn't we maybe beat feet out of here before the cops show up? I mean, you just got out of one scrape with them, Sarge. I don't think we can afford another one right now."

Bolan nodded and looked at Corsack. "Is there some place we can go that won't draw attention?"

"That would depend," she said. "You got any wings?"

Grimaldi smiled. "Funny you should ask."

WITHIN AN HOUR, Grimaldi had Bolan and Corsack off Unalaska and headed to the port city of Adak.

"So, maybe you should explain this to me," Bolan suggested.

"What's to explain?" Corsack asked, batting her eyelashes.

"I don't do coy, lady." Bolan frowned. "You picked me out of a crowd. You had me pegged as out of place right off, and that's not something that would be easy for anyone to do who didn't have a real practiced eye. And you seem to know a lot more about what's going on around here than even military officials. So spill."

"I'm not *with* them, if that's what you're suggesting."

Bolan shrugged. "I never suggested anything. But you have to admit that I'm right."

"You're right," Corsack said. "Okay, I'll level with you. Something really strange has been going on in Adak for the past year. And let's just say your assessment of my insider knowledge of the military and what's been happening is correct. Although I promise you I didn't come by my information dishonestly. Or at least I didn't come by it with the intent to use it for harm. Just the opposite, in fact."

"That much I can believe," Bolan observed. "But I inferred from your earlier remarks about the plane that disappeared that you were taking this a bit personally."

"My husband was killed in the line of duty." Corsack took a long pull from the beer Bolan had given her, just one of the few refreshments stocked in the jet's onboard refrigerator unit. "He was a signals officer at Elmendorf-Richardson."

"How long ago?"

"Not long enough." Her eyes glistened. "Damn it, but I miss him."

Bolan cleared his throat. He understood, although he didn't say it. He knew it didn't make a bit of difference if he understood or not, because it didn't assuage the grief and hurt. The men and women of America sacrificed a lot to serve in the military, especially in this day and age, and Bolan felt they weren't appreciated nearly as much for their sacrifices as they should have been. "Okay, here's the straight story," Bolan said. "I work for the US government in an unofficial capacity. Call me a freelancer with connections."

"The White House?"

"Could be. So that's what I can tell you. Hell if it's not all I can tell you."

"It's enough," she said. "After being married to a military man for so many years, I've learned the details aren't nearly as important as the people willing to do the job, day in and day out."

"So, what was your idea?"

"I'd guess you were at Mookee's trying to break in," she emphasized the last words with midair quote signs.

"I figured if anyone had the information I needed it would be local residents," Bolan said. "The military has competent investigators, but they're outsiders. The people who work up here aren't going to let them in easily."

"You're right about that. My plan had originally been to take you to a guy I know who could have gotten you a cover working the docks at the Adak port. Now it looks like we'll have to do this the hard way."

"I'm not sure I like the sound of that," Bolan said.

Corsack frowned. "I wish there was another road to

go down, but I'm afraid there isn't. I just hope you're as tough as you look."

Bolan's eyebrows rose. "You want to read me in?"

"Most of the guys who work and live on Adak are natives, or they know somebody with pull. Everyone who *wants* to work there who isn't related to someone in the Onalash Corporation has to earn the respect of those who serve on Haglemann's union."

"That's what I was originally shooting for," Bolan interjected. "Until we got picked off on the way to wherever you were taking us. So who's this Haglemann?"

"Davis Haglemann. He's the local union boss."

"I can tell you don't particularly care for him."

"Now *that* would be an understatement," Corsack replied, blowing a strand of hair out of her eyes. "Haglemann's not exactly someone you want to run afoul of. He's nothing more than a thug—well, maybe more like the boss of thugs. The guy doesn't have enough gonads to do his own dirty work. He puts that into the hands of his union reps."

"Sounds like an awfully big organization when you consider the population on Adak Island. What does it run these days, about two thousand?"

"And some change. I see you're well informed."

"I try."

"Well, whatever else you might know, you probably don't know that everything happens in Adak on Haglemann's whim. If he says jump, everyone asks how high, and nobody questions him. Except a select few of us, and he just tries to either bribe his way out of it or simply ignore those of us who protest conditions. Truth be told, things are actually pretty good on the island. We all have nice houses, and nobody's homeless or starving."

"Poverty and social disorder isn't good for business," Bolan said in a matter-of-fact way.

"Right," Corsack agreed. "That's why he does his best to keep up appearances and keep any widows or less fortunate appeased."

"And how exactly does he manage that?"

Corsack snorted and executed a dismissive wave. "How doesn't he manage it? Everything from bigscreen TVs to low-interest loans to cold, hard cash."

"You mean bribes."

"Yes, I do mean bribes."

Bolan's eyes narrowed. "Sounds like someone who likes to exploit the less fortunate."

"He's a bastard—real son of a bitch."

"Tell me more about him."

"He owns the only exclusive country club on the entire island. It's right there at Nazan Bay, which is where all the main docking and port facilities are located. The weather's only good enough between April and October for freight services. The remaining months are basically down time where people mostly stay indoors, drink and screw each other by a roaring fire." She added quickly, "Not to sound crude, just telling you like it is."

Bolan nodded. "And it's exactly that kind of seasonal rotation that gets you a city with a lid on it."

"Or a whole island. It also keeps out any of the undesirables, or so that's what Davis calls them."

"Any thoughts about whether he'd sell out his own people to a terrorist group?"

"He doesn't have any of his own," she replied. "He's

a business entity through and through, and not the least bit interested in the problems of the locals. He's practically turned that town into a police state. And nobody has enough money or power to stop him. Most people just look the other way, as long as they got food in their bellies and roofs over their heads. Anyone who makes too much noise gets told to leave and a free one-way ticket out of paradise."

"Why have you stayed?"

Corsack downed the last of her beer and sniffed before replying. "Guess I'm just the beat-up, stubborn old serviceman's widow and not willing to give up. Not yet, anyway."

"Not so old," Bolan said with a gentle smile.

"Sweet of you to say," Corsack said. "But you're not really my type."

"Noted," Bolan said, wholly unoffended by Corsack. Actually, he liked her. She was tough and spoke her mind, and he admired her convictions. The two of them were more alike than he'd originally thought.

"So you were telling me about this alternate plan to get me on the inside."

"Yeah," she said, crumpling the beer can in her hand and tossing it in a nearby wastebasket. "But you aren't going to like it very much."

Nazan Bay, Adak Island

"WHAT DO YOU MEAN you don't know what happened to them?" Davis Haglemann shouted into the receiver. "How the fuck do you lose one out-of-towner who stands out like a sore thumb with one of our locals?"

"I'm sorry, sir," the voice on the other line said. "Somehow they managed to escape both tries."

"Quit whining like a little girl." Haglemann sighed and sat back in his chair. He could feel the swell of anger in the form of blood pooling at the base of his neck. The doctor had ordered him to reduce his stress. Screw the old bird; he didn't know what he was talking about, anyway. Haglemann had been pumping the guy's old lady off and on for months.

"I'm sorry, sir."

"And quit saying you're sorry! You *are* sorry…a sorry bastard. You said he was with that Corsack bitch?"

"Yes, sir."

"She may bring him back here," Haglemann said. "And nobody enters or leaves this island without me knowing about it. If they do come here, I'll take care of it. Just keep your eyes and ears open, and if he does show up again, take him out. Immediately. And try not to fuck it up again. Got me?"

"Yes, sir. Thank you, sir."

Haglemann slammed the phone into its cradle with an angry wheeze. He stared at it a moment before letting his eyes meet the bemused gaze of the red-haired, swarthy man seated before him. If he hadn't needed Vladimir Moscovich quite so badly, he would have shot that stupid smirk off the Russian's face.

"What are you grinning at?"

Moscovich's expression didn't wane. "You really need to take these things a bit less personally, my friend. You'll live longer."

"Let's get something straight, Vlad," Haglemann said. "We're not friends. You got that? We're business partners, and that's it. Furthermore, how I choose to react to my own people and problems is none of your fucking business!"

Moscovich raised a hand and shook his head. "Don't take offense so easily. I meant nothing by it."

"You meant something by it, all right. You're trying to make it sound like I can't do my job, and you're patronizing me. So just cut it out before I decide to toss you out of here on your ear myself. And don't think I'm too old or too weak to do it. I don't give a rat's ass about your connections or your personal score with America. We've got a strict business deal here, and you only got to worry about keeping up your end of it."

Moscovich appeared to study his fingernails and look unconcerned. "How you handle security is your business, yes. But if that handling compromises my people or mission, then I have a direct interest in its outcome. *Da?*"

The Russian mercenary's expression turned flinty, and he did nothing to hide that challenging countenance when returning Haglemann's own iron gaze.

The union boss tried to pretend as if it didn't bother him, but it did, and Moscovich *knew* it did, and that only pissed off Haglemann more. Part of him wished he'd never made a deal with the Russian, but he needed the guy if he planned to keep the resources isolated on Adak.

Haglemann decided to take a different tack. "Do you realize, *comrade*, that it had never been the desire of the natives to have a union?"

Moscovich visibly bristled at the slur behind Haglemann's use of that arcane word. "Now who's being insulting?"

Haglemann continued without missing a beat. "It

took everything I had to get the corporation to even negotiate with my people. Fortunately, the workers prevailed, and now I've got more money than I know what to do with."

"What's your point?" Moscovich asked.

"My point is that I was running things here long before you brought along your little network, and I'll be running things here long after you're dead and buried. And the fact is it was your little activities here and that gadget you've developed to crash instrumentation on military planes and vessels that's created the panic to start with. Soon this place will be crawling with military investigators, not just one or two government agents from who-knows-what agency."

"Your cooperation isn't really necessary," Moscovich replied. "And I find it more than interesting that one man has managed to escape your people not once but twice. Even the police you have on the payroll in Unalaska cannot seem to keep tabs on him. The sheer ingenuity and elusiveness of this man reminds me what happened a number of years ago in New York City."

"And what was that, pray tell?" Haglemann asked, making a show of yawning and looking at his watch.

"A similar matter and not without serious consequences to my associates, to be sure." Moscovich shrugged. "Although they were not so careful, and they led this particular man right into the very heart of St. Petersburg."

"And what happened to this man?"

Moscovich shrugged. "Nobody seems to know. He disappeared and was never heard from again. We think perhaps he may have been eliminated by a rival or an ally. We have many allies, as you know."

Haglemann nodded. "How could I forget, as often as you remind me?"

"He may also have gone into hiding, being the coward he was." Moscovich rose. "In any case, it's as you've said. This is your problem and not ours. I would appreciate if you took care of it quickly and quietly, and don't make it become ours. I have little time for these distractions."

"Just make sure you keep to your end of this agreement, and that the payments come on time from your—" Haglemann mimed quote signs "—many allies. I'll take care of this issue, I assure you. Because, despite what you may think, I'm still top dog around here."

Moscovich waved casually as he left Haglemann's office. "Fine. Let us hope you don't get neutered while pissing on the neighbor's tree."

When the door closed behind him, Haglemann muttered, "What a prick."

CHAPTER FIVE

They were near a dockside tavern similar to the one Bolan had visited on Unalaska when the roar of a crowd reached them.

Bolan thought Corsack would lead him into the tavern, but instead she made a beeline off the main path and headed for a short, squat metal building that looked to be some sort of small warehouse. The main door to the building was cracked, and the noise had come from there. "Is this the part I'm not going to like?" Bolan asked as they approached.

"Yes," she said with a wicked grin. "But don't worry— I'll protect you."

"Who's worried?" Bolan asked.

They passed through the small crack where the massive doors parted, and Bolan realized it wasn't a warehouse but a small plane hangar. Just on the inside of the door two burly men stopped them, nearly identical with their towering heights and rippling biceps adorned with tattoos, scars and other marks of dubious origin. They relaxed when they recognized Corsack, who just tossed her head at Bolan. The men parted like mechanical pillars to admit the pair.

Beyond them the crowd had formed in a circle, and Corsack had to push and shove a path to the edge. A massive rope, thick like the kind used to moor freighter ships, lined the inner circle. Three men occupied the center, two circling each other attired in nothing but shirts, pants and plenty of blood. The third, the referee, kept watch on them.

The two fighters had been searching each other for an opening when Bolan first laid eyes on them, but now one had obviously seen an advantage and attempted to seize it. He went low for a single-leg takedown, but his opponent countered by driving an elbow into his spine. The blow missed direct contact, glancing off the right shoulder blade at the last moment. That was good for the attacker, Bolan knew, because the counter might otherwise have paralyzed him.

Men and women all around them shouted, one very close to Bolan's right ear. He could almost feel the crowd's bloodlust. The fight continued for several minutes, neither of the fighters really gaining much of an advantage, until one of them finally scored a lucky punch to the jaw that dazed his opponent. Seeing how the blow rocked the guy's head, he immediately followed with another and another. Finally, a well-placed haymaker floored the dazed fighter, and the crowd erupted into a mixture of cheers and groans. The referee knelt, made a quick inspection and declared the fighter left standing a winner by knockout.

The cheering resumed for another minute, but then it passed, and the noise died to excited chatter as the crowd dispersed. Some moved away with swaggers, and others with dejected expressions. From this alone, Bolan could tell the winning betters from the losers. Corsack didn't move, and he waited patiently beside her for a sign. She continued to scan the area around the roped section, searching for someone specific. Finally, she nodded and gestured for Bolan to follow.

The two made their way down to the rope barrier, shouldering through the spectators who were now rushing to get out what appeared to be the only main door. Eventually, they arrived at a point that seemed to serve as the entry and exit for the participant fighters. Bolan sized up most of the men and the couple of females present, but none of them seemed extraordinary. Two of the fighters parted at the last moment, accompanied by their managers, who were obviously pocketing the winnings, to reveal a metal-gray card table.

An old man, with a grizzled countenance and gray-white hair that seemed to erupt from his head in shocking tufts, sat at the table. Three formidable types, all built similarly to the pair at the door, stood behind him like stone-faced statues. Bolan's eyes noted the metal lockbox on the table next to the old man. The guy sat calmly counting a massive wad of cash. Bolan wondered why Corsack hesitated, but then realized she was waiting until he'd finished counting.

He finally completed his task, loaded the cash into the lockbox and secured it. He then passed the box to one of the men behind him with a grunt before rising from the table. Once he was on his feet, he looked at Corsack.

"Well, hello, Maddie. Haven't seen you down here in a while."

"Hello, Otto."

The old man nodded toward Bolan. "Who's your friend? I don't recognize him."

"He's new in town."

Lustrum sighed deeply and shook his head. "And

naturally you thought you'd bring him here to me. Honestly, Maddie, you really need to stop picking up strays. People are starting to talk, you know."

"Talk about *what*?" Corsack remained impassive, but there was no mistaking the icy tone.

"Let's save that conversation for a more private venue," Lustrum replied with a deflective wave. "For now, what can I do for you?"

"My friend needs work."

Lustrum gave Bolan the once-over. "Looks strong. Capable. You're willing to vouch for him?"

"I am."

"And he understands what's required in order to earn a place among us?"

Bolan had been patient as long as he could. "Talking about me as if I'm not here doesn't really work for me, friend. I'm good to speak for myself. Just what exactly is it I have to do to get some work?"

"You can start by showing a little more respect… *friend*," one of the bodyguards said.

Lustrum raised a hand. "Easy, Rov. There's nothing wrong with showing a little backbone. We need more men like this here on Adak."

"Like what?" Bolan asked.

"Tough men, resourceful men. Working on the docks is a hard life. If you don't—"

"I think you misunderstand," Bolan said with a cool smile. "I'm not here to become a dockworker. My talents lie in other areas."

"I see." Lustrum looked at Corsack. "I think, Maddie, you've brought your friend to the wrong man. I'd be more than happy to get him work here at the port. But that's it. I can't relegate him to any other position."

"Can't or won't?" Corsack asked.

"We're at a critical juncture right now. Davis doesn't want to risk any more poor decisions. His business concerns are under scrutiny."

"Davis doesn't run things at this end, Otto," Corsack pointed out. "You do—or at least you did."

Lustrum's expression went hard, but there was something more to it than that. Bolan understood what Corsack was trying to do, and he had to admit the lady knew her stuff. Bolan wasn't sure exactly what Lustrum did, but from what Corsack had just said, there was some relationship between Lustrum and Davis Haglemann. Chances were good this would get him on the inside if he played his cards right.

"Okay, Maddie. Okay." Lustrum scratched the back of his neck. "You've done me a lot of favors over the years, so maybe I owe you one. I'm willing to give your man a shot here. But *no* way am I letting him into one of the crews overseen by Davis. He works for me or not at all."

"Fine."

Lustrum returned his gaze to Bolan. "Of course, the only question remains is, are you up to it, Mr.—?"

"Mike Blansky. Depends. What do I have to do?"

"If you want to work for me, I've got to know you can hold your own, no matter what." Lustrum turned to the man who'd lipped off to Bolan earlier. "Rov, you seem to have taken a personal shine to Blansky here. I think I'll give you the opportunity to put him to the test. His mettle against yours until one of you stays down."

Bolan chuckled. "You want me to fight *him* to prove myself?"

"That's right." Lustrum grinned.

Bolan looked the man called Rov in the eyes. He saw the killer instinct there, understood it because he'd seen it before. But the soldier saw something else; an uncertainty that he knew he could exploit. Rov might have acted tough, maybe even been tough, but he was young, and that meant he didn't have the experience that the Executioner did.

"Fine," Bolan said. "It seems a little sadistic, but I'm willing if he is."

Without hesitation, Bolan turned and ducked under the rope barrier, glancing to ensure Rov was following. It wasn't the way he would have preferred to get on the inside, but he had to play the role if he was to gain the trust. Whatever had been going on in this region of the world the past few days, Bolan was sure Davis Haglemann and his people had something to do with it. Or at least they were involved somehow, if he were to believe even half the things Corsack had told them on the flight.

Rov came under the rope from the same point Bolan had, but instead of squaring off he lunged at the Executioner with surprising speed, arm already cocked to land a punch. The soldier sidestepped in time to take the blow to his right shoulder, thankful he had since the blow landed hard enough to cause pain. Had it connected, it most likely would have broken Bolan's jaw. Bolan waited until the last moment when Rov's impetus carried him past, then stuck out his foot and dropped to his side with a slap against the thin mat. He executed the leg sweep perfectly, and Rov went down like a ton of bricks. The soldier immediately regained his feet and waited for the next attack to come. He didn't have long to wait.

Rov got to his feet and charged low, encircling his beefy arms around Bolan's waist in a body-block tackle. The soldier had no way to move out of the line of attack and had to go down with his opponent, but at the last moment he twisted so that Rov would land on his back. He used the brief opportunity in the superior position to drive a palm strike into the man's sternum just below the notch of the breastbone. The air left Rov's lungs as the strike winded him. He gasped and wheezed, trying to suck in air, finally jostling Bolan out of position with a buck of his hips. The Executioner tried to maintain superior position, but his thighs couldn't find purchase and he came free.

Rov moved with surprising grace and speed, gaining the top role and driving his forearm against Bolan's throat. The Executioner tried to break the choke, even knowing that brute strength would never accomplish it—especially not with Rov using all his weight behind it. The only way to counter such a move was to gain leverage, and he knew exactly how to achieve it. The Executioner wrapped his right hand against the hand of the forearm holding him down and drove his thumb into a pressure point, a move meant to distract more than debilitate. Hot, stale breath gushed from Rov, who was already sweating profusely at straining to hold his adversary down. The distraction did its job, enough so that Bolan could get his left arm snaked into the crook of the elbow.

Twisting his body and using the motion of his hips to put strength behind the joint lock, the maneuver broke the choke hold and took Rov off balance. Bolan continued the twist until he'd executed a full-on arm bar with enough pressure to bring Rov's elbow to the point of snapping. The soldier used that leverage to pry off his adversary and continued the motion until he'd regained his feet. Rov tried to break free by yanking his arm, but Bolan now had him in a jujitsu hold that proved very difficult to counter, unless one was well-experienced in such tactics.

Every time Rov tried to move, Bolan applied more pressure to remind the bigger man of his precarious situation. Despite the pressure on his arm, Rov continued to resist his opponent until the Executioner thought he might have to break the man's arm. Finally, Bolan extended the technique so that he could maintain the hold while actually driving Rov's force toward the ground. In that moment, gravity did the rest until Bolan had Rov's right arm pinned to the floor and a knee in the back of the man's neck. He tried to rise, but his position proved so unwieldy that Bolan had little trouble holding the man pinned to the ground.

The soldier finally looked in Lustrum's direction. "He's not going anywhere. I can hold him this way all day. Are we done?"

Lustrum thought about it for a minute, while Rov continued to shout and curse, the sounds almost unintelligible. He knew if Lustrum declared Bolan the victor that it would not only mean they had to accept him, but Rov would lose face and reputation in front of his peers. That didn't matter to Bolan. Even if it had gone another way, or he beat Rov without disgracing him, he'd have to watch his back all the same. This was a closed society, just as Corsack had said, and no matter how this ended, Bolan would still be considered an outsider.

"Tell me we're done!" Bolan commanded.

"You're done," Lustrum said.

Bolan released his hold, and Rov produced a small grunt of relief.

As the pair climbed warily to their feet, and Bolan started to turn, the reflection of light on metal flashed in Bolan's peripheral vision. Rov was charging once more, but this time he held what looked like a fighting knife in fist. Bolan's reflexes saved him from being gutted like a fish, the blade whistling past as it narrowly missed his midsection. Bolan managed to grab hold of Rov's wrist as it went past. He locked the elbow and yanked back while simultaneously driving the meaty portion of his forearm against Rov's elbow. The bone snapped with an audible pop, and the knife jumped from fingers numbed by nerve damage.

With a guttural roar of pain, Rov managed to draw a Beretta Tomcat pocket pistol with his other hand.

Before his opponent could make a move to fire the weapon, Bolan swung him in an arc, then ducked through and executed a throw that landed the guy on his back. He twisted down on the damaged arm, locking the shoulder to the floor, before stomping one boot onto Rov's throat. Pink, frothy blood spewed from the man's mouth as the cartilage and bone cracked beneath Bolan's heel.

The Executioner stepped back, breathing heavily with the exertion and sudden charge of adrenaline, watching with a flare of anger tinged by sympathy while the light left Rov's eyes. Quickly and inevitably, Rov's breathing slowed to a stop.

Bolan turned to look at Lustrum who sat with his two remaining bodyguards. They had seemed to watch the entire thing with utter impassivity.

"It wasn't supposed to be like this," Bolan said.

"Couldn't end any other way, Blansky," Lustrum replied.

Bolan's eyes shifted toward Corsack, and she gave him a sad half smile. He could tell behind that small gesture she felt tortured by what he'd been forced to do. Part of Bolan understood it, and they shared a moment in that glance, but it still stung his sense of fair play. Rov had been silently challenged and committed to a fight, one that couldn't have ended any other way unless he risked disgrace.

"So you got what you wanted," Lustrum said. "What are you crying about? Rov wasn't going to let you live, and he wasn't going to give up. If he'd allowed you to shame him, he would have found a time to reclaim his honor or he would have been forced to leave."

Lustrum rose slowly from his chair and turned to leave. "Relax, Blansky. Nobody has to know it was you. The waters of Nazan Bay run cold and deep. Heh. Yeah, many untold stories at the bottom of that puppy. Many stories."

Bolan thought he could hear almost a cackle as he watched the old man saunter away accompanied by his two bodyguards. He stared at Rov's motionless body one last time before turning on his heel and heading toward Corsack.

"I'm sorry," she whispered. "I didn't know he'd do anything like that. He's always just…well, I mean in the past he—"

"Forget it," Bolan said. "I did what I had to do. Rov

didn't leave me any choice. And this is too important to worry about right now."

Corsack just nodded.

"Now what happens?" Bolan asked, watching Lustrum make his way toward the exit.

"He'll be in touch," Corsack said, laying eyes on Lustrum, as well.

"When?"

"Soon. Or as soon as he can check you out." She lowered her voice and continued, "So I sure as hell hope whatever you got set up wasn't done in a slipshod manner, or we're going to have bigger problems than we've got right now. Otto likes me, but he won't hesitate to come to my house in the middle of the night and cut both our throats."

"Maybe I should go back to the plane and wait," Bolan said.

"No, it's much better if you stay at my place," she replied. "You go back there, it's going to look suspicious."

As they made their way out of the hangar, Bolan remarked, "You were right about one thing."

"What's that?"

"I didn't like it."

CHAPTER SIX

Maddie Corsack's place was Spartan but comfortable. The house wasn't very large—it looked like one of the smallest of the similar houses on the block—but it didn't lack a woman's touch.

"It doesn't seem as if you've lived high off Haglemann's proverbial hog like your neighbors," Bolan observed with interest.

Corsack shook her head. "I take the payments. Haglemann calls them dividends, supposedly from investments of our union dues. But I don't spend any of it on myself. I donate it to a fund for widows of servicemen killed in action."

"Nice."

"I'm sorry for what you had to go through," she said hesitantly, canting her head in the general direction of the docks. "Back there, I mean. I know you didn't want to have to do what you did. You're not a cold-blooded killer."

"How do you know that?"

"I see it in your eyes. I think you actually care about other people. I think it's why you do what you do. And you clearly didn't want to kill Rov. He left you no choice."

"I'll move past it," Bolan said. "But thanks for your concern. I'm more interested to know how much you know about Rov. And about Lustrum."

She nodded. "I call them the Red Scourge. I know, it's not very PC of me, but then I've never been known for my tact."

"So both Rov and Lustrum are Russian?"

"No, not Otto. But Rov is definitely Russian." That piqued Bolan's interest. The very low population on Adak, along with the high use of Alaskan native laborers, would have eliminated the place as a melting pot. Yet here was a business magnate, a union boss, operating with complete autonomy and using Europeans and Scandinavians as little more than thugs.

"How long have you known him?"

"A long time. Lustrum took over as chief of operations down on the docks for Haglemann's various corporate ventures about eight years ago. Haglemann's like a spoiled rich kid, and Lustrum, while he may try to be tough, is little more than another one of Haglemann's errand boys. The way he goes panting after the guy sometimes is sick. Of course, he uses the thugs to enforce things and ensure they're done his way, since nothing he does is in the interest of the workers. Other than the kickbacks and money he puts in everyone's pocket. He somehow has managed to keep it all legal and aboveboard. And as long as people are getting paid, they're willing to look the other way."

"These union thugs he's using—is that the job Lustrum's going to recruit me for?"

"I don't know for sure," Corsack said with a shrug. "But it's probably a good bet. He'll either stick you on a dock crew or he'll have you working security at the private club."

"He has a club?" Bolan asked.

She nodded. "It's really Haglemann's club. Haglemann's got everything here. He's practically turned this into his own private island."

"So where do we go from here?"

"Well, I assume someone has developed some sort of background identity for you."

Bolan nodded.

"If it's not too clean, you should be okay. Lustrum will definitely check it out, and when he's satisfied he'll be in touch."

"No offense, and I appreciate the insight, but I can't just wait around here for something to happen."

"You may not have a choice," she replied.

"There's always a choice."

"If you jump the gun on this, Mike, it could blow up in your face."

"Listen to me," Bolan said. "There are two US military assets missing, not to mention more than a hundred service members. Now, I think Haglemann had something to do with it, and even if he didn't I'm betting he knows who did. If those men and women are still alive, I owe it to them to get results as soon as possible."

"So, what are you going to do?"

"What I do best," Bolan replied. "But I have some questions first, and you're the only one who can answer them."

VLADIMIR MOSCOVICH PLANNED to kill Davis Haglemann. Not right away—he needed the guy at the moment to keep the workers in line until he could accomplish his mission. But the time was coming soon, and when it did, Moscovich would act on it. For now, he had to entertain the liberal bastard's whims and avoid doing anything that would arouse suspicions. If anything, the Russian understood that Haglemann commanded a much larger following. He knew the area better, and he had greater resources from which to draw.

Moscovich and his fifty men would be no match for the hundred or so guns at Haglemann's disposal.

"Granted, they don't have our experience," Moscovich told his second-in-command, Alexei Vizhgail.

"But what they lack there they make up for in sheer numbers. That is not a battle I think we can win."

"Agreed. It has always been my contention that we must avoid a fight if we're to complete our mission."

Indeed, it was critical that they finish what they'd started. The technology had now been used twice with very favorable results, and those back at headquarters in St. Petersburg were pleased with his reports and progress. But it still meant little this far north.

"Maybe it won't have to come to that, my friend," Moscovich said.

Once they were in the sedan and headed for the plane awaiting them at the harbor, he said, "Yet these small tests feel like a hollow victory, despite our success. I want to take this much further, to make the Americans pay for what they did to us. Well, at least what one American had done. *One man!* It is still almost unthinkable to me!"

Indeed, it had been difficult to believe even when he'd first learned of it. Famed network leader Yuri Godunov, head of the organization's operations in New York City, had masterminded a brilliant plan to overtake America's banking systems. Thanks to a cowardly hacker who'd managed to get himself captured, the plan was exposed and all the players were either captured or destroyed. Somehow, a lone government agent had managed to penetrate the Godunov family security and wreak havoc from the inside out. The trail eventually had led this enigmatic killer back to St. Petersburg where he'd murdered both Godunov and an NSA asset they had managed to turn, Gregori Nasenko. The pair had been shot dead in their downtown office, Nasenko in the head and Godunov in the back as he'd attempted to flee.

"Executed in cold blood" was how Moscovich's masters had described it.

Those words had haunted him for the next few years. He'd been childhood friends with Stepan, Godunov's nephew, who had also allegedly met his demise at the hands of the mysterious American agent. These events had affected him deeply, and when the opportunity to get revenge came, Moscovich jumped at it.

They arrived at Adak Port, the hive of activity for Nazan Bay. Of course, it was dark and there wasn't much happening at that time of night. By the time they reached their destination in the nearby Rat Islands it would be daylight again, a common occurrence in this part of the world. Many thought that it was cold and dark most of the time, but, in fact, the opposite was true. At least from the aspect of sunlight. The more northern the territory, the more hours of daylight. Of course, even more sunlight could not stop the bitter cold and storms, but that was hardly news.

This environment didn't bother Moscovich or his men. They had trained for it in some of the coldest regions of Russia. They were used to it, knew how to survive in its inhospitable embrace, and they were all the better prepared for it. Of course, their base of operations was another matter entirely.

Within minutes of arriving at the port, they were aboard their motor launch and traveling at high speed across the Bering Sea. Thanks to Haglemann's influence, they could come and go at will without having to jump through hoops. They didn't need any clearances, naturally—it wouldn't do to slam into another boat just to protect their autonomy—but it was better than attempting to travel by aircraft. Especially since word had it that the military had turned most of the area into a no-fly zone. But nobody questioned them, and no customs or police agents showed up to inspect their boat. Not that it would have mattered. Haglemann had the Adak police department under his thumb, too. They operated independently, but they didn't really concern themselves with Haglemann's specific business interests.

Greed. The entire show was run by greed, and Moscovich had been trained to take advantage of that selfish desire, particularly among American citizens.

The boat reached the island four hours later at a makeshift dock nestled along the southern fringes of the Rat Islands. Moscovich and Vizhgail left the dock and headed toward an outcropping, making their way behind the rocks and eventually reaching the entrance to a cavern concealed behind a wall of brush. Mounted to an oval frame of aluminum tubes was a heat-scattering material designed to diffuse the signature that marked it as a heat source.

They had landed on Semisopochnoi Island, though their team had taken to calling it Semisop for short. The fact that it was uninhabited was one of the main reasons for choosing it, but also because it was highly challenging terrain for outsiders to negotiate. At only three-hundred-sixty square kilometers it had four peaks that were between seven hundred and almost thirteen hundred meters. Its last volcanic eruption, in Mount Cerberus, had occurred in 1987, more than one hundred years after the previous one. However, its magma chambers were still quite active and not as viscous, so they tended to flow much faster and build up gases at a higher rate, too. All in all, it wasn't the safest place to be, but it was abandoned and drew very little attention outside the scientific community. Nobody would bother them there—nobody would even bother to *look* for them there, so Moscovich was convinced they could conduct their work undisturbed.

So far, he'd been right. Semisop also had the added advantage of being a perfect prison, as could attest the group of military personnel who sat under round-the-clock guard while jailed behind giant fishing cages.

After Moscovich and his team had successfully used the new jamming technology to down the plane— there had been no survivors—they'd tested its efficacy against the USCGC *Llewellyn*. The device had performed with spectacular results, although Moscovich didn't really pretend to understand all the technical achievements behind it.

All he knew was that they now had a fantastic weapon to use against the Americans.

Of course, there had been some survivors aboard the cutter that they had been forced to take prisoner. Moscovich didn't fancy himself a soldier, but he also wasn't a cold-blooded killer. He did not murder unarmed personnel, be they American military or otherwise. He sought only to further the ambitions of his people by stripping America of her identity and her wealth. If he could do that, nature would do the rest, as history had repeatedly shown its abhorrence of a vacuum. Then again, the prisoners hadn't proven to be much bother. Once the key troublemakers had been dispatched by Moscovich's group of commandos, who'd been schooled in the finest tactics by former Spetsnaz and GRU trainers, the remaining navy personnel had fallen in line quickly.

Moscovich and Vizhgail moved past the group and advanced deeper into the cavern until they reached the main operations area. The lights were powered by long-life battery cells, which were recharged using a series of small diesel generators. They had plenty of potable water hauled in regularly from Port Adak, along with food and other supplies that could last them a month, maybe two if they had to ration.

They could have operated here perhaps indefinitely. But it was damn hot, the result of molten lava that rose through natural vents in the dense basalt and rock. The operations supervisor, Benyamin Tokov, one of the toughest and smartest men he had ever known, greeted them with a curt nod. "How did it go?"

"Not well," Moscovich replied. "I had to exchange the usual pleasantries with Haglemann."

"I wish we could just kill that sloth. He's a thorn in our sides."

"We can't let him deflect us from our mission. And I'm more concerned about the recent reports from his people on Unalaska."

Tokov's brow furrowed. "What happened?"

"Apparently not twelve hours after our operation

against the cutter, a man showed up at the main station. His flight was last minute, unannounced and not a regular scheduled courier or freight hauler. Naturally, Haglemann was suspicious and ordered his men at the airport on Unalaska to check it out."

"Ultimately, there was a conflict, and Haglemann's men got their collective asses handed to them," Vizhgail added.

Tokov frowned and locked eyes with Moscovich. "That sounds almost like—"

"Yes," Moscovich cut in. "That was my thinking, as well."

"Could it be a coincidence?"

"I don't know," Moscovich said. "But it moves up the timetable, regardless. Haglemann won't be able to keep this newcomer out for long. Eventually someone will come to Adak and begin asking questions, and that will inevitably lead them to us. We have to move before that happens."

"But the sub is still a month or better out."

"We're going to have to ask for it to come sooner, then."

Moscovich turned to Vizhgail. "Alexei, make contact with them and take care of it."

When Vizhgail left them, Tokov guided Moscovich out of earshot of the technicians and guards. "I would assume if this *is* who we think it is, you don't plan to let him leave alive."

Moscovich put a hand on his shoulder. "Don't worry, my brother. I would move Mount Cerberus if it meant I could have the pleasure of dispatching this man. We will find him and eliminate him if that fool Haglemann cannot. I swear it on my last breath."

AFTER BOLAN LEFT Corsack's house, he returned to the plane where Jack Grimaldi waited for him. The pilot could see from the grim look on Bolan's face that things hadn't gone well.

"What's wrong?"

"A lot," Bolan replied. "If my suspicions are correct."

"Doesn't sound good."

"It's not. Do you remember the mission I took a few years ago in Boston? The one that led to that terrorist operation against the banking system?"

Grimaldi frowned as he pondered the reference. He scratched his neck and finally replied, "Yeah, I think so. Wasn't that when the Russian Business Network tried to use one of their computer hackers to develop a system that would run amok inside the framework right there on Wall Street?"

"One and the same," Bolan said. "And I have a feeling it's the RBN behind this current situation."

"What? How's that possible?" Grimaldi looked skeptical. "I mean come on, Sarge, I trust you all the way. But don't you think that's a bit of a stretch? I don't see how the RBN could have the resources to pull off something like this, never mind a motive."

"The motive's unimportant. And the evidence the RBN's behind this is overwhelming." Bolan told Grimaldi the story of his encounter, leaving out none of the details. He concluded his narrative by saying, "The RBN may not have the resources alone to do something like this, but you can bet they would if they're manipulating Davis Haglemann in some way. The guy's practically established his own empire on Adak, and he's done it right under the nose of the US government."

"And you think the RBN's been keeping it quiet in exchange for…?"

"A port free of customs inquiries," Bolan said. "They can come and go as they like on Adak as long as Haglemann's in charge. And meanwhile all the traffic looks legit, so nobody asks any questions. He's paying the top brass big money to keep quiet."

"So he gets rich and the RBN gets what?"

"That's the answer we don't have," Bolan said. "Yet."

"Okay, let's assume you're right. What's the plan?"

"Corsack was able to give me the lowdown on information relative to a private club Haglemann runs here. I'm going to poke the bear and see what happens."

Grimaldi chuckled. "Poke the bear—no pun intended, of course."

"Of course," the Executioner replied.

CHAPTER SEVEN

As soon as darkness fell, Bolan geared up and left the terminal. The only transportation available was a motorcycle, a cold venture for this time of year, but beggars couldn't be choosers. The Executioner wore a thermal-insulated black suit, along with boots, goggles and a full mask to protect Bolan's lungs from breathing icy winds. The Beretta rode in well-oiled shoulder rigging, and the .44 Magnum Desert Eagle occupied its usual place of honor on his right hip. Finally, a carbine version of the FN-FNC was slung across his back. Manufactured by *Fabrique Nationale de Herstal*, the FNC had proven a versatile and trustworthy companion on many of Bolan's missions. This wouldn't be any exception, especially since Bolan had no idea what he was up against and had almost no intelligence to go on.

The Executioner made his trip to the clubhouse unchallenged and parked his motorcycle in an unpaved area between two run-down buildings. It surprised him that a guy as allegedly fastidious as Haglemann would permit such structures to exist anywhere near his club. The club itself was modern, laid out with plenty of space, and attractive. A small flight of flagstone steps led to the grand entrance, which consisted of heavy double doors of carved wood and a generous overhang.

Bolan withdrew night-vision goggles and scanned the terrain. He could make out only a little behind the fuzzy, gray-green rendering. There wasn't much light to speak of, even when the NVDs were set at the highest level. At least the infrared seemed to be working, and Bolan could see the remnant heat signatures from at least four separate figures. Bolan had suspected from what Corsack told him the place was a hard site, and this only confirmed it. If this had been the security or the job for which Lustrum had Bolan in mind, the Executioner could do worse going in.

Yeah, it was time to shake things up a bit and see just how deep Haglemann and Lustrum had thrown their hands in with the RBN.

YORGI ZAKOFF HATED the Americans and cursed the day he'd been forced to work with them—especially *this* crew. When Moscovich had first ordered him to stand in for Lustrum, Zakoff had obeyed without question. After all, there were certain sacrifices that had to be made if they were to achieve their goal of visiting retribution on America. But now, having spent the past few months working with Lustrum's guys, a bunch of uneducated dockworkers who were neither as tough nor as smart as they thought themselves, Zakoff had just about reached his limits.

Seeing Rov die at the hands of the newcomer hadn't done anything to improve his mood. He couldn't believe that Lustrum would have even entertained the notion just because some dumb bitch had asked him for a favor. Not that it had been all Lustrum's fault. Rov should have waited until another opportunity to take the American, a place and time of his own choosing.

Attacking the guy after it had been declared finished had been foolish, and now Rov was dead. Not that Zakoff didn't hold Lustrum responsible. When the time came, he'd find a way to pay back Lustrum and the newcomer.

"Jeez, Otak, would ya play a goddamn card already," Hans said. "My legs are falling asleep waiting on your slow ass!"

Melburn, the other native worker who'd been born on Unalaska and raised on Adak, let out a guffaw. Consumption of too much beer had already started to slur his words. "He probably lost count, Hans."

Zakoff shook his head as he watched the three stevedores play cutthroat spades. They'd invited him to sit in, but he'd refused—just another reason to dislike these men. They were supposed to be security for the club, but instead they liked to drink beers and play cards all night. He'd pointed it out to his boss once, but the team leader had just thrown it back in his face, advising that nothing ever happened, anyway, and nobody was stupid enough to cross Davis Haglemann. After that, Zakoff didn't broach the subject again, instead musing that even if they did encounter trouble, they probably wouldn't be able to handle it if they were stone-cold sober.

The thought went through Zakoff's mind just a moment before Hans's head exploded from the bullet that went through his skull. Gory aftermath splattered Hans's teammates and their card table. Otak and Melburn reacted with rather incredible speed, considering they had been drinking, let alone they had never encountered anything like this before. On the other hand,

Zakoff had been trained for years to respond to just a situation like this and he acted as training dictated. The Russian whipped out his .357 Magnum SIG Sauer P239 pistol and went for cover.

Melburn and Otak had jumped from their seats and looked for their own shelter, but only Otak succeeded. Melburn caught a round in the side that punctured a lung before lodging in his heart, and a second ripped away the better part of his jaw. Melburn's body was slammed sideways, and he landed on the flimsy table, which collapsed beneath his weight.

Otak turned at the last moment, a move that would ultimately save his life as another round came through the window and clipped his left arm but a millisecond earlier would have entered his back at the level of his heart. Otak went down, shouting with pain and grabbing at the messy, bloody wound left in the wake of the bullet. He lay on his good shoulder near the overturned table, whimpering like an injured dog with frozen horror blasted into his expression.

Zakoff could only shake his head at this. What a pathetic bunch Vizhgail had lumped him with—two were dead because of their ignorance, and the third was a coward. Zakoff was so angered by Otak's response and annoyed at the whining that he aimed his pistol and fired point-blank into the man's face. That wiped the stupid expression off Otak's face and shut him up, which satisfied the Russian's outrage with immense satisfaction.

He crawled from the room, and as soon as he reached the safety of an inner corridor he scrambled to his feet and headed toward the nearest phone to call for reinforcements.

SCRATCH TWO, MACK BOLAN thought as he peered through the optic sight attached to his FN-FNC.

Bolan watched carefully but didn't see any further movement. The other two who had been visible through the window were either hugging the floor or had already managed to crawl out of harm's way. In any case, they were no longer in range, so Bolan would have to go inside and pick them off. He entertained the thought of just leaving, but that wasn't an option. He planned to send a clear message to Haglemann, and sniping a couple of guns wouldn't really be enough to shake up the guy. No, this first contact had to be more…spectacular.

The Executioner climbed to his feet and rushed the club, mounting the flagstone steps two at once until he reached the massive covered porch. He wouldn't have much time. If the reports from the rifle didn't bring Haglemann's personal police force on the run, then the survivors inside would surely call for backup. Bolan needed to make his statement before that happened, since a skirmish with any sort of significant force would bring more attention than he wanted.

Bolan shattered a glass window with the metal folding stock of his weapon, then lobbed a smoke grenade through it. The bomb popped a moment later, and a loud hissing noise ensued as the smoker filled the foyer with a gray haze. As soon as the grenade kicked off, Bolan shot the lock off the door and pushed through. He swept the surrounding area with the muzzle of his carbine, ready to meet any resistance, but nobody showed to challenge him.

The Executioner proceeded through the foyer and into the main seating area of the club. Davis Haglemann had chosen to ally himself with the Russian Business Network, or at least Lustrum had, and the lives of American military had been snuffed without regard. That and that alone was unacceptable to Mack Bolan, and he planned to send a clear message that said as much to Haglemann and the Russians.

Bolan navigated his way to the kitchen, and as he walked through, a flash of movement drew his attention toward one corner. A lone, armed assailant broke cover and angled for a good shooting position. He might have succeeded had it not been for Bolan's reflexes. Two rounds burned the air near Bolan's head as the soldier took cover. He swung his weapon into target acquisition and triggered a few short bursts, but none hit the target, who darted from his place and headed toward concealment behind a long, stainless steel preparation counter.

Bolan snatched the NVD goggles off his face and set them at his feet. He then dropped to his belly and crawled along the back side of the counter, moving slowly and carefully to prevent making noise that would allow his enemy to pinpoint his location. They guy's eyes had obviously adjusted, and there was enough gloom that the NVDs no longer gave Bolan a tactical edge. Stealth would be the key to securing a victory here, a truth that proved out a moment later when Bolan detected the shadowy figure emerging from his spot and heading directly toward his position. A dim hood light presented a silhouette, and Bolan quietly reached to his hip and withdrew his Desert Eagle. From that prone position he extended his arm, aimed center mass and squeezed the trigger. The proximity of the shot actually drove home with enough force to flip the target on to his back.

The ringing in Bolan's ears took a minute or so to subside. He ignored it as he frisked the body for identification, lifted what papers he found, then set about the task of rigging the joint to blow. Being in the kitchen would make it simple enough. The Executioner located several propane storage tanks and packed them with C-4 plastique from his satchel. He primed the high explosive for detonation on a timer and set it to eight minutes, then made his exit out the rear and circled back to the spot between the two houses where he'd left his motorcycle.

As Bolan expected, the reinforcements arrived right on schedule—it looked to be a mix of civilian vehicles along with an Adak police vehicle. As the collection got out of their cars, the club suddenly went up in a massive blast and a whoosh of red-orange flame that had to reach heights of a hundred feet or better. Under the cover of the explosion, fire and secondary blasts, Bolan kick-started the motorcycle to life, and within thirty seconds he'd departed the area completely unobserved.

He'd sent his first message to Davis Haglemann. Now it was time to wait for the reply.

Stony Man Farm, Virginia

"THE RUSSIAN BUSINESS NETWORK?" When Barbara Price nodded, Hal Brognola shook his head. "I knew we hadn't heard the last of them, but I didn't think they had these kinds of capabilities."

"Frankly, Hal, neither did I," Bolan replied. "Godunov and his cronies demonstrated they had significant resources when they tried to take down Wall Street. But in order for them to pull off something like this, they'd have to be in bed with members of the Russian government. And they're apparently in bed with Davis Haglemann, too. They come and go here on Adak as they please."

"Barb," Brognola said, "what's the Russian government's *official* position on the RBN?"

"Well, of course, they officially disavow any relationship with them, although they've never officially taken any sort of direct stance."

"Such as?"

"Well, such as declaring them a terrorist organization, for one. The RBN started as more of a cybercrime organization than any other. They would stand up internet services and hosting for just about any criminal organization around the world, be it identity theft, child porn, financial scams or whatever. But their organization has since grown."

"Any evidence they're linked to the Russian government in some way?"

Price smiled. "You mean outside the president's ties to St. Petersburg?"

"Intelligence I picked up over time indicates members within the RBN might have ties to high-ranking politicians within the Kremlin," Bolan said. "In fact, those ties could be familial."

"Not to mention there's strong evidence they've got their hooks into the FSB," Price added. "Their alleged Storm network is still active, and it's said to be growing more powerful all the time."

"Is there a chance they could have used that to attack our military assets?" Brognola asked.

"Better than a chance," a new voice interjected.

Brognola and Price turned to see Aaron "the Bear" Kurtzman wheel into the room. The man may not have had use of his legs, but that wrestler-like body was as strong and solid as it looked, and the mind within a cornucopia of information and intelligence. Kurtzman's technical genius, coupled with the keen combined intellect of his crack cybernetics team members, had saved the lives of all the field operatives for Stony Man at one time or another, not to mention proving an effective tool in the Executioner's own private war against terrorism.

"Sorry for my tardiness," Kurtzman said. "But as soon as I got Striker's coded message I began to dig into the latest happenings by our Russian friends."

"What have you got?" Bolan asked.

"There's little reason to doubt the Storm network couldn't pull off something like this," Kurtzman said. "Of course, it's not like they've left a clear trail of bread crumbs for us."

"But you think they did use their systems to sabotage US military targets?" Bolan asked.

"Absolutely."

"Can you explain how they managed to do it?" Price said.

"Possibly, although it would be mere speculation," Kurtzman said. "Mind you, I have no proof yet, and I don't know that I can get any."

"Speculate, anyway," Bolan suggested. "I'd like to have some idea of what we're up against, so I know how to respond."

"Okay. In a nutshell, I think they used a wireless network to jam communications between various military stations and the missing assets. How they managed to do this, I can't really tell you yet. Like I say, they didn't leave any sort of trail."

"Okay, so they jammed communications," Brognola said. "But to what ends? Did they destroy the vessels or merely abscond with them? And if the latter scenario, how were they able to make something as big as a plane or Coast Guard cutter disappear into thin air?"

"I don't think they did," Kurtzman replied. "I mean naturally, you can't just make something that size fall off the proverbial radar with magic. But by cutting communications in an area as remote as the Bering Sea, they've killed the lifeblood of effective operations. If vessels and planes can't talk to one another, that's a big problem."

"Agreed," Price said.

"So they cut off communications and then what?" Bolan asked. "Crashed the plane? Blew it out of the sky? Landed it remotely on some neighboring island?"

"Any of the above," Kurtzman said.

A deathly silence enveloped the room.

"That kind of technology would be dangerous enough in the hands of a legitimate military force," Brognola stated. "In the hands of terrorists, it's unthinkable."

"It is definitely too great a threat to ignore," Price said.

She looked at Brognola. "Hal?"

"Ordinarily I'd run this by the Man first," Brognola said. "Get his take on it before committing to any kind of action. But this time around, Striker, you're where we are not and able to take action. And it seems you already have a handle on what's going on from what you've told us so far. I'm inclined to go with whatever operational objectives you propose at this point."

"If the RBN has a technology even remotely capable of doing what Aaron's just said, it's critical we find and destroy it as soon as possible."

"And how do you best think you can accomplish that?" Brognola asked.

"I sent a message to Haglemann earlier this morning," Bolan said. "I thought the best tactic would be to wait for his response to see if I could get on the inside of the organization. Now, I don't think we have that kind of time. I think they crashed that plane and I think they sank the *Llewellyn*. And if they boarded the cutter before sinking it, they might have taken hostages."

"What makes you think so?" Price asked.

"Well, cutting communications is all well and good," Bolan said. "But in order to be effective, they would have needed a way to actually take control of those assets once they jammed communications. That means a physical means of some type to commit the sabotage, whether sneaking a transceiver aboard or uploading some sort of computer virus."

"So you think they had someone's cooperation."

"Exactly. Specifically, someone on Haglemann's payroll."

"It sounds as if you have a plan already forming," Brognola said.

"I do. And if the RBN's responsible for killing hundreds of service personnel, I'm going to make it my personal business to wipe them out. Permanently."

"You'll have our full support, then, Striker," Brognola said. "Get these bastards where they live, and do what you do best."

"You can bet on it, Hal."

CHAPTER EIGHT

Adak Island

As soon as Bolan arrived at Maddie Corsack's house, she ushered him. "I was so worried about you."

"What's wrong?"

"There was trouble at Davis Haglemann's club this morning. Big trouble. Somebody torched the place. You wouldn't happen to know anything about that?"

"I might," Bolan said. "But why worry about me?"

"Lustrum called. He said he wanted to offer you that job and told me to get in touch with you. I'm supposed to let him know as soon as I reached you."

"Funny thing to have his attention when his boss's club just went up in smoke," Bolan replied. "Don't you think?"

"I guess."

Bolan nodded. "What else did he say?"

"Nothing much. Just that when I got hold of you to have you come here and he'd meet you."

"It's a setup."

"Why would it be? I thought your objective was to get inside Haglemann's organization. Isn't this what you wanted to happen?"

"In spite of the fact I tried to be careful, they figured out I was behind what happened at the club," Bolan said. "Lustrum choosing now to reach out to me was no coincidence."

"So why would he reach out to me?"

"He's betting on your allegiance to him and Haglemann, maybe? I don't know."

"Fat chance!" she replied with a snort. "Lustrum knows damn well there's no love lost between me and Davis, that's for sure."

"Well, then he may be gunning for you, too."

"Wait. What do you mean by that?"

"His wanting you to call him when I arrive here is a possible pretext for killing you, as well."

"Now wait a minute, Blansky. Lustrum's a pain in the ass, maybe, but he's no cold-blooded killer."

"You need to open your eyes, Corsack," Bolan said. "Maybe Lustrum isn't a killer, but he's got killers working for him. And those men I encountered at the club were working alongside a terrorist organization known as the Russian Business Network. Ever heard of them?"

Corsack shook her head.

"Well, I don't have time to go into all of the particulars. What I *can* tell you is they're not a nice bunch. They're terrorists, very adept at committing cyber-crimes like child pornography and identity theft. A few years ago, they tried to make a play for America's financial infrastructure. I can't go into details, but I can tell you that they have the resources to pull it off, and I barely came through it when I stopped them once before. Now, they might have been responsible for the deaths of countless military personnel. And I can assure you, I won't let that go unanswered."

Corsack sat slowly on her couch and put her head in her hands. She let out a soft moan, and when she looked up, her eyes were pooled with tears. "I don't believe this. I mean, I knew Lustrum and Haglemann were no angels, but I didn't think they would do anything like this."

"Most of the people on Adak probably didn't, either," Bolan said gently. "This isn't your fault, Corsack. No matter how in tune you might be with this community, you couldn't have seen this coming. Nobody could."

Corsack wiped the tears from her face, then rose and headed to the coffeepot. She poured herself a cup, offered one to Bolan, who accepted, then appeared to come to a decision.

"I may not agree with everything you're doing," she said. "I might not even say I believe what you've told me about Lustrum and Haglemann. But I do know you're not a cold-blooded murderer or a liar. So I guess that's going to have to be good enough. For now."

"So you'll help me?"

She nodded. "Just tell me what you want me to do."

"First, call Lustrum and let him know I'm here and we're waiting."

"But I thought you said it was a trap, that they'd come for you."

"That's exactly what I want them to do. I've started to shake them up, and I want to keep them off balance. It's the only way to get to Haglemann, and Haglemann is my ticket to finding out where the RBN is holed up."

"It's definitely not here on Adak. I can tell you that much."

"I'm sure you're right," Bolan said. "But I don't know where they're operating, and Haglemann's probably the only one that has the information."

"What about Lustrum?"

Bolan shook his head and frowned. "Doubtful. Lustrum's a lackey, despite what he might want everyone to think."

"Possibly," Corsack agreed. "But one thing he isn't is stupid. There's no way he's going to believe I'd set up a friend."

"Well, then, you're just going to have to sound really convincing when you call him. I gathered from your conversation last night that you've got a little bit of leverage."

The remark produced a laugh from Corsack. "Hardly! Oh, he's got a little crush on me, I suppose. I let him take me out to dinner once—at Haglemann's club, as a matter of fact. But that's the extent of it."

"Maybe it's time to play that card in your favor."

"Only if you think there's no other way."

"I don't know if there's any other way of not arousing his suspicions," Bolan said. "But you could tell him you have information about the hit on the club. And you could tell him you think I have something to do with it, and you don't think it's right I should get away with it."

"In other words, make it sound like you used me."

"Exactly."

"But isn't that really what you're doing, anyway, Blansky? I mean, I'm not an idiot. I know you're asking me to turn on the only real life I've ever known."

"Listen, Corsack," Bolan said. "You've already done more than your fair share to help these people. I don't believe you're so naive you don't know how things work in the real world. Just make sure that whatever you do you're doing it for the right reasons, the reasons that make sense. Personally, I won't ask more of anybody than that."

"Fair enough," Corsack said. "Now I'd best make that call."

Bolan nodded. "We'll be ready."

THREE VEHICLES, A LIMO with one sedan in the lead and another bringing up the rear, pulled to the curb in front of Corsack's house less than thirty minutes after she made the call.

Bolan had to admit he hadn't expected them quite that soon, but he was ready for them all the same. He made a quick count, peering at them through the corner of the curtain, and then keyed the small microphone with an earpiece. "Striker to Eagle."

"Go, Striker."

"They're here," Bolan said. "Make some noise."

"Roger that."

A moment later, a flash caught Bolan's eye and a flaming trail made an arc high into the air before bursting into a flash of light that lit the gray morning sky. The starburst surprised the half-dozen or so men who had emerged from the sedans, and they involuntarily reached for firearms beneath their jackets. As with the crew at Haglemann's club, Bolan knew that these men weren't equipped to take on somebody like him.

Grimaldi followed the starburst round with a hail of autofire, the rounds chewing up the ground around the men while not actually hitting any of them. Bolan checked his watch and counted down thirty seconds before bringing his own autorifle into action. He ordered Corsack to stay on the floor one last time, then climbed to his feet and headed for the front entrance. He waited until he heard a lull in the firing, then burst through the front door, leveling his weapon and triggering several volleys on the run. When he reached the closest man who was prone on the ground, he grabbed him by the shoulder and hauled him to his feet.

"What the hell are you doing?" Bolan demanded. "Get behind some cover!"

Another volley of rounds chewed up dirt near Bolan's feet, and the Executioner forced back the grin. He hoped Grimaldi's aim was off from his usual accuracy. The Stony Man flier might have held down a primary job as a pilot, but he was also a trained and experienced combatant when the need arose and had proven as much time and again.

Bolan came upon a second guy. It was Lustrum. He tugged the guy to his feet the same as the first. He half dragged, half carried the older man along with him as he triggered another volley in Grimaldi's general direction. Bolan reached one of the vehicles, a limousine, with his prospective employer and none too gently shoved the man into the backseat.

"Get the others and let's go!" Bolan ordered.

A few of the men had pulled pistols, but nobody fired since they couldn't really tell where the shots were coming from. The man looked as if he might challenge Bolan, but when Lustrum started screaming at him to take action, the guy opted to shout orders for his men to withdraw. They could argue the virtues of who was in charge later. The guy verified that the men had returned to their vehicles before jumping into the seat facing Bolan and Lustrum. Within a few seconds, they were secure and speeding from the scene with a screech of tires and smoking rubber.

Lustrum pulled a handkerchief from his coat pocket and mopped his brow. He then looked at Bolan who sat in the seat next to him. The Executioner ejected the magazine of blank rounds, made a show of inspecting them, then slammed it home once more.

"What the hell was that about?" Lustrum asked.

"You tell me," Bolan said.

"You mean…you didn't… The club, that wasn't you?"

"No," Bolan replied simply.

"There's been a big mistake, Blansky. A *big* mistake!"

"Meaning?"

"We thought for sure you were the one who hit the club."

Bolan shook his head. "I knew you had me pegged from the start, Mr. Lustrum."

"Huh? Whad'ya mean by that?"

"You figured out I wasn't just some local looking for honest work."

Lustrum was a little off at first, but then the light dawned on him, and he quickly changed expressions. "Well, yeah, of course."

"I was sent here to protect the club. And you. I was sent to protect all of Mr. Haglemann's assets."

"To protect *us*? Sent by who?" demanded the other guy Bolan had saved from a faux destruction.

"Our mutual Russian friends," Bolan said quietly as he engaged the safety on the carbine.

A brief and panicked silent exchange occurred between Lustrum and his guy. The man then raised the pistol he still held and leveled it at Bolan.

"Hey, what's with the hostilities?" Bolan asked. "I just saved your ass back there, and you point a gun at me? I'm not the one who blew up your club, friend, and obviously I wasn't the one shooting at you."

"You seem to know an awful lot about what's going on here for hired help," the pistol wielder said with an expression that Bolan read as unconvinced.

"Dumyat, put that gun away!" Lustrum snapped.

The guy called Dumyat looked surprised at first but finally complied, keeping one eye on Bolan at all times.

Lustrum gave Bolan his full attention. "So, let's suppose you're telling me the truth. Why the hell would the Russians send you, an American, to do their work? Why not one of their own?"

"It could be because there was some trouble on Unalaska yesterday morning," Bolan said.

"How come I didn't hear about it?"

Bolan shrugged. "What your boss chooses to share or not share with you is none of my affair, Mr. Lustrum. I'm just here to do a job and get paid. Once the job's done, I'm gone, and you can do whatever you want."

"Does Davis know about your assignment?"

Bolan shook his head. "I've never even met Mr. Haglemann. I think our mutual benefactors would prefer to keep my involvement as quiet as possible."

"Why would they want to do that?"

Bolan jerked his thumb over his shoulder and replied, "Because of what happened back there. Somebody's been poking their nose into whatever you have going on here. Again, that's not really any of my business. I was brought in to…fix the situation. There are a lot of people starting to look at Adak in the course of this most recent emergency, and it's my job to stifle their curiosity."

"What emergency?" Dumyat asked with a scowl. It was hard to tell, though, since a sneer was what seemed to be more of his usual expression.

So Haglemann wasn't keeping his men apprised of what was really going on. Unless Dumyat was really sharp and knew how to play coy well, which Bolan highly doubted, it seemed Haglemann hadn't been completely forthcoming regarding his relationship with the Russians. Was it possible Corsack had been right all along? Were Haglemann's people merely pawns in a grander scheme? If so, what did they figure was the real relationship between Haglemann and the Russians? Perhaps another business venture to make them all wealthier. Until he knew for certain, Bolan couldn't risk killing any more of Lustrum's men.

There had already been enough bloodshed at the moment.

"I think we should go straight to Davis and get this all worked out right now, boss," Dumyat said.

Lustrum considered the suggestion for a long time, looking at Bolan with thoughtful assessment. Finally he said, "Yeah, I think you're right. We need to find out what's going on."

"I think it's better I do it alone, then, first," Bolan said.

"And why's that?"

"Because if you take me in there, he might think you're the reason for all of his problems. Letting an outsider in so easily won't go well with Haglemann. But if I go in and explain you had nothing at all to do with it, that I'm here at the request of his business associates, your name stays out of it, and he thinks you got it all under control."

"You make a good point," Lustrum said.

"But, boss—!"

Lustrum's face reddened. "I said he makes a good point, Dumyat! Now shut up!"

Dumyat fell silent, but the muscles in his neck and jaw twitched visibly.

Lustrum looked at Bolan. "Okay, Blansky. You got it your way. I'll get you a meeting with Davis this morning."

Bolan nodded.

"But if you cross me, Blansky, I'll cut you into fish bait and dump your carcass in the bay. We've got a good system here, and I don't need you screwing it up. My men, the workers here, they come first. You understand?"

"Perfectly," the Executioner replied.

Semisopochnoi Island

COMMANDER LOUIS DUCATI sat in the corner of the massive steel cage and watched the activities around him with unwavering interest. A good part of his diligence was so he'd be able to provide intelligence if anyone managed to make contact with him or a member of his crew. He'd done everything he could to keep up their spirits through the ordeal, an especially difficult task given nobody would have classified Ducati as socially adept. He loved his crew, to be sure, and gave full attention to their needs and requirements. He wanted them to have the very best in their careers and personal lives.

He'd never remotely suspected that concern would extend to a circumstance like this.

What he hadn't been able to figure out yet was how their captors managed to cut off communications, or why they'd chosen to sink the *Llewellyn*. It didn't make sense. They'd also killed the security team members but left the remaining crew alive, except for the first officer who had attempted to resist and was killed in a hail of gunfire. Ducati couldn't get the images from his mind, watching as Gareth Keller's body jumped and twitched under the dozens of bullets that had struck him. Ducati had never been in action, not once during his entire career in the USCG.

Maybe this was all his fault. If he'd been more experienced, perhaps he would have been better equipped to repel the men who had boarded his ship. It burned as he swallowed back the bitterness and the complete sense of worthlessness. A good commander would never have let the enemy take his ship.

Don't think like that, he scolded himself. Hold it together for the rest of your crew.

Indeed, Ducati had attempted to remain strong and vigilant. He'd already appointed his operations officer to second-in-command, and he'd been coordinating with his other command staff to come up with plans of action if he could find a way out of their makeshift prison. So far, their situation looked bleak. Ducati couldn't get a handle on what their captors had planned.

What he didn't know was much more than what he did. The soldiers and their leader spoke in Russian. One of his communications officers had confirmed as much, since she spoke Russian. She hadn't been able to catch much as the captors were careful not to speak about anything specifically. They'd been given water but no food, and they'd only been permitted one at a time for bathroom privileges on a timetable. When they were being put in the cages—the twin, steel monstrosities could only have been constructed once inside this massive cavern, since the entrance they'd come through would not have allowed access in whole—two of the men had resisted, and they'd been beaten severely. Both men had regained consciousness, and Ducati had sternly warned the rest of the crew after the incident not to resist unless escape was a strong possibility.

They'd lost enough good men and women, and he didn't intend to add to the body count.

Ducati thought he'd identified the leader, someone his communications officer had thought they called Vlad, but that was it. There was another one who had accompanied the leader everywhere, and he was certain that one went by Alexei. He didn't have any other names. He estimated more than thirty-six hours had passed since their encounter with the Russians, although he couldn't be one hundred percent sure about it. Everything metal or electronic had been taken from their persons. They'd even removed the metal rank insignia from the officers because the sharp ends could be used as a weapon.

At best count, their captors numbered somewhere in the area of twenty, and they were all armed. The guards alone carried sidearms and machine guns of various makes. Ducati couldn't put his finger on their origins, though. No specific Russian terrorist groups came to his mind, and these men didn't really act like military troops, anyway. More like criminals. Thugs. It just didn't make sense.

"Sir?"

The voice of his new XO, Chris Rastogi, resounded

in his ears and shook Ducati from his ruminations. "Yes, Chris."

"I just finished talking with Corbett."

Ducati reached into his memory and quickly brought up a mental image of Corbett. He was the senior officer they'd left in charge of the crew in the other cage.

"What's the story?"

"They're all fine except for Gross, sir."

Petty Officer First Class Jeff Gross. The name immediately came to mind, a fine enlisted man and consummate leader. He worked the engine room as a shift supervisor.

"What's wrong with him, XO?"

"Can't be sure, but he's not doing too well, according to Corbett. Got sweaty skin, and his color isn't so hot, either."

"It's no wonder," Ducati said, wiping the sweat from his brow with the back of his sleeve. "So damned hot in here, it's a wonder we're all not dehydrated. Unless he's got some sort of complication that's surfaced from his bowel problems. You know, he was recently on shore leave for intestinal inflammation, but they released him with a clean bill of health."

"He says it's nothing like that, sir. He's just feeling sick to his stomach, and the last piss break he said it burned. And he swears it's not a woman."

The bit of crass humor actually brought a grin to Ducati's face. "I'm sure it isn't. Maybe he's not drinking enough water. I'll see if we can get some extra, but if our captors aren't feeling particularly beneficent we'll have to ration some extra for him next round. Meanwhile, let Corbett know I'll see what I can do."

"Aye, sir."

It seemed good fortune might be on their side, because as Ducati was about to call on a guard to get someone, the leader of the group happened to walk from an adjoining cavern that led to what might be anybody's guess. Ducati flagged the attention of the man by waving his arms and calling out. At first it looked as if he planned to ignore Ducati, but then he seemed to think better of it and decided to approach. "Are you in charge here?"

The man said nothing at first, instead choosing to reply with a smug grin.

"Speakee English?" Ducati tried.

"You're rather flippant for a military officer," the man said. "And, yes, I speak English quite well."

Ducati had to agree, although he noted the heavy Russian accent. "One of my men is sick. I was wondering if I could request some extra water for him. I think he may be dehydrated."

"You have all the water you're going to get. I won't give extra and let one of *my* men go without."

"Well, then, you may have to cart a dead body out of here soon."

"Come again?"

"It's blasted *hot* in here, man! You can't expect us to sit here with only water and no food and survive for any length of time."

"Perhaps your survival isn't part of my plan."

"Well, if you'd thought to kill us, I would have assumed you'd done it by now," Ducati challenged. He knew it wasn't good to rebut the guy, and being sarcastic probably wouldn't buy him any good will. Still, he had to let the guy know the terms of the situation. "If you want me to keep these people quiet and not give you any trouble, you have to work with me. Be reasonable."

"Be reasonable? Like your countrymen were reasonable with my people, perhaps? I do not think you would care much for that type of reasonability, Mr....?"

"Ducati. My rank is commander with the United States Coast Guard. But then, I assume you already knew that, so I'll skip reciting all the rest of it like service number and current billet, and so forth."

"I see you're not a foolish man," he replied. "My name is Vladimir Moscovich."

"And you're in charge here?"

"I am."

"When are you going to let us go? Or do you plan to ever let us go? After all, you just gave me your name, and if it's your real name you'll never let me leave here alive knowing it."

"I've not decided yet," he replied. "And you knowing my name, well, I know yours, and it's only fair, yes?"

"I suppose."

"Besides, knowing my name won't be of much good. When this operation is through, I will most likely be dead. And if I die, it is reasonably assured that you will perish along with me. In fact, it's likely you'll perish even if I live."

"Why are you doing this?" Ducati demanded. "Do you realize what you've done is an act of war? America won't stand for this!"

"I don't imagine it will," Moscovich said. "But then, I don't really care. You see, it makes little difference to me. America has made a mistake sending its agents to interfere with my organization."

"And what organization is that?"

"It's hardly important. What is of importance is my mission, and I will accomplish it this very day. There is nothing you'll be able to do about it. As to your fate, I will most likely not decide this. I will instead let the commander of the submarine that's on its way here now decide this. I'm sure you would rather appreciate one military man deciding how to deal with another and its crew. No?"

As Moscovich turned on his heel, Ducati said, "What about the water?"

Moscovich stopped, and it seemed as though his shoulders hunched. Finally he turned to one of his men and jerked his head in the direction of their cage. Ducati didn't know what it meant, but when he glanced over at his communications officer and saw the look on her face, he knew it wasn't good.

A moment later, two guards appeared in front of the locked gate of the steel cage. A third opened the padlock attached to the chains, and the two men stepped inside. Each grabbed one of Ducati's arms and dragged him forcefully from the cage. Rastogi rushed forward to engage them, but the guard standing by struck him in the side of the head with a well-aimed butt stroke from the stock of his SMG. Rastogi's head reeled from the blow, and his body toppled backward into the waiting arms of several crew members.

Ducati immediately shouted for Rastogi and the others to stand down, adding as he was dragged away, "Just keep your heads, people. That's an order!"

CHAPTER NINE

Adak Island

Jack Grimaldi had watched helplessly as the enemy drove away with Bolan, even though it had been their plan from the beginning and had come out exactly as Bolan hoped. The Sarge could take care of himself, he knew, but that didn't mean he wasn't concerned about his old friend. Their relationship had been forged through many years combating some of the worst evil imaginable.

As soon as the guns had cleared out and the convoy departed, Grimaldi packed the assault rifle and other gear in the hard gun case he'd bought. He then packed it in the trunk of the vehicle that Corsack had managed to borrow from a friend on the docks, climbed behind the wheel and immediately proceeded to Corsack's house. He didn't worry about anybody looking for him; neither did he worry about the cops showing up. The last place anybody would think to look for him would be Corsack's place, which was exactly why Bolan had executed the plan the way he had.

Once he was inside with the equipment, Grimaldi sat at the small kitchen nook. He took the cup of hot cocoa Corsack offered him.

"So, what's next?" she asked after shoving the mug in front of him.

Grimaldi nodded his thanks and said, "Now we wait."

"Seems to be sort of what I've been doing a lot of when it comes to Mike."

That brought a chuckle from Grimaldi. "When you know him as long as I have, you get used to it."

"How did you get all wrapped up in this?" she asked.

"That would be something I can't discuss."

"No, of course not."

"You, however, got involved in this under rather strange circumstances."

"Not really," she replied. "I'm just a working girl. I care about this place, which is a hell of a lot more than I can say about Haglemann and his cronies."

"And you think that most of the other people on the island don't really know what they've been up to?"

"Right. Especially the part about these Russians. What's the story with these guys, anyway? They sound like nothing but thugs."

"They are thugs," Grimaldi replied. "But there's a little bit more than that. They have resources and connections. We put them down once before but apparently not hard enough to keep them down."

"And so this time around, it'll be different."

"Oh, yeah. This time it'll be permanent."

HAGLEMANN'S ESTATE WAS nothing short of magnificent. The grounds were extensive, the house constructed from the finest materials and the landscaping exquisite. And from what Bolan saw as they passed through the security at the front gate, it boasted a top-of-the-line electronic surveillance system. Coupled with the pairs of sentries patrolling the perimeter, it would be a challenge to penetrate the grounds undetected.

The Executioner wasn't impressed; he'd gotten into and out of more secure facilities than this. For one thing, he was certain Kurtzman had provided him with a bag of tricks that contained nothing but the best in surveillance countermeasures. Moreover, a roving guard typically meant regular intervals in the patrols. Human habits were the greatest detriment to security. The guards were uniformed, which made it easy to pick out friend from foe. No, this place wouldn't pose much of a problem for Bolan. It would all just come down to a matter of striking at the right place and the right time. A short stint inside the organization would provide him with all the information he needed.

Now to size up Davis Haglemann.

The convoy came to a stop beneath an overhang that extended from the main entrance. The men climbed from the cars, but only Lustrum, Dumyat and Bolan were permitted to enter the estate. The others were instructed to wait there under the watchful eye of the three men who guarded the front door. Another man, who wore a navy-colored wool suit and walked with the casual saunter of a guy packing a heavy pistol in shoulder leather, led them through the front entrance into a neighboring den. A hearth of chiseled granite and framed by mahogany polished to a mirror finish reflected the crackling flames of a cozy fire.

Two of the walls were lined with books, and a bearskin rug sprawled across the floor. A variety of ancient firearms, including a flintlock rifle, were mounted against another wall. Bolan studied the room with feigned interest as Lustrum and Dumyat took seats in some nearby, high-back chairs. A baby grand piano occupied another corner of the room, as did an old, Elizabethan-style desk.

Haglemann might have been scum, but he had impeccable tastes when it came to looking like a man of success and prestige. Bolan intended to see to it that he crammed all of that false pretense down the man's throat until he choked to death on it. They waited nearly twenty minutes, adding to Haglemann's brooding mystique of self-importance, before the guy finally decided to show himself. He wasn't much to look at insofar as he didn't possess striking good looks or even a regal bearing. He had an aura of eccentricity, if Bolan could have assigned any descriptor, and even that stunk with the laundry list of improprieties and dastardly business dealings attributed to him. He was little more than an overgrown, spoiled rich kid who had manipulated circumstances in the region to his benefit. He played at being the head of a powerful union and attempted to make it look that he had the best interests of the citizens on Adak at heart, when in actuality he couldn't have cared less.

Davis Haglemann wasn't what he pretended to be. Bolan had seen men of this type many times, and he knew *exactly* what kind of man Haglemann was. He wasn't a man at all, really, but just another head on the monster Hydra that gained strength by preying on the weak and helpless and weary. He was just the kind of man who represented what Bolan had spent all of his life fighting.

"Otto," Haglemann said with a nod to Lustrum.

"Mr. Haglemann," Lustrum replied. He cleared his throat. "Good morning, sir. I'm sorry to drop in so unexpectedly, but I thought you'd want to meet this man right away."

Haglemann looked in the direction Lustrum gestured and took notice of Bolan for the first time. Bolan watched for any recognition on Haglemann's face, but the tycoon remained impassive. At least he wouldn't have to shoot his way out of here, not at this moment, anyway. That would make his job much easier, although Bolan wouldn't let that cause him to underestimate Haglemann. Underestimating an enemy, any enemy, made an enemy dangerous.

"And who are you?"

"His name is—"

Bolan cut Lustrum off as he stepped forward and extended his hand. "Mike Blansky, Mr. Haglemann. I was sent here to solve your little problem."

"Really?" Haglemann's voice sounded uncertain even as he willingly shook Bolan's hand. "And what problem might that be?"

"The one that started on Unalaska."

Haglemann's eyes got a little wider, but he otherwise managed not to react, and Bolan knew he'd struck a nerve. "I'm not sure what you mean."

"Maybe you are," Bolan said.

"Maybe I'm not." Haglemann looked at Lustrum. "What the hell's going on here, Otto?"

"I sort of had the same question, Mr. Haglemann," Lustrum said.

"Pardon me?"

"The job that got done on the club—this guy didn't do it," Lustrum said.

Haglemann's eyes narrowed, and he turned to look at Bolan. "Is that right?"

"That's right," Bolan said. He dropped casually into an overstuffed suede chair and propped his feet on the matching ottoman. "In fact, I was sent here to prevent it. I just didn't get here in time. Our mutual friends, well, they thought he'd come after you personally."

"What friends?" Haglemann said. "I don't think you really want to discuss that publicly."

"Why not?" Lustrum demanded. "That's why you had us bring you here. Isn't it? So Mr. Haglemann could explain—"

"What? What the fuck are you talking about?" Haglemann's face flushed, and he started spitting. "Who are *you* that I should explain myself to you? Get the fuck out of here right now, Otto, while you can still walk out of here under your own power! And take Dumbshit with you."

"It's, uh, Dumyat, sir."

"Who gives a shit! Get out!" He looked at Bolan. "You stay, because you got some definite explaining to do."

"Gladly," Bolan replied.

The two men made haste to leave, not as much to follow orders as to merely extricate themselves from the suddenly malevolent presence. Corsack had warned Bolan that Haglemann was prone to sudden fits of temper, and there were even rumors among his inner circle that he took medication to control it because he wasn't exactly right in the head. After witnessing the exchange, Bolan had to wonder if the guy was off his meds. The weight of the Beretta 93-R in his shoulder leather felt comfortable. None of the security outside had even frisked him, just assuming that the FN-FNC he'd turned over to them was his only weaponry.

That kind of slack attitude would only make Bolan's job easier when the time came. If he acquired the intelligence he needed on the Russian Business Network, he would most likely take out Haglemann here and now under the noses of his security team. Nobody would even take notice, given Bolan had the subsonic rounds loaded in his pistol.

Haglemann went to a nearby credenza and poured himself a drink. "Can I offer you something, Mr. Blansky?"

"No, thanks."

Haglemann poured a tumbler full of brown liquid Bolan assumed to be whiskey or brandy, from the tint. One look told him Haglemann was probably a brandy man, although he might also enjoy Scotch whisky. Haglemann took several large swallows and studied Bolan for a time.

"So tell me why I shouldn't have you killed here and now."

"It wouldn't put you in well with my boss. Or should I say bosses?"

"And who exactly is it you work for?"

"Come on, Haglemann," Bolan said, rising to his feet and shoving his hands casually in his pocket. "You don't really think I'm going to start dropping names. We both know that our mutual interests are fond of the color red. Isn't that good enough?"

"Afraid not," Haglemann said. "You could be playing me for a sucker."

"Like you're playing those Podunk guys like Otto Lustrum and his bruisers? Those guys aren't gangsters." Bolan produced a mocking laugh. "We both know they couldn't protect their own mothers, let alone your assets. Hell, they just let somebody walk onto your island and blow up your club. And my boss isn't going to be happy when he learns two of his men are dead."

"I thought only Zakoff was at the club."

"What about Rov?"

"What about him?"

"Killed yesterday. Neck broken and stabbed to death."

"What? How did *that* happen?"

Bolan shrugged. "Something about some kind of brawling they do near the docks. I guess your man Lustrum there runs the gambling action. The same guy who blew up your club managed to get a bout in the ring and killed Rov."

"That dirty, stupid shit!" Haglemann downed his drink and set the tumbler roughly on the credenza, completely unconcerned it would mar the surface. "I told him to keep that stuff under control."

"Well, it doesn't look like he's doing that," Bolan said. "And now two of your associate's people are dead, and your operation is at risk. That's why I was called in. I'm a specialist at these kinds of problems."

Haglemann scowled. "I told Moscovich I didn't need any of his help. Looks like he ignored me."

"Out of his hands," Bolan lied. "I was brought in by his people in St. Petersburg."

"Why's that?"

"Because this isn't the first time this particular individual has interfered with their operations."

"You mean this has happened before?"

Bolan nodded and folded his arms, looking at the floor reflectively as he spoke. "Yeah, a few years ago. They got an operation squashed in New York City. My people tell me they think it's the same guy, since they never could figure out who did them in."

"Well, you won't have to worry about Otto. He'll be in the bottom of the bay by tonight."

"Actually, no," Bolan said. "I need him. For at least a little while longer."

"Why?"

"Because he's got the manpower. This guy is tricky and moves around a lot, which is why it's been so hard to nail him." Bolan shook his head. "In fact, he hit us today when Lustrum came to pick me up at Maddie Corsack's place."

"You know Maddie?"

"Old friend."

"From where?"

Bolan's smile contained frost. "Now, that's not really important. Is it?"

"It's important to me, asshole!"

"Look, Mr. Haglemann," Bolan said in a cool, quiet tone as he took a few steps in the man's direction. "I've got no fight with you. But I also don't work for you. I'm a free agent, and I don't put up with any nonsense. You want to run your show, you're entitled to do it how you like. But when it comes to me, you'll keep a civil tongue in your head or I'll save us all a lot of trouble and put a bullet right here."

Bolan reached out and tapped Haglemann's forehead with a rigid finger, adding, "You hear me?"

The action so surprised Haglemann he didn't know how to react. He stepped back and looked at Bolan with utter surprise.

"Now that we got that settled, I need to know that if I ask for any support from you, I'll get it. After all, it's my job to keep you alive, and I think I can do a much better job than Otto and his boys. Do we have an agreement?"

Haglemann said nothing at first, still obviously stunned by the fact Bolan had just threatened him in a way nobody had ever done before. Oddly, Haglemann seemed to have suddenly gained a new respect for Bolan. It was exactly what the soldier counted on and the reason he'd chosen this role from his camouflage arsenal.

"Sure," Haglemann said. "Have it your way. I don't give a shit just as long as you get this bastard. He's already killed more than a half-dozen of my people."

"Good. Now, the first thing I'm going to need is a solid set of wheels," Bolan said. "Something fast but tough."

"Like what?"

Bolan shrugged. "SUV or a Jeep, maybe."

"How about a Hummer?"

"That'll do just fine," the Executioner replied with a smile.

CHAPTER TEN

Behind the wheel of a late-model Hummer, Bolan had
to wonder exactly what deity had been looking over
him. He'd half expected a guy as shrewd as Davis Haglemann to figure him for the enemy, in which case
he might not have left Haglemann's property alive.
Yet he'd managed to drive through the tall front gates
unchallenged.

He expected Haglemann to put a tail on him, at
least, and yet as he turned on to the road and headed
for Corsack's place, he didn't get the sense anyone was
following him so far. Haglemann had even agreed to
explain Bolan's involvement, give some sort of cover
story, which led Bolan to conclude that Corsack had
probably been right. If Lustrum or his thugs found out
Haglemann was actually working alongside members
of the RBN, the union boss would lose all support. It
would probably also mean his life, since they wouldn't
see any reason to trust a guy like Haglemann.

Bolan shook his head at the irony of that.

Men like Lustrum shouldn't have been trusting a
guy like Haglemann to begin with. Haglemann was a
businessman, a *rich* businessman at that, and he had
no background or experience as a working stiff. Bolan
couldn't understand how he'd been able to gain the respect of the men and women on Adak who toiled and

slaved through the long days. Their lives weren't easy, and yet they stuck it out year after year, and just like Corsack had said, they couldn't imagine going somewhere else. This was their home and they gave a damn, and a guy like Bolan, who had never really been able to call any place "home" since he'd first taken on the Mafia all those years ago in Pittsfield, could understand that.

Haglemann wasn't anything like them, and yet the residents here had embraced him for a few extra bucks and a big-screen television. It didn't make sense to Bolan, and he realized in that moment it was most likely because they didn't really know what was going on. They had become victims of Haglemann's greed and avarice just like those who had suffered at the hands of his allies.

Bolan waited until he was out of sight of Haglemann's residence before reaching beneath his jacket and whipping the secured phone into play. He dialed Stony Man by entering a series of special codes, and in just seconds he had Price on the line.

"How's it going?" she asked.

"I managed to get inside Haglemann's guard," Bolan said, "and talked to him personally."

"You think he bought it?"

"Hard to tell."

Bolan's eyes flicked to the rearview mirror as he made a left-hand turn on to the road that would take him to the docks. As he did, another vehicle pulled off a side road and took up a position of considerable distance behind him. Bolan knew what it meant, but he figured there was no need for alarm. At this point, it would only make sense for Haglemann to put somebody on him to watch his movements.

"I'm confident he thinks it's the RBN who sent me," Bolan continued. "He's got plenty of witnesses, Lustrum included, who will verify that I was fighting on their side when the shooting started. As far as Haglemann's concerned, I saved Lustrum's ass, and I kept his involvement with the Russians quiet. He even lent me one of his vehicles."

"Any chance it's wired?"

"Doubtful," Bolan said. "It belongs to him personally, and he wouldn't have had time to bug the vehicle. If I thought he had me bugged, I wouldn't be calling you."

"Of course, I should've realized that," Price said. Bolan could hear the weariness in her voice. "Sorry."

"Forget it. So, with Haglemann on board, all I have to do is set up the rest of it."

"Have you figured out how you're going to do that?"

"I have a tentative plan, but it's going to take a lot of help on your part. Haglemann's definitely working with the Russians. What I don't know is exactly who or what the background is. That's where I need your help."

"What do you need?"

"Get me all the information you can on the name Moscovich. No first name, so you'll have to see if you can tie that into whatever intelligence is currently on hand regarding the RBN. Next, I'm going to have to get a better understanding of how they took out our military assets. Especially the cutter. That's a very big ship to make just disappear. If they sank the vessel, there should be some hundred bodies or more that went down with her."

"The first part will be easy," Price replied. "The second may be a much tougher order. The military has taken sole responsibility for the investigation, and we might not be able to get the inside loop without directly involving the White House."

"I know it's sketchy, but I'm going to need all the intelligence I can if I hope to rip this thing apart from the inside. Also, I'm going to head back to Unalaska for a short while."

"Are you going to get help from the deputy chief again?"

"I have no choice. She's my only subject-matter expert, and before she let me go, she promised to keep her ear to the ground."

"Why not just call her?"

"I would under normal circumstances, but there's no question Haglemann and the Russians have got operatives working there, and I plan to prevent this from happening again. That's the biggest threat. Haglemann's not going anywhere right now, anyway, so it's better to play it cool."

"Understood. We'll get on it at this end."

"Out here," Bolan said, and he cut the connection.

The vehicle behind was keeping a consistent interval between them. If Bolan slowed, the pursuer followed suit. Same story for when he increased speed. That was the tough thing about roads on a place like Adak. They were long and open and had little traffic, which made vehicle surveillance nearly impossible to pull off. Bolan pulled his cell and dialed another number via a code.

When the familiar voice answered, Bolan said, "Looks like I'm going to need to call on your services again."

"Just say where and when," Jack Grimaldi replied.

Stony Man Farm, Virginia

WHEN BARBARA PRICE got the call from Bolan he gave her just one name: Moscovich.

Price took this information to Aaron Kurtzman who jumped on it and began a sweeping search for that name and any ties it might have to the Russian Business Network. As with most things, Kurtzman approached the situation like an attack dog on a thief. Normally, Price left him to his work and waited for Kurtzman to bring her the information, but in this case she chose to pull up a chair and watch and wait in the Annex's Computer Room.

Within an hour, Kurtzman had gleaned everything he could, and Price contacted Brognola, who had stayed at the Farm and taken some time to get a few hours of shut-eye. When she told him what they'd found, he said, "I'll be in the Computer Room in fifteen minutes."

True to his word, the Stony Man chief arrived a short time later and took a seat at the small briefing table where Price and Kurtzman were putting the last touches on their information to present to Brognola.

"That one name from Striker opened a whole new world to us," Price began.

"What about his suspicions regarding the Russian Business Network? Is there any evidence they're at the heart of this?"

"Plenty," Price said. "Striker was dead-on in his assumptions, although I can't really say I'm all that happy he was right."

Brognola nodded. "Yeah, it's usually never good

news, but at least we have some idea of what he's up against. So, what did you learn?"

Price nodded at Kurtzman who tapped a key, and the image of a young, handsome man was projected on one of the large monitors on the wall opposite.

"This is Vladimir Moscovich," Price said. "The picture is about eight years old, taken around the time Moscovich was a student at St. Petersburg State University."

"Impressive education for a criminal," Brognola said.

"You only know the half of it," Kurtzman interjected.

"Moscovich holds a doctorate," Price continued. "And given that the university is a federal state-owned institution and the oldest college in Russia, there's little doubt about the ties between the RBN and officials within government. The other interesting thing is that the source of funding for his education was never identified."

"No financial trail?" Brognola asked, looking in Kurtzman's direction.

The cyber wizard shook his head. "If there's anything the RBN has proved adept at, it's hiding money. That's how they built their organization to begin with."

Brognola sighed. "Okay, so let's assume the money just came from the RBN. They financed Moscovich through school, and he, in turn, works for them in whatever scheme they've cooked up. So, what else do we know?"

"Well, Striker says that Haglemann most definitely talked like Moscovich is heading up whatever the RBN has planned. He's convinced Moscovich is operating on another island, and his people have somehow managed to conceal their activities. He's also convinced the RBN is getting some support from Russian military."

"Not good," Brognola replied. "How did we come about that tidbit?"

"Reports on Russian military asset movements," Kurtzman said. "Somehow, a Russian submarine was on maneuvers in the present area of concern a few months back, but nobody thought anything of it, so the information got buried."

Brognola could feel his chronic condition coming on, so he whipped out a roll of antacids he kept in his shirt pocket, popped three and chewed furiously. Around the mouthful he said, "And why the hell did nobody think it was important?"

Kurtzman shrugged. "Who knows? Maybe because the sub was operating in international waters and didn't cross into US boundaries."

"The Aleutian Island chain represents the northernmost geographical point of US territories," Price pointed out. "We have no reason to patrol them with any sort of significant military force. The Coast Guard has always been able to handle the region with relative ease."

"And of course," Brognola finished, "the Russian government would utterly deny any complicity in activities that involved sabotage of US military vessels or planes."

"Naturally," Price said. "Acknowledging any such activities would be deemed as acts of war."

"It would appear we don't need the Russians to make any such official declaration," Brognola said. "The RBN seems to be doing just fine in this covert war they've decided to launch. What about the technology they've developed? Is it really possible they have the means to do what Striker proposed they have?"

"I think there's little doubt at this point," Kurtzman replied grimly. "But there's still some part of the picture we don't yet have, although I think the new information regarding Davis Haglemann is going to shed a whole lot of light on that situation."

"In what way?"

"In the case of flight 195B *and* the *Llewellyn*," Price said, "what the RBN accomplished in shutting down communications and computerized control could not have been done without some sort of device having been planted aboard those vessels."

"Both that plane and the cutter had been at Adak within the past few months," Kurtzman added. "And all of the operations at Nazan Bay are overseen by the union workers Haglemann represents. He's the head of the union and the sole intermediary with the corporations that employ those crews."

"So someone had to be present on the plane and ship in order for the Russians to succeed in what they were doing?" Brognola asked.

"Precisely," Price said. "Striker thinks that's proof enough Haglemann's behind the RBN gaining access, and he's also complicit in these acts of terror. I agree with him."

"As do I," Brognola said with a sigh. "Which also means I'm going to have to inform the Oval Office. The President isn't going to like to hear that a prominent American businessman is in cahoots with Russian terrorists, and that an American service member might be involved. And he won't be pleased to know that we have considerable evidence the RBN now has Russian military support."

"He may not like it, but he can hardly be surprised," Price said. "The Russian president and his advisers have been trying to push our buttons for years. This seems exactly like a way to do it without having his name directly involved."

"Agreed," Brognola said. "So, have we found anything that could help Striker locate where the Russians are hiding?"

"Since we don't have any physical evidence, like wreckage or a location for the *Llewellyn*, it's been very difficult to collect that kind of information," Kurtzman said. "Neither satellite nor infrared imaging has been of help since there's so much volcanic activity in the area. Moreover, much of the Aleutian Island chain is uninhabited."

"I'm afraid Striker's pretty much on his own with this one," Price said. "If we come across anything, we'll of course feed it to him immediately. Right now, he's got his hands full playing a role, and he'll just have to come by his information the old-fashioned way."

Brognola nodded. "He's been there before. Do we have anything at all we can send that will help him?"

"Well, the information we've collected on Vladimir Moscovich should help point him in the right direction," Price said. "And we're forwarding everything we know about Haglemann, including his contacts, business interests, assets, the works."

Brognola nodded. "When I report this to the Man, I'll request an executive order to freeze all of his accounts and business dealings. That will at least ensure no further outside contamination."

Price smiled. "And maybe put him into the spirit of being much more cooperative?"

"Can't hurt."

"The information on Moscovich should definitely help, too," Kurtzman added. "Rumblings from CIA and other sources have actually indicated Moscovich has some personal involvement in this."

"In what way?" Brognola inquired.

"The RBN was none too happy after Striker broke up their little plan to wreck the financial industry a few years ago. Moscovich's movements and activities for the past year are strong indicators this endeavor has been his primary focus."

"Then four months ago, Moscovich dropped off the radar," Price added. "An NSA agent lost him in St. Petersburg, and they haven't seen or heard from him since."

"Funny," Brognola said. "There are very few people who could get out of Russia in such a covert fashion."

"That was our assessment, as well. Bear and I are convinced Moscovich could only have pulled off something like that with the support of the government. Or at least high rankers inside the Kremlin. Insiders tell us that after what happened to Yuri Godunov and his associates, the very top echelon inside the RBN became very interested in finding out who toppled their plans."

"Do they know it was Striker?" Brognola asked, concern in his voice.

"Probably not," Kurtzman replied. "You know that we take great pains to keep his identity under wraps. But there are others tied to this indirectly who could expose him and his position."

"For example?"

Price sighed before replying, "FBI Special Agent Marquez, for one."

Brognola nodded as the name brought back a few memories. At the time she'd first Bolan, Marquez had been an NYPD detective first grade with the Organized Crime Unit. As a result of her assisting Bolan, or maybe more like as a consequence, she'd been recruited to a position of special agent within the RICO task force of a New York field office. Later, she'd transferred out West—Brognola couldn't recall where exactly—where she continued serving to this day with complete distinction. During all that time, she'd never revealed much of what she knew about Bolan. "Do we have reason to believe she's a potential target?"

"There's been no evidence of that so far," Price said. "She's currently assigned to the FBI headquarters in Denver. As near as we can tell, the RBN doesn't know of her involvement, or potentially even of her whereabouts."

"Which makes her an unlikely target, then," Brognola said. "But I'm glad to see you're covering all the bases."

Price nodded. "Striker had us dig into Moscovich's background because he thinks it will help him draw him out, make him show his hand before he's ready. The more he knows about Moscovich, the better he can protect his role with Haglemann."

"But I thought he already had Haglemann's number?"

"He does. The only problem is, Haglemann has influences far and wide. He may have already discussed the RBN's goals here with Moscovich. Or the Russians might still be keeping Haglemann totally in the dark on their true purpose."

"We don't even know what it is," Brognola interjected with a tired swipe at his eyes. "And there's no reason to think Haglemann's people aren't in the same boat when it comes to Haglemann."

"That was Striker's thought, too."

"Okay, I think I have enough to give the Man. I know it goes without saying, but proceed with forwarding to Striker everything you have on Haglemann and Moscovich. I completely trust his judgment on how to handle it from there."

"What about Marquez?"

"Put our local people on alert to keep an eye on her. But tell them to use caution and not get too close. Marquez isn't stupid. She'll spot a surveillance operation quicker than you can snap your fingers."

"Understood. We'll keep a respectful distance."

CHAPTER ELEVEN

Adak Island

Mack Bolan was within view of the docks when Grimaldi sprang the surprise. The pilot's aim was incredibly accurate as he fired more than two dozen rounds from the M60A4 heavy machine gun. The bullet holes in the shiny new Hummer would paint a very convincing picture for Haglemann and help with the Executioner's credibility. Fortunately for Bolan, all those rounds hit either the backseat or rear fenders, and he grinned at the thought of Grimaldi working behind the machine gun with unbridled enthusiasm.

Bolan waited until he'd reached his planned stopping point before going EVA. He brought the FN-FNC to his shoulder and snapped off several short volleys of blanks before making a break in the direction of the plane. The vehicle that had been following him increased speed and came to a halt immediately behind his. Four men toting a variety of assault weapons emerged from it as Bolan rounded the corner of a large building that was the first of several clustered along the wharf.

Bolan withdrew the magazine of blanks and replaced it with a hot one loaded with the real deal. The soldier continued along the waterfront until he found a break in the buildings, then turned into an alley that doubled as a service road. He spotted what he'd hoped to find, a ladder that granted roof access—he'd remembered seeing it when he first arrived with Corsack. Bolan slung the FNC, jumped to grab the first rung of the ladder and then effortlessly scaled the twenty-foot height.

Bolan made the rooftop. He could hear Grimaldi exchanging fire with the four enemy gunners, but he had to be careful in his ascent due to the roof's steep angle. Eventually he reached the peak, and as he'd hoped, it granted him a perfect view of the scene on the road but kept him distant enough the enemy wouldn't be able to make him out with the naked eye. He sighted the assault rifle on their position, then adjusted the angle slightly for drop and windage. With the skill that came from years of experience, Bolan stroked the trigger. The bullet left his weapon at a muzzle velocity just short of 3,200 feet per second and reached its target in a heartbeat. The gunner's head exploded under the impact and showered the man near him with blood and gray matter.

Bolan acquired the second target, took a deep breath, then let half out before squeezing off his shot. The round struck the man in the forehead, cracking bone and driving him back a step before his corpse hit the pavement.

The Executioner lifted his head from the stock of the FNC and watched with grim satisfaction as Grimaldi dispatched the other two gunners. One fell under a volley of 7.62 mm rounds that nearly gutted the guy and tore his intestines to bloody shreds. The second caught two rounds in the chest and a third had his shoulder nearly severed from his torso. The man staggered a moment or two, apparently struggling vainly to take in air since the rounds had perforated his lungs.

Bolan sighted in and triggered a mercy round.

He moved backward on his knees and elbows to descend the roof, a sort of half scurry and half slide, until he got a foothold on the top rungs of the ladder. He quickly made his way to ground level, whipped out his cell phone and contacted Grimaldi.

"Nice work," he said. "Put on the finishing touches, and I'll meet you at the plane."

Grimaldi acknowledged Bolan's orders, and less than a minute later as the Executioner trotted along the waterfront in the direction of the plane parked at the makeshift airfield, he heard the explosions from Grimaldi launching a pair of 40 mm HE grenades at the Hummer and the enemy's sedan. Secondary explosions resounded, and Bolan noted how eerie the docks were. Nobody was working, no activity, and Bolan wondered at first but then remembered that it was a Sunday, and everybody was off.

It was just as well, since he would have preferred this particular action to go unobserved. It also kept the bystanders out of the way. He checked his watch and realized the numbers were running down. He'd have to locate the people Haglemann and his RBN allies had on Unalaska, neutralize their operations and get back to Adak in the next twelve hours. It wouldn't do to leave the mess behind and disappear, although the cleanup activity would keep Haglemann's people busy long enough. With luck, by the time they realized Bolan hadn't been in the Hummer when it was destroyed, he would be back on Adak Island and ready to carry out the final phase against Moscovich.

What troubled him most was that he didn't know the location of the Russians' base in the Aleutians. He couldn't believe for a moment they were operating here on Adak. The island was too small for them to have a secret base, and too open to discovery. He also didn't believe they had established a secret area on Unalaska for many of the same reasons. That left a whole chain of islands that were too vast and inhospitable to search randomly. It could take months or even years, even if he had access to military resources.

And that was the other bad part of the situation. American service personnel were missing, possibly killed or even taken prisoner, and their time would be running out. Not to mention the military was on high alert and investigators would soon be crawling through the entire island chain once they got a handle on what was going on. Bolan meant to see they never had to face it—the military needed to keep its focus on doing what it did best, and the Executioner planned to make sure they could do that.

Yeah. Mack Bolan was about to conduct a total war against the Russian Business Network. And in the next twenty-four hours, only one victor would emerge.

Unalaska

DEPUTY CHIEF BRENDA SHAFFERNIK had a problem on her hands. It had started as a small problem but quickly turned into a big one. The two officers she'd sent to keep an eye on Mike Blansky hadn't reported back, and all attempts to reach the pair had failed. So two officers were missing, Blansky was in the wind and Meltrieger was asking some uncomfortable questions. Not that she could blame him. The chief was on edge, the council was on edge—hell, everybody was on edge from the top brass to the officers on the street.

Shaffernik wondered if she'd fallen for a sucker play, letting Blansky convince her that he worked for the government. She dismissed the thought nearly as soon as it came into her mind. There was no doubt about Blansky's legitimacy. His cover was just too perfect to be anything but made up, and his timing of arrival could not be chalked up to mere coincidence. Shaffernik had managed to find the flight that had carried off the mysterious Blansky. The flight plan stated Anchorage as the destination, but no corresponding flight had ever arrived. Shaffernik didn't have near the clearance or clout to query any of the other dozens of airports scattered along the Aleutians. Not even the chief could have solicited that kind of cooperation, and particularly not in the current climate of mistrust.

At least the military had permitted air and ship travel to resume, but the entire area between Alaska and the Aleutians was replete with Coast Guard water and air patrols, and two combat wings on regular flyovers out of Joint Base Elmendorf-Richardson. Meanwhile, with the recent events in Unalaska, Meltrieger was asking her to enforce law and order while the place was crawling with antsy tourists, demanding government inspectors, agents from probably a half-dozen of the big-initial outfits, and workers who just wanted to do their jobs and be left alone to drink or sleep away their off-hours.

A cop's job was never done.

And then at that point when it seemed most overwhelming, her thoughts would go oddly back to Blansky, a handsome guy who was determined to do his duty.

If she was a normal gal, she'd flirt a little and see what happened. But she wasn't a normal gal and never would be. She was a cop through and through, just like her dad and *his* dad before him. After their parents had died, just within a few years of each other, Shaffernik's only other close relative, her sister, had met a wealthy rancher, moved with him to Wyoming and gotten married. She only heard from her a few times a year, and even then it seemed as if their conversations were superficial and distant. It was probably why she had thrown herself into her work with such earnestness.

A rap at her door brought her out of her reverie. She gestured for the knocker, her day sergeant, to enter. When he poked his head through the door she said, "What's up, Kabunuck?"

"Two men from the Defense Intelligence Agency are here, ma'am. They want to speak with you. They asked for Chief Meltrieger, but he's ind—"

Shaffernik nodded. "Yeah, yeah, I know. Send them in."

She rose to greet the men as they entered, eyeing them studiously. They were G-men, no doubt there, with the polyester suits, patent-leather shoes and stock can-do-no-wrong swaggers. Shaffernik shook their hands in turn and directed them to the pair of seats in front of her desk. Once Kabunuck had closed the door behind him, the taller of the two men spoke.

"Thanks for seeing us on such short notice," he said with a rather disarming grin.

Shaffernik just nodded and gestured for him to continue.

"We understand you're busy, so we'll get right to it. You've been informed of the military plane that went down early yesterday morning?"

"Of course," she said. "I've heard about little else since it happened. Military shut down all traffic on and off this island. It was very inconvenient."

"Sorry to hear that. I'm Special Agent Wexler and this is my partner, Special Agent Philbin. Unfortunately, I can't be too concerned about your troubles since the loss of American military personnel under these circumstances must take priority."

"I know," Shaffernik said. "And I'm not really meaning to sound like I'm beefing about it or to be disrespectful. I have great respect for our military, and I assure you I'm just as distressed by what's happened as I'm sure most everyone else is."

"Thanks."

"But we are rather busy right now, so if you could get to the purpose of your visit, I'd be obliged."

"Of course. We've been assigned to investigate any events here on Unalaska that may have occurred that you would deem unusual. This includes any reports that were filed, and any and all information on the party or parties involved. We'd also be appreciative if you could provide us with any of your opinions as to the nature of these incidents, and any arrests."

"And," Philbin interjected, "we'd like to know of any suspects you held or currently are holding, and to talk to those individuals on a case-by-case basis."

Shaffernik sat back and brushed a strand of hair out of her eye. "Well, now, that's a pretty tall order, isn't it? Most of that information will take some time to pull together, since it's been nothing but chaos here since the no-fly zone was instituted. Not to mention we got a whole lot of detainees I had to release on PR since our jail couldn't hold them."

"Is that common?"

"Lawlessness isn't normally common around here," Shaffernik said. "Although there was recently a Marine battle cruiser parked off our shores, gentlemen. You have to admit that's not exactly normal, either. Those kinds of things tend to make people nervous. And when a bunch of laborers from an Alaska native regional corporation start feeling nervous, they tend to get into trouble they wouldn't normally get into. So, yeah, there's been a bit of a change in climate here, and I've had my hands full."

"What kind of trouble?" Wexler asked.

"Several brawls down at the docks, for starters."

"In the bars?"

Shaffernik nodded and replied matter-of-factly, "Some. But we've also had one in the workplace. Like I said before, people are nervous."

"There's no reason for anybody to worry if they aren't guilty of anything," Wexler said.

"People get nervous around the police these days, gentlemen," Shaffernik pointed out. "Or haven't you been reading the newspapers?"

"Well, I—"

"Look," Shaffernik cut in, "I don't mean to sound uncooperative, but I don't have the resources presently available to pull off policing duties and assist you. You can utilize anyone Sergeant Kabunuck can spare, but that's about the best I can do."

"We understand this isn't the best timing," Philbin said.

"Any cooperation would be greatly appreciated," Wexler added. "There is just one other item we'd like to discuss."

"What's that?" Shaffernik asked, leaning back in her chair.

"It's our understanding that some sort of shooting took place in Unalaska yesterday."

Shaffernik chewed at her lower lip as she stared at Wexler, knowing her hesitation in reply already gave it away. How had he learned about *that* already? The details hadn't been leaked to anyone in the press, and as far as she was aware, Meltrieger hadn't communicated it because he really didn't know anything. And he didn't know much about it because Shaffernik had advised they were still looking into it.

"There was an incident involving firearms that took place yesterday, correct," she finally said. "It's still under investigation."

"What happened?"

"The details are muddy," she said.

"Could you summarize?"

"As I said, it's still under investigation. I don't want to speculate until I have the facts."

Wexler smiled and shifted in his seat, visibly trying to hold himself in check to prevent an uncomfortable situation. Despite the fact they were within their jurisdiction to make these inquiries, it never helped federal agents to alienate local law enforcement. "Could you at least give us a summary of the incident?"

Shaffernik sighed and then folded her arms. "Several men in a truck were reported shooting what appeared to be automatic weapons into the air. We immediately dispatched deputies to the scene, and upon attempting to apprehend the suspects, a gun battle ensued. My deputies were forced to defend themselves and ended up shooting several suspects."

"And where does the case currently stand?"

"I have a bunch of dead men slabbed at the coroner's office, and we're attempting to identify them right now. We're also trying to piece together what happened, how they managed to smuggle weapons on to Unalaska, and why they chose to fire on my officers."

"Is that it?"

"We also made an arrest, but that individual was subsequently released."

"Why?" Wexler interjected.

"Turns out he was an innocent bystander," she replied with a shrug. "He had nothing to do with those men. He just happened to be in the area at the time of the incident."

"And so you released him?" When she nodded, Philbin pulled a photograph from his pocket and handed it to her across her desk. "Is this the man you arrested?"

The photo was a somewhat blurred image that appeared to have been taken from a security camera. Shaffernik did her best not to show any emotion if it was a picture of Blansky. She half expected it to be, and she turned out to be right. She looked carefully for a moment, desperate to decide whether or not she should admit it was him. On one hand, if she lied and they caught her in it, she could lose her job and her badge. They'd also charge her with interfering in a federal investigation, and that could land her in prison. If she admitted it was him, however, what would happen to him and his cover? Would he go to jail? Would they try to apprehend him, or would they inform her he was actually a criminal and he'd neatly pulled the wool over her eyes?

Finally, she made her decision from something deep in her gut, some instinct.

As she returned the picture she replied, "I—"

There was a rap at the door. It opened a moment later, and Kabunuck poked his head inside. "Ma'am?"

"We're in the middle of something here, Sergeant Kabunuck," Shaffernik said.

"I know and I'm sorry, but we have a situation."

"What now?"

"Some kind of disturbance on the docks. There's at least a dozen men engaged in a gun battle, and the person who called it in states it sounds like automatic weapons fire."

"Send everybody we have!" Shaffernik said, jumping to her feet. She turned to the agents. "Sorry, gentlemen, but I'm afraid we'll have to cut this short. I'm needed."

"We'll come with you."

"I'd prefer you didn't," Shaffernik said as she buckled her gun belt.

Philbin's grin lacked any warmth. "We'd prefer we did."

"In the spirit of cooperation and all," Wexler added.

"Are you both armed?"

"Of course," Philbin said.

"Fine, come on. You can ride with me."

CHAPTER TWELVE

Grimaldi landed the rented seaplane at Unalaska's dock area, and Bolan was debarking when the trouble started.

Like the smaller wharf front at Unalaska, the docks were devoid of workers, so there were no bystanders in the immediate vicinity. It made for the perfect place to set up an ambush, and it seemed the enemy had decided to take advantage of the situation. This time, however, the gunners weren't locals armed with pop guns. These individuals showed up with full-sized assault rifles and apparently plenty of ammunition to spare, because they didn't hesitate to send sustained salvos of autofire in Bolan's direction.

Only by diving off the pier did Bolan manage to save his skin. Despite the midsummer weather, there was no such thing as warm water in that part of the world. Bolan's teeth instantly started to chatter as he gulped deep breaths of air to keep from passing out at the shock to his system. He immediately began to swim, powerful arms and legs propelling his body through the choppy water that lapped against the underside of the docks. Bolan spent several minutes in the water. It quickly started to sap his strength, but he would not allow his mind to succumb to the sleepiness. His conscious mind ebbed like an evening tide, threatening to overtake him with sweet darkness, and Bolan fought it with every fiber of his being.

Eventually, he reached a ladder along the side of the dock, used to access smaller boats, and hauled his body out of the water. His clothes and boots were waterlogged, and he knew the Beretta 93-R tucked beneath his left arm would be completely useless now that it was soaked. Firing a pistol that had been exposed to the elements in such a way was not only dangerous— it would most likely jam after he fired the first shot.

Fortunately, as Bolan risked a glance over the top of the dock, he saw that Jack Grimaldi had sprung to action and was laying down significant cover fire from an M16A3. Nestled beneath the fore-grips was a familiar cylindrical shape, and Grimaldi was using it with full effect. The first 40 mm HE grenade he triggered from the M203 landed squarely between two of the three vehicles that had been carrying the hit squad. It exploded in a fiery blast that took out a trio of gunners, blowing their appendages in every direction and consuming the effective range area with superheated gases in a dazzling, fireworks-style display of destruction.

Grimaldi ducked beneath the wing of the seaplane, slammed home a second grenade and came up just long enough to aim. He was poised to let it loose when several police vehicles rounded the far corner of the docks and sped toward the scene. Bolan waved him off, then ran for the cover of a stack of crate palettes nearby. The flimsy wood wouldn't necessarily protect him, but it would conceal him from his enemies, and it was difficult for them to hit what they couldn't see. As it was, the arrival of the cops had diverted their attention, and they no longer seemed concerned with killing Bolan.

Grimaldi saw the break, reached into the plane to grab the weapons satchel, then ran like hell to get to Bolan. He dropped behind the crates with his friend, setting the satchel between them and presenting the Executioner with a grin. "Cavalry to the rescue."

Bolan nodded his thanks as he withdrew an M4A1, this one a carbine, sighted over the top of the crates and began to trigger controlled bursts. Two of the enemy fell under the soldier's marksmanship before they realized if they stayed they'd be trapped in a cross fire. Grimaldi followed suit and managed to get one more man with a 3-round burst that included a head shot before the survivors piled into their vehicles and drove out of there in a big hurry.

A number of police vehicles that had closed the gap headed in pursuit, but two more stopped. Bolan ordered Grimaldi to stay hidden, confident the cops hadn't seen the pilot, and then left concealment and started running toward the stationary police vehicles. He'd held on to his rifle, but he had it pointed up and away from the police, the grip resting on his right shoulder and his left hand high in the air.

Two uniformed officers jumped from the sedan and drew on him. Bolan continued his approach but slowed and kept his hands in a neutral position. A second vehicle, an SUV, screeched to a halt behind the first. The driver who got out was an immediately familiar face, and one Bolan had hoped to be seeing again. She had her pistol out, but she didn't point it at him. The two men riding with her, however, were another story. Bolan pegged them immediately as federal agents, even as they drew pistols and sighted on him.

"Hold up!" Shaffernik said to them and the two

uniformed officers. "Everybody, stand down! He's a friendly!"

The officers immediately obeyed, but the two agents weren't quite so accommodating. One said, "Friendly? Until we know better, this guy is a suspected terrorist!"

Shaffernik shook her head. "I know him, and he's not a terrorist. The guys that just ran from here are the terrorists. Now, you're in my jurisdiction, and I'm telling you to put your guns down."

"We don't have time for this," Bolan told the two men. "If you won't trust me, then at least trust her."

The men exchanged glances and slowly nodded to each other in agreement.

As they lowered their pistols, Bolan took a few closer steps and said, "Nice to see you again."

"You, too, Blansky," she said with a smile.

"Any chance we can use your wheels?"

"Your chariot awaits," she replied. She shouted orders to the other two officers to follow her, then they piled into her SUV and left, Bolan riding shotgun, with the two Feds in back. Shaffernik got the current location of the chase underway and then headed in that direction. She mumbled something about knowing a shortcut and told her passengers to brace themselves.

"The ride's going to be bumpy," she said, turning suddenly off the hardtop on to a rutted path that barely passed for the definition of a trail.

"I thought you said you didn't know this guy," one agent said to Shaffernik.

"I never said that," she replied. "I was about to answer, then we were interrupted."

"So, then who the hell are you, mister?"

"The name's Mike Blansky," Bolan replied. "And I'm on your side, you can be sure of that."

"How do we know?"

"Because the crew that just tried to blow me away are Russian terrorists, most likely part of the Russian Business Network."

"What?" Philbin shouted. "Are you talking *the* Russian—?"

"Yeah. A full-blown mercenary team trained and financed by top RBN leaders in St. Petersburg."

Wexler said, "What kind of proof to do you have? Ouch!" He rubbed his head and yelled, "Dammit, lady, slow down a bit. So, Blansky, how do you know this is the RBN?"

"Because I've been up against them before, and I know how they operate."

"You think…" Philbin's breath caught in his throat. "Are you saying it's the RBN behind the crash of 195B?"

Bolan nodded as he watched the rough ride ahead of them. "And the disappearance of the *Llewellyn*, too. It's also possible that they've take the Coast Guard personnel prisoner."

"And what about the ship?"

"I don't think they sank it. It's too valuable. I believe it's hidden."

Wexler snorted. "Ridiculous! The military hasn't found one single bit of evidence to suggest anything of the sort happened. Not to mention the fact there's been no response from any of the normal signals we should be receiving from the vessel."

"Which is exactly the point," Bolan said, pausing to grab the hand bar on the A-frame as Shaffernik went over a particularly nasty bump. "My contacts have already determined beyond any doubt the RBN was able to disrupt all signals to and from the *Llewellyn*. And in order to do that they didn't act alone. One of the men we're chasing may well have the answer to our questions."

"If we can take one or more of them alive," Shaffernik interjected.

"Right. That's going to be the real trick. And if these are members of the RBN, they won't go quietly. Your officers could be headed into real trouble."

"I've already told them to proceed with caution."

"So, Blansky," Philbin said. "Exactly what agency did you say you were with?"

"I didn't," Bolan replied.

"What are you, then?" Philbin pressed. "DHS or something?"

Shaffernik exchanged amused glances with Bolan before she spoke on his behalf. "He's the 'or something.'"

They continued on the road in silence for the next few minutes until topping a rise. The road dropped off, but on the far side of the rise was an expansive, rolling slope that seemed downright smooth in comparison to their jaunt thus far. Shaffernik braked and reached under the seat to retrieve a pair of binoculars. She scanned the road that curved below and eventually stopped and handed the binoculars to Bolan and pointed to four vehicles moving along a gravel road.

"There they are. Everybody, hang on!"

Shaffernik stomped the accelerator, and the SUV leaped to life, bouncing and jouncing its way down the hill as it gained speed. At one point, Bolan saw a glint of metal on light, followed by a smattering of muzzle-flashes.

"Looks like they're not going to give up without a fight," Bolan observed. "Are your people well-armed, Shaffernik?"

"Not against automatic weapons. We keep shotguns in front-seat racks of some, and two sets of extra protective body armor in the rear of every squad. But nothing like they're using." She nodded toward Bolan's weapon. "*Or* you."

"Tell them to back off," Bolan said.

"What? Those men are some of the most capable—"

"It's not about capability," Bolan said. "It's about being able to fight fire with fire. I have the capacity to do what they can't."

"But the bystanders—"

"Are out of the way," Bolan said. "Now, please do as I say."

Shaffernik hesitated a moment, and Bolan thought he might have to get stronger with her, but then at the last moment she picked up her radio and gave the order for her men to back off the chase. By that time they'd closed on the vehicle, and the trio of police units that had been pursuing their quarry were no longer visible. Bolan reached to his belt and withdrew his cellular phone, one of the few things he carried that was waterproof. He'd had the phone enhanced by Hermann "Gadgets" Schwarz, Able Team's electronics wizard, giving him the ability to reach assistance even against the most unforgiving elements.

Bolan dialed a number that would cut directly into Grimaldi's communications. Fortunately, the pilot had had enough foresight to lease a helicopter from the airport at Unalaska and stash it in a terminal in case they needed it. He would have taken his pickup truck and headed directly to the terminal hangar and prepped the chopper on the off chance Bolan would call for help.

When Grimaldi answered, Bolan said, "Striker here. Were you able to get airborne?"

"Roger that," Grimaldi replied.

"What about the plane?"

"Fortunately, none of the shooting seems to have touched it. At least not that I can tell. Apparently they were too bent on getting to you that they didn't care much about your mode of transportation."

"Thank lady luck for small favors, eh?"

"Really. At least I can get us back to Adak without a problem. Would have been much different if they'd shot us up. I can't fly a plane with a bunch of holes in it."

"I'll stay connected. Come down on my signal and be ready. We have some vermin to hunt."

"Do you happen to be in a police SUV?"

"That's us."

"Already got you in sight. Stand by for pickup."

Bolan acknowledged with an affirmative before signing off. He had to admit operating on a land mass as small as Unalaska made things much easier when it came to flight operations. The entire island covered only a thousand square miles while the city shared the tip of Unalaska Island and all of Amaknak Island, to include Dutch Harbor. That made it very easy to get from one point to another in an extremely short period of time.

"Stop here," Bolan said.

Shaffernik brought the SUV to a screeching halt. "Now what?"

"I'm leaving," Bolan told her.

"On foot?" Wexler inquired from the backseat.

"I have a ride on the way."

Bolan turned to Shaffernik and asked, "Where does this road lead?"

"Uh, I'm sure it ends up at a cluster of abandoned port buildings on the edge of the bay. It's the only road in or out, if I don't miss my guess."

Bolan nodded. "That's probably where they've been hiding. Here's what I need you to do. Get your people together, as many as you can spare. Make sure they're armed, and get there with them as quick as you can."

"What are we looking for?"

"You should know it when you see it."

"Now, wait just a damn minute," Philbin said as Bolan climbed from the SUV.

The agent exited afterward and reached out to grab Bolan's shoulder. The soldier reached up and twisted Philbin's hand as he pivoted his body and executed a hip toss, slamming the agent to the cold, hard, dusty ground and knocking the wind from his lungs. Bolan twisted Philbin's arm before the agent could catch his breath and put one boot against the man's shoulder.

"First rule, don't touch," Bolan said. "Second, I'm here with the approval of some very influential sectors within the federal government. Sectors that operate well above your pay grade—" he nodded toward Wexler "—your partner's pay grade and even that of your superiors. Last, not a single one of you are equipped to handle roughly a dozen or more Russian terrorists armed with military-grade ordnance and explosives. I am. So let's have no more nonsense. Understand?"

Bolan then removed his boot and hauled the guy

to his feet in one yank before shoving Philbin toward the SUV.

Wexler had been so stunned by the swiftness of the incident he'd barely had time to react, and Shaffernik had just sat there and looked on with an expression of unbridled amusement.

The Executioner turned and ran toward a patch of open ground, cutting through the high grass as fast as his waterlogged boots would carry him. He reached the LZ just a moment before Grimaldi touched down and then proceeded to the chopper, where the pilot left his seat and quickly helped the soldier aboard.

"You okay?" he shouted over the rotor wash.

"Tired and cold!" Bolan said as he took the hand Grimaldi offered and hauled his bulky frame into the cramped fuselage. "But alive!"

Grimaldi nodded and then pointed toward a roll that Bolan immediately recognized as a clean black suit. He began to strip out of his soaked civilian clothing as Grimaldi made his way back to the cockpit. He toweled dry as quickly as possible, and by the time the pilot got the chopper off the ground, Bolan had mostly donned the heavy-duty, skintight black suit. He had no idea how many men he'd be going up against, but he wouldn't be effective if he collapsed due to hypothermia. Once he'd stuck his feet into a new pair of combat boots, he pushed forward to the cockpit. Bolan tapped Grimaldi and pointed toward the cluster of abandoned buildings along the bay, just as Shaffernik had described.

The pilot tossed a quick nod and salute, then Bolan went about getting rigged up for war. He first slid into a shoulder harness where a new Beretta 93-R was nestled in the holster. He then buckled on the military web belt that supported a holstered .44 Magnum Desert Eagle and spare magazines. Lastly, he reloaded the M4A1 carbine and pocketed a few Diehl DM51 grenades. A pair of smoker grenades also hung from the harness. He didn't know if the forces he encountered in his assault would number only those who had escaped at the wharf or if they'd have reinforcements awaiting him. The M4A1 would be perfect for this kind of job, although Bolan wouldn't have dismissed using the FNC out of hand. Unlike most modern arms, the M4A1 utilized the more familiar safe/semi-auto/full-auto configuration. Moreover, it had become a favorite of Special Forces and counterterrorism units because it packed the wallop of an M16 but had a compact profile with its Mark 18 CQBR—close quarters battle receiver— which made it perfect for doing the building-by-building sweep Bolan had in mind. The soldier respected it on those grounds alone.

One thing didn't make sense, and Bolan thought furiously, trying to find some justification. The RBN had operated out of this point with relative obscurity. Stony Man was convinced their operations had been months in the planning. Why now would they risk revealing themselves? Did they consider him that much of a threat, or was it something more ominous than that? Bolan had to wonder if the RBN was about to unleash some sort of master plan and they weren't taking any chances. Well, the Executioner had a remedy for that, and he was about to administer it.

"Get ready!" Grimaldi shouted after circling a couple of times to give Bolan a view at all angles.

They hadn't spotted any of the vehicles they'd been

chasing, but that meant next to nothing. Shaffernik had been clear that the road they'd used to escape led solely to this point, so the RBN terrorists had to be hiding there. It was the only thing that made sense and explained how they'd managed to work so long without being detected.

Grimaldi brought the chopper to hover just above a flat patch on the outskirts of the building cluster. Bolan waited until it steadied, then dropped the five or so feet to the ground, shoulder rolled and got to his feet. He made a flat run to the corner of the nearest building as the chopper pitched up and away.

CHAPTER THIRTEEN

Semisopochnoi Island

Louis Ducati had always considered himself an intelligent man, but at that moment he couldn't understand the motives of his captors.

Without asking any questions at all, they had proceeded to strip him to his briefs, tied him to a chair and submitted him to regular beatings. One of his teeth had cracked, and two more were loose. He couldn't feel the swelling in his lips, but whenever he tried to speak it sounded muffled to him. He could no longer see out of his left eye, swollen shut as it was, and whenever he breathed deeply, his ribs hurt from where they'd worked on his chest and sides.

Since they hadn't interrogated him in any way, Ducati chalked it up to punishment, a way of demonstrating to the disheartened crew that these people were in charge and it wouldn't do any good to resist them or ask for special favors. That's what worried Ducati most, the safety of his crew. He was still feeling inadequate for allowing them to take his ship. He should have resisted them, but when he'd seen how quickly they had neutralized the commando unit and security officers, he'd figured any attempts at armed resistance would have gotten them killed. Most of his people hadn't fired a weapon outside their basic training and subsequent requalification exercises, all of which took place on a controlled range.

And why was it so blasted hot? The cavern had felt like a furnace ever since they'd been brought here. Ducati could only assume they were near pockets of active lava. The Aleutians were filled, in fact, with regular volcanic activity—activity that had practically built the island chain. For their captors to have chosen such a hazardous environment didn't make a lot of sense.

The door slammed open, and Ducati barely had the strength to lift his head. He prepared himself mentally for another beating and squinted his one good eye to look into the eyes of the leader. Ducati thought for a fleeting moment that he saw what looked like compassion in the man's expression, but in the end he surmised it was a mixture of amused sympathy. After all, he'd probably been the one to order this treatment, so Ducati hardly had a reason to think the man would now have empathy for him.

Ducati jumped in spite of himself when the man barked some kind of orders in Russian he could not understand. Two more men appeared who had been obscured behind the big form of their leader. He prepared himself for more blows, but they never came. Instead, the men untied the leather straps and hauled him to his feet. They got under his arms and assisted him into a nearby chamber where they lifted his body and dumped him into a metal tub filled with very warm water.

One of them handed him a bar of soap and ordered him to clean up while another disappeared down what passed for a corridor. The network of underground caverns here was extensive—Ducati had to admit the

choice of his enemies to use such natural terrain was
no less than ingenious. From what Ducati had observed
since they'd brought him to his makeshift cell, they
were well equipped with plenty of supplies. He had
also observed some computers and other electronic
equipment, a setup very similar to the kind he'd once
seen in a mobile radar station in the Yukon, one that
was used by search-and-rescue teams.

Ducati figured there was little point in fighting the
small reprieve he'd gotten, so he cleaned his wounds
as gently as possible, the rehydrated blood leaving the
water muddy brown. After he'd finished washing, they
took him out of the tub and threw a towel at him. He
dried off as best he could, his every muscle screaming
in protest as he bent to try to dispel most of the water
from his legs. The guard threw his uniform at him and
gestured that he should get dressed. It took him more
than five agonizing minutes just to get on his pants and
shirt. Putting on the shoes and socks would be next to
impossible without assistance, but he didn't figure he'd
get that kind of attention.

The other man returned with a green plastic bag
that Ducati recognized as military rations. He took the
bag when offered, leaned against the edge of the metal
tub and reached in. He half expected to be bitten by
a snake or stung by a scorpion but instead found only
a few different foodstuffs wrapped in vacuum-sealed
packages. At least he didn't have to worry about them
trying to poison him. He was beginning to feel better, realizing that because they'd allowed him to clean
up and get into his uniform that for the moment they
weren't going to execute him.

They allowed him to eat, a painful experience at

best, before they took him back to the room where they'd tortured him. He was reluctant to sit in the chair that he could now make out had a bit of dried blood on it, convinced they were only fortifying him so they could inflict more punishment. Instead, they sat him roughly in the chair, but he noticed immediately they did not restrain him. He let out a sigh of relief that whistled through his broken nose. He couldn't remember the last time he'd been able to breathe through it with his mouth closed.

The leader stepped in and folded his arms. "Before we return you to your cell, I wish to explain to you the seriousness of your actions. You're alive only because I wish you to be alive. No other reason. My men and I are not barbarians, and we do not commit cold-blooded murder. But I thought you might like to know the man you asked mercy for is actually the one responsible for your undoing."

Ducati could hardly believe his ears. Was this guy actually talking about Gross?

"I don't believe you."

"Believe me or not," the Russian leader responded. "It makes no difference. We have extracted him from your group, so he will pose no more of a nuisance. As for you, we will return you to your crew now as an example of our resolve. No further pleas of mercy or complaints from you or your officers will be tolerated. If there are any further transgressions, I will cut off the head of your most junior crew member, and their blood will be on your hands. Do you understand?"

Painful as it was, Ducati nodded and resisted the urge to protest. He also decided not to inquire about Gross. To even think he would be responsible for the death of another crew member made him want to be sick. He couldn't be sure what this Russian pig had meant by Gross being responsible for their undoing. He was thoroughly convinced the terrorist would make good on his threat if Ducati pressed, so he erred on the side of keeping quiet.

After their exchange, the leader nodded at his two men, who got Ducati on his feet and assisted him back to his cell. Ducati could see the worried faces of his crew even as they shoved him roughly into the cage, but he immediately put up a hand and just nodded that he would live, and they should not speak at all about it. First thing he needed to do was rest, so he found a point at the very back of the cage and sat slowly on the ground, assisted by a few of his crew. The corpsman in the group did a quick assessment and whispered encouragement before turning him over to Rastogi.

"How are things, XO?" Ducati muttered, head leaned back and eyes closed. He was fighting nausea and didn't want to bring up the meal. He'd eaten too damn fast.

"Not good, sir. A lot of our people are starting to feel sick. I don't know if it's the lack of food or just heat exhaustion."

Ducati fought back another wave before rubbing his suddenly dry tongue against his lower lip, a painful act that sent a shudder through him. "What about Gross?"

"Oh, I don't know his status. A little while after they took you out of here, they came and got him."

"How long was I gone?"

"Six, maybe seven hours. Sir, what do they want with us? Do you know?"

Ducati shook his head slowly. "No, I just need to rest right now, XO. Can we talk about it later?"

"Yes, sir, of course. Rest…"

But Ducati had already succumbed to the sweet embrace of slumber.

"YORGI IS DEAD?" Vladimir Moscovich said.

Tokov nodded. "The word just came in."

"How?"

"Some sort of attack on the American's club."

"Haglemann?"

Tokov shrugged. "I guess. Whoever is running the island."

Moscovich cursed and slammed the side of his fist against a nearby cavern wall. "He probably entrusted it to the local one, Lustrum. He isn't worth a shit! Haglemann told me he had everything under control!"

"Well, it would not appear the bastard does. And we've now lost another good man."

"What about Alexei? Is he aware of this?"

"I have been unable to raise him."

Moscovich scowled. "Why didn't you tell me that before?"

"Because we only just recently heard about Yorgi, and when we attempted to contact Alexei we couldn't raise him."

"When was his next scheduled check-in?"

Tokov looked at his watch. "Right now. In fact, he's missed it."

"This isn't good."

"I agree," Tokov said. "And no disrespect, Vlad, but this thing is starting to get out of hand. We are going to have to accelerate our plans and get out of here."

"Were you able to contact the sub?"

"Yes. The captain has informed me, it will take them at least sixteen hours to arrive."

"Good," Moscovich said. "I think we can hold out that long."

"I'm not so sure."

"What do you mean?"

"There's no question the Americans are ramping up security along the major islands. There have been entirely too many delays in executing our plans, and if we wait any longer we risk complete failure in our mission. We cannot delay any longer, Vladimir! We must move now."

Moscovich didn't really want to admit it, but he knew Tokov spoke the truth. They'd spent too much time testing the system, and now they risked discovery. Such a thing would not only undermine the efforts of the Kremlin, but it put enmity between his people and the government. They couldn't afford to make enemies of the FSB, let alone the Russian military. If they called for extraction and the submarine arrived, and the US military detected them, not only would their plans be laid waste but it would endanger their sole source of naval support. His master wouldn't be happy, and neither would those sitting on the power base in Moscow and St. Petersburg.

Moscovich looked Tokov in the eyes and rested a hand on his friend's shoulder. "That's what I love about you, comrade. You're not afraid to tell me the truth no matter how unpleasant it might be. Very well, let's prime the devices and get ready to pack up. By this time day after tomorrow, we will be well on our way to the United States. And then we shall have our revenge.

"In the meantime, I want you to keep trying to raise

Alexei. We have to tell him it's time for the team to leave Unalaska and get back here."

"What about the rumors of the American there?"

"From what you've told me, it sounds as if he's no longer on the main island. He's probably managed to get to Adak. That's most likely who hit Haglemann. This individual must now become a secondary consideration. We can no longer risk waiting on them to locate him."

"And what if it is...*him*?"

"Then I will deal with him personally," Moscovich said. "For now, you have stated your case and well. So let's proceed under the assumption the original plan remains in place."

Moscovich wheeled and marched out of the makeshift operations center, a cold feeling in the pit of his stomach. Alexei Vizhgail was as reliable a soldier as Moscovich had ever served with. If he'd missed his check-in, that didn't bode well for his mission or his men. Moscovich had opted to send Vizhgail to Unalaska with more than half their force to see if they could neutralize the threat from whatever American agencies had placed the individual or individuals responsible for eliminating the first team of locals from Haglemann's private force.

Granted, the local authorities on the island didn't have a clue what was happening, since the American military intelligence agencies had essentially instigated an information blackout. If they had been smart, they might have had more success locating Moscovich and his men had they solicited local cooperation. The fact they would choose to shut down all but the most essential operations and route all traffic in and around the Aleutian Islands through a central checkpoint was precisely the reaction Moscovich had said it would be.

This entire plan had been his brainchild, something only the highest officials within the Network and government had known. The Americans had much bureaucracy, but they weren't entirely impotent, as their success in bringing down Yuri Godunov and his attempt to create a financial empire within the American banking system had proven. But that didn't change the fact they still followed protocols whenever an incident was declared an act of terror. Those protocols were what Moscovich had determined on his own, with very careful study, could be used against them.

But as he'd been told by Bea Nasenko, the heir-apparent to the Nasenko holdings within the Network: "The mission must take priority to any personal aspirations of vengeance, Vladimir. We cannot afford mixing business with our passions. Take heart in this that there will be plenty of time to exact retribution."

What had not stood out to Nasenko or her associates was that Moscovich couldn't think of any better vengeance than this. By demonstrating their ability to disrupt military communications, they had struck a blow at the very heart of American might. No longer would they be victims to the whims of a corrupt, power-hungry government that thought itself inviolate. Moscovich cared nothing for Nasenko's philosophy or the Russian president's personal ambitions. Everyone had ambitions in the elite of Russian society. Even Moscovich had ambitions. Ambitions weren't enough. There had to be more, and Moscovich intended to prove through this mission that superior tactical thinking could achieve a multitude of goals.

Moscovich entered an adjoining cavern to the one where they'd kept Ducati. Seated there sipping a sweating bottle of ice-cold Baltika No. 3 was Petty Officer First Class Gross. Moscovich thought him little more than a cretin, his belly and bank account full as a reward for his treachery. Any man who would sell out his own country was dog shit in Moscovich's best estimation, but a necessary evil in this line of business. Gross had been the one to secretly obtain and plant the device aboard the USCG cutter that allowed them to cut communications—a great find, indeed, given his access to a large working part of the vessel.

"I trust you're comfortable."

"Yeah, I guess," Gross said, sitting up a little in a halfhearted attempt to show some deference.

What a weasel, Moscovich thought, but he said, "I've returned your commander to his cell."

"He's not my commander," Gross replied. "I never really liked that guy. Kind of a pain in the ass. You know what I mean?"

"No, I don't."

"Well…" Gross seemed to think better of it and just waved the subject away. "It doesn't matter much now. I heard your boys gave him a good smackdown. Frankly, he's had that kind of beating coming. I'm surprised somebody hasn't already done it."

"If you thought him so deserving, why didn't *you* do it?" Moscovich asked, tempting his unwanted guest.

"Are you kidding? And wind up in the brig? No, thanks, man. I don't need that kind of trouble. Speaking of which, what's the deal here? Are you going to arrange some way for me to get out of here? I sure as hell don't want to be anywhere nearby when you guys do your thing."

"It's being taken care of," Moscovich said. "We keep our word. When we make a deal, we consider that sacrosanct, and I strongly advise you do the same."

"It doesn't matter one way or the other to me what you do. I just need you to get me as far as Anchorage. I can take it from there."

Moscovich fought the urge to pull his pistol and shoot that smug, obnoxious look right off the American's face. He knew traitors were a necessary evil, but he didn't like working with them. If they would turn on their own country, how could they be trusted? It was one of the greatest enigmas for a man with his sensibilities. Sure, Moscovich was a hardened soldier and freedom fighter, but he was also educated. He was comfortable with tactics and planning, and he'd found that approach suited him since he nearly always got better results, and his work had a desired outcome. In many regards, it was why the Nasenko family had sent him to see this plan through.

If he could make it come together—if he could get his men to pull it off and work together to achieve their goals—the RBN would be restored to its former glory, and Moscovich would rise to a level equal to or even surpassing those in St. Petersburg. He might even be put in charge of all operations in the West. So for now, he would put up with Gross.

"You need not worry," Moscovich said. "You'll be on your way soon."

Yes, he thought. Very soon.

CHAPTER FOURTEEN

Unalaska

Even as Grimaldi lifted the chopper up and away from the scene, enemy combatants seemed to come out of the woodwork like termites. A trio of terrorists armed to the teeth began to shoot at the chopper, apparently oblivious to the fact that one of their opponents already had boots on the ground. The Executioner was like the black wraith of Death, a frightening specter adorned with multiple tools of war.

Bolan knelt, using the corner of the building as cover, raised the M4A1 and fast-sighted down the rails. He flipped the fire selector to full-auto burn and squeezed off a series of two short volleys. The first caught the lead terrorist full in the chest and drove him to the ground as the 5.56 mm rounds pummeled his vital heart and lung tissue. The man's body twitched only a moment before his nervous system succumbed to death. The second volley went high. The soldier immediately adjusted his aim, holding low, and triggered a third burst that cut the legs out from under his target. High-velocity slugs shattered bone and tore flesh. The initial skirmish had reduced the team to one, and that man was now occupied with dragging his screaming, bleeding comrade off the battlefield as quickly as possible.

Bolan let him tend to his teammate, unwilling to shoot a guy in the back who at least had the decency to help a friend rather than run away or ignore his plight in favor of trying to kill an enemy that had just bested him in pretty narrow odds. The Executioner kept one eye on the retreaters even as he broke cover and ran for the next adjacent building.

Given a choice, the Executioner wouldn't have done a search of this nature, but he knew the enemy had obviously decided to make their stand here. Bolan also had to consider the timing factor. He didn't know how long it would take Shaffernik to get her people together and get to this site, but he didn't think it would take long. She was a competent police officer, and for the most part her people seemed equal to the task set before them. Bolan didn't want cops to fall if it could be helped. At least the fact there were no bystanders to worry about was one small grace he could appreciate.

Bolan pushed on.

"THIS IS INSANE!" Wexler announced. "We should call the military."

"There's no time for the military to mobilize," Shaffernik said. "And anyway, I've already advised our support staff to notify them that there are possible terrorists at that location."

"And you're trusting the word of this Blansky on it?" Philbin said, rubbing his shoulder self-consciously.

"I am."

They were in the armory at police headquarters. The two men were watching as Shaffernik geared up for their operation at the abandoned buildings. Already, police units were mobilizing. Shaffernik had contacted

Meltrieger and requested permission to deploy and call up the reserves. Meltrieger had balked, until Shaffernik explained the sudden arrival of the military investigators and the probable relationship between the terrorists and the disappearance of the Coast Guard cutter. At hearing that, he immediately granted her carte blanche to put the ball in play and promised whatever support and resources she would need.

Meltrieger was a stickler for procedure, but he wasn't a politician. He hated red tape, and that was exactly the reason Shaffernik had come to work for him as his deputy chief.

"I ought to have that asshole brought up on charges," Philbin mumbled.

"You grabbed him," Shaffernik countered as she secured her flak vest. "If it had been me, I probably would have done the same thing. And you guys may be federal officers, but we're responsible for policing and the safety of all citizens here in Unalaska. If you want to try superseding that, you better get a court order. Now, you're welcome to come along with my team, but I have my orders, and I'm going to follow them. So decide now what you're going to do."

Wexler and Philbin looked at each other, but each knew that Shaffernik had a point. She was in charge by authority and necessity granted under the law, and it wasn't their place to attempt to override that. For now, the best they could do was to cooperate and hope to hell this tough cop knew what she was doing.

"Fine," Wexler finally said after a nod from Philbin. He attempted to look as contrite as possible. "We'll do it your way."

"Good," she replied. "See my tactical guy over there,

and he'll get you fitted for some body armor. Unless you have equipment of your own."

"We do," Philbin said. "It's out in the car. I'll go get it."

When Philbin had departed, Wexler decided to take the opportunity to ask some questions. "So how did you really run into this Blansky guy?"

"He showed up and told me about his investigation into the disappearance of flight 195B and the *Llewellyn*."

"So when he came to you he had firsthand knowledge of those events."

"He seemed to."

"And you didn't check him out?"

"Of course I checked him out. And everything I heard and saw led me to conclude he was on the up-and-up."

"Do you believe his story about the Russian Business Network being behind all of this?"

Shaffernik stopped the checks on her equipment and sighed. What the hell did Wexler want, and why was he probing her so hard? She knew one thing for certain. If she showed doubt or expressed any sort of hesitation, guys like Wexler and Philbin would use that to make her start second-guessing everything. That would, in turn, make her seem indecisive, and they could use that against her. Not to mention it would undermine whatever Blansky was attempting to accomplish here, and Shaffernik happened to believe the guy was who he said he was.

"I don't know anything about the Russian Business Network," she said. "Not really. All I know is that so far Blansky has been right. And I also know he cares about people, and he's looking out for the best interests of our country. So that's good enough for me. Frankly, I think it ought to be good enough for anybody who has the same goals as he does for an outcome that doesn't involve any more missing or dead service members."

"But he's suggesting that a member of the US Coast Guard is a traitor!"

"I never heard him suggest that," she said. "All I heard him say was that *somebody* had to be working on the inside in order for the Russians to hijack something as large and secure as a Coast Guard cutter, not to mention neutralize a crew of approximately ninety service personnel plus a full security team aboard."

"Yes, okay, fine. Maybe you got a point there." Wexler scratched the back of his neck contemplatively. "But what about this story that there's a businessman, a sympathizer with the RBN?"

"I don't know about that," Shaffernik said. "What I *do* know is I wouldn't put it past them. The guy in charge on Adak Island is a man named Davis Haglemann. He's a union boss, with big-time business interests and very well favored among the corporate interests. Here in Alaska, things aren't as cut and dried as they are other places.

"People here don't make as much money, and a good many of the native people are living at or below poverty level. Haglemann's made their lives better, as I hear it, and that's going to buy the dude some loyalty. *But* I also know that people here tend to be fiercely patriotic. They don't want their home exploited any more than we do, and it's just possible Haglemann's been pulling the wool over their eyes, because it will gain him something."

"Well, I guess we'll find out soon enough if your faith in this Blansky guy is well-founded."

"I guess we will," Shaffernik replied. "Suit up as soon as your partner gets back. We're leaving in five minutes, with or without you."

THE FIRST BUILDING Mack Bolan entered smelled of dust and disuse, with an interior as black as night. That was fine with him, since he wanted to move without being seen and clear each location as fast as possible. The soldier advanced through the almost labyrinthine halls of the massive structure that seemed to be a combination of warehouse space and offices. The night-vision device aided him greatly as he swept along the darkened corridors with the M4A1 held at the ready.

Bolan was about halfway through the second building when he encountered the enemy. They had set up a site in an open floor area that looked as if it had at one time been some type of cafeteria. From his vantage point on a second-floor landing that overlooked the zone, the Executioner counted four armed men crouched behind various objects of cover. He could see the gray-green halo generated by each individual and realized just in time that those men were wearing NVDs, as well.

Another heartbeat passed, and between the two moments he saw movement. They had spotted him despite his attempts to be stealthy, and only by going prone did he avoid the plethora of hot lead burning the air just above his head. Bolan crawled backward out of the fire zone as fast as possible, then rolled to one side and unclipped a Diehl DM51 grenade from his web belt. Bolan yanked the pin and tossed the grenade over the railing. At a three count he got to his feet and sprinted down the corridor in the opposite direction.

He'd reached the steps just as the grenade went, descending them two at a time. The debris still rained on the room as Bolan pushed into the area and searched for his targets. He got the first one before the man, who had obviously been disoriented by the unexpected blast of the grenade, could get his bearings. Bolan's 3-round burst hit the man full in the skull, shattering his night-vision goggles and causing his head to explode in an eerie spray.

Bolan swung his sights on to a second target and triggered two short bursts that slammed into the terrorist's chest, driving him into a long, stainless steel serving counter. The man toppled to the floor in a noisy clank of metal on metal.

As the pops died from the suppressor on his weapon, Bolan heard the shuffle of feet. He turned and knelt. The air where he'd been standing a moment before came alive with a full-auto burst. He tracked his weapon on to a point just below the muzzle-flashes. The weapons used by his enemy had flash suppressors but apparently they weren't the style designed for CQB, and they pinpointed location with deadly accuracy when aided by NVDs. The soldier triggered a sustained burst. The enemy gun ceased firing, and the body of the gunner crumpled to the floor a moment later.

Bolan held his position and tracked the area in front of him. He then swept to his left flank and right, looking for the fourth target, but no threat emerged. After a full two minutes of waiting, the Executioner slowly rose from position and began to search the area. Eventually, he found the fourth man who had apparently taken a large part of the grenade blast, because his stomach looked as if it had been torn open. The soldier moved on, pulling the NVDs from his face just before he emerged into the daylight of Unalaska. There were still a number of buildings to search, although he was confident he'd done a good job of chipping away at the RBN forces in this location. A dozen or so had first assaulted them at the docks, and Bolan was aware he'd neutralized nearly all of that force. An entire army could have been hidden here, but he doubted the Russian terrorists had that kind of manpower. After all, there was evidence to support the theory a Russian sub had smuggled them into the region, and that would have severely limited their numbers.

No, they'd have just enough to get the job done. Whatever else the RBN had planned, it wouldn't involve a big group. If Vladimir Moscovich was in charge of this little shindig, and Bolan had little reason to doubt otherwise at this point, Moscovich fit the profile of a guy who would martyr himself for the cause no matter what sort of lunacy that might seem. In any case, Shaffernik would soon arrive with reinforcements, and Bolan knew he still had targets to locate.

Yeah, the numbers were running down, and the Executioner planned to make sure it was a doomsday countdown for his enemies.

ALEXEI VIZHGAIL FELT a cold lump in his throat as he looked at the worried expressions of what remained of his team. Five men. That's what he had to complete the operation. It wouldn't be enough, and so now he was left with the only option available. They would have to cut their losses and attempt an escape, right under the nose of the American dog who had proven himself a cunning and deadly opponent.

Vizhgail had never considered himself a man afraid to die, but that didn't make much difference at this point. If they hoped to escape with their lives intact and still provide enough of a distraction that Vlad Moscovich could complete his part of the operation, they would have to abandon their efforts with the cutter. So far they had stripped the vessel of a good number of pieces of vital equipment they would take with them and deliver to their own military intelligence people.

If we survive, Vizhgail thought.

"Take a look around," he told his men. "What you see is all that remains of our team. The rest are on Semisop and will hold things in place until the submarine comes to get them. Our communications equipment has also been destroyed, so I cannot raise Vlad or Benyamin. And soon our enemies will engage us."

Kirillov, one of Vizhgail's lieutenants who had a bad leg wound and had been dragged to safety, gasped, "There's only one man. Surely…that does not equate to being surrounded."

"Would that be the one man who managed to wound you and kill another of our men?" Vizhgail asked. "Or the same man who destroyed the club belonging to that dog, Haglemann? And need I remind you that the detachment I sent to ambush this American has neither returned nor reported in yet? We're *through*, men! We have nothing left to fight for and very little resources to fight with. Our action is a holding action, then, and our mission is to attempt to escape and rejoin the others."

"How will we do this, sir?" Anatoly Bruschev asked.

Vizhgail shook his head. "The rest of you are going to leave. I'll stay behind to distract the Americans. While they're occupied with my plan, you will use the motor launch we brought here to escape."

Bruschev started to open his mouth as if to protest but then shut it. Vizhgail couldn't help but sympathize, despite the fact he didn't really hold out hope for any of them to survive. He already considered his own life forfeit, and chances were the Americans had already begun a process of closing the noose. All they could do now was salvage the situation and implement survival rules.

"What about the ship?" Andrei Polakoff asked. "Should we sink it?"

Vizhgail shook his head. "We're out of time. And we don't have the ordnance to do so even if we had time. No, you have your instructions. Take the tech we salvaged off the cutter and head for the launch. And do it now—you'll need extra time with Kirillov injured. Bind his wound. He looks like he's about to bleed out."

The men looked hesitant but eventually broke away and prepared for their departure. Even as the darkness of the building swallowed them up, Alexei Vizhgail had already set about the task of preparing for his encounter with the American. If this was the man who had taken down the Godunov-Nasenko regime, Vizhgail would consider it an honor to die bringing him down once and for all.

CHAPTER FIFTEEN

Adak Island

"How does this happen?" Davis Haglemann demanded. "Can somebody tell me how the hell this happens?"

Otto Lustrum stood frozen in place and tried to keep his knees from shaking. Blast it all, but he didn't like this rich, entitled shit, anyway! He never really had. He didn't like the way Haglemann made him feel, and he didn't like the guy's business practices. When Haglemann had appointed Lustrum foreman over the entire labor force on Adak, the veteran dockworker had been indecently grateful. He'd built a thriving community of devoted workers and taken very little for himself. Oh, sure, so maybe he'd pinched a few bucks here and there in his gambling operation, but who the hell cared? Everybody got his or her entertainment, and he collected a cut of the action for providing it. He was a businessman just like Haglemann. It's not like the two were that much different.

"You were supposed to keep an eye on this guy!" Haglemann snapped. "Now he's probably dead, and that leaves my ass hanging out there in the wind. Well, frankly, I'm not looking to get my head blown off just because you're an idiot!"

"Davis, try to understand," Lustrum pleaded. "We

put some guys on Blansky just like you asked. How were we supposed to know the psychopath he was supposed to be protecting you from would take him out?"

"You shoulda known!" Haglemann slammed his beefy fist on his desk. "You shoulda *goddamn* well known it. Now I'm up shit creek without a paddle. Well, you be sure this fuck-up isn't going to go unnoticed, Otto. I've got to hire on extra security to watch my ass because you couldn't do this one simple thing."

"What I want to know is, what's the story with these guys you're doing business with? Why all the intrigue?"

"Intrigue? Jeez, Lustrum, have you lost your mind? This isn't the 1950s, you know. The cold war is over! I can do business with whomever I like! And anyway, that's none of your concern. You work for me."

"I work for the people!" Lustrum said. "My people, which are obviously not anybody you care about, Davis."

"You get the hell out of here, Otto! Get the hell *out*!" Haglemann pointed toward the door of his office. "You get out of here and don't ever let me see your face again, or it will be the last time. You understand?"

Lustrum started to open his mouth and then clamped down on his words at the last second. The five men who moved off station were very large and all armed. They were top-shelf protectors hired a long time ago as Haglemann's personal security force, and they were mean customers. Lustrum was getting on in years, and he doubted he could best even one of these men, let alone all five.

"That's fine, Davis. But understand *this*—we're through and double through. Whatever shit comes down from this, don't come crawling to me. You're on your own!"

"Get the fuck out of here!" Haglemann screamed with such apoplexy Lustrum thought the guy might throw a clot right there.

Lustrum left the house, jumped into the backseat of his limo and fumed all the way down the winding drive that led from Haglemann's estate. It would sure as hell be the last time he darkened the guy's door, of that much he was certain. It was also a given he'd be cut off from any additional money or resources. It was a good thing he'd managed to bank a large part of it in offshore securities. Lustrum had to wonder if it was time to leave Adak Island. He was tired, and the past forty-eight hours it seemed as if everything had gone to hell.

The other problem was this Mike Blansky. Lustrum wondered if the guy was more trouble than he was worth when Maddie Corsack had first introduced them—his gut had told him there was something off about the guy. Blansky had killed Rov, who Lustrum now suspected wasn't everything he appeared to be, either. That wasn't half as disturbing as Zakoff, the guy he'd assigned to work with the boys who oversaw club security. Whoever had taken them out was a professional, and Lustrum was beginning to wonder why there'd been so much trouble since Blansky had shown up on the island.

There was somebody who could shed light on that particular subject, and Lustrum had decided even as he left Haglemann's he wanted to talk to that someone. It was time to have a long heart-to-heart with Corsack and get to the bottom of this whole thing. Lustrum had already lost at least a dozen men, decent and hardworking men with wives and, in a few cases, even a kid or two. How was he supposed to explain that? Haglemann had originally promised the widows would be taken care of, but how did Lustrum know that? Especially now that he was on the outs with the labor boss. The idea of reconciliation was unlikely—Haglemann wasn't known to be a forgiving man.

But Lustrum still had a few cards up his sleeve. Besides, he didn't think anyone had broken the news about Blansky to Corsack. He'd thought about waiting since they hadn't yet confirmed Blansky was dead, given it would take some time to identify the bodies. All of them had been severely burned by the explosion. But they had found the charbroiled remains of several men around the two damaged vehicles, one of them the Hummer Blansky had borrowed from Haglemann. Chances were pretty good the mysterious Mike Blansky was dead.

Lustrum didn't know the exact nature of Corsack's relationship with the guy, but he was betting it was romantic. She might not take the news too well. Still, Blansky had saved Lustrum's life, and he at least owed the guy that much if nothing else. And once he'd gotten it straight in his mind, Otto Lustrum would decide his next move.

"DEAD?" CORSACK REPEATED in a choked whisper. "Are you sure?"

Otto Lustrum folded his hands and tried to look as contrite as possible. Corsack wasn't sure she bought it—hell, she wasn't much sure of anything anymore. It was possible this was just another trick. Things had transpired very quickly over the past twenty-four hours. It was possible Lustrum had discovered Blansky was behind the attack on the club, or maybe even Haglemann. Perhaps it was really Lustrum who'd murdered Blansky, and now he was just trying to cover his own ass. But to what ends? He didn't *need* Corsack's help or support, so he wouldn't benefit from lying to her.

None of it made sense. The pilot she knew only as Jack had left on very short notice, claiming to have been in direct contact with Blansky. He'd gone off in a hurry to help the big guy, in fact. Had he been too late? And if Blansky really *was* dead, as Lustrum was now telling her, what had happened to Jack? Why hadn't he returned to her? Had he been killed, as well?

No, it just didn't make any sense to Corsack at all.

"We don't have all the facts yet, but it doesn't look good," Lustrum said. "It's going to take the coroner a lot of time to identify the remains. There were four bodies on the scene. I'm sure at least a couple of those guys are our own people."

"Why?" Corsack asked. "Why would they have been our people, Otto?"

Lustrum shook his head. "I was just following Davis Haglemann's orders. He was the one who told me to keep my eye on Blansky."

"Did he suspect Mike of something wrong?"

"No, no. Nothing like that. Just the opposite, in fact. He told me Blansky was about the only guy he trusted. Said Blansky was some kind of friend to some of Mr. Haglemann's associates…or something like that. I don't know. The details are fuzzy! And as usual, Haglemann keeps me in the dark half the time!"

Lustrum sighed, and Corsack could see he was conflicted. She'd never believed he was guilty of all the horrible things for which Blansky accused him. She'd meant what she said about the people on Adak Island. They were generally good people who were struggling to make the best of a very difficult situation. Some had wondered why anybody would want to ever live in such a remote place, but after having spent so many years there, Corsack didn't wonder. All told, life was pretty simple on Adak, and when things were going right it was a good place to be.

Corsack came to her decision, took a deep breath to calm her nerves and charged in. "Blansky isn't who you think he is. Or maybe he *wasn't*... I don't know."

"What are you talking about?"

"I'm talking about Davis," Corsack said, fighting back the tears as the impact of what she'd heard about Blansky's potential demise set in. "You've chosen some pretty poor allies in your time, Otto."

"You mean in Haglemann?"

Corsack nodded, and now the tears started a steady fall down her cheeks. "Davis is a crook and a filthy traitor."

"Traitor to *what*?" Lustrum said, abruptly taken aback by Corsack's reaction. "What has he done?"

"He's a traitor to you and me and everybody here on Adak. It was Blansky who destroyed Haglemann's club, and it was Blansky who set up the ambush here. He had to do it!"

"Who is he?"

"Some kind of secret agent with the government? CIA, maybe, or Special Forces? I don't know for sure. But what I do know is he's one of the good guys," Corsack replied.

"And how do you know that?"

"Because since I met him the bad guys have been trying to kill him. Don't blame him, Otto, and please, forgive me for betraying you. I didn't want to believe it at first, but Blansky was able to show me proof Davis is working with these Russian terrorists or whatever they are."

The dawning light of realization began to spread across Lustrum's face, as if he'd always known. He'd been aware that everything wasn't on the level with Haglemann's business, but he'd turned a blind eye to that out of greed. Something definitely changed in his expression at that point, his posture becoming a bit stiffer and his lips tightening as he came to the conclusion that nothing was as it had appeared to him.

"Are you telling me it was Blansky who all this time has been killing these good men?"

"That's just the point, Otto. It isn't Blansky who killed them. Yeah, okay, sure, maybe he pulled the trigger, but he sure isn't the one who led them to do it. They killed themselves because of their own faulty decisions."

"That's bullshit, Maddie, and you know it!"

"Is it, Otto? Is it really all that hard to understand? You and so many of your friends, you sold out to Davis Haglemann a long time ago. You are the ones who decided to look the other way while he lied and cheated his way into being nominated the head of the union. How else could he have risen to power so quickly? You know as well as I do that nobody can do what Haglemann's done, or get as far as he's gotten, without the people of Adak Island backing them. You know that!"

"You took the money, too, Maddie," Lustrum grumbled.

Corsack nodded slowly and tried to swallow the bitter truth of his words. "Yes, I took his filthy money. And I'm so ashamed of it now. I'm ashamed to have taken one red cent from Davis Haglemann. But I was broken and scarred after my husband died. I deserved that money—I had it coming to me for the sacrifices I made. But if I could, Otto, if I could, I'd give back every dime now."

"I'm ashamed to admit it, but so would I," Lustrum said. He looked wistfully and unseeingly, just so he didn't have to meet Corsack's shaken gaze. "I'm a frustrated, tired, broken-down old man, Maddie girl. I've done a lot of really bad stuff in my life."

"You can find forgiveness," Corsack interjected. "You *can* make it right."

Lustrum snorted. "I don't want forgiveness. Forgiveness is completely subjective, Maddie. What I want is to kill Blansky, but that got taken away from me. So I guess I'll have to settle for killing Davis instead."

"And then what, Otto?" Corsack protested. "Are you going to run away and leave the rest of us here to pick up the pieces? Is that your answer? Commit cold-blooded murder and then just run away? Because if that's your plan, you'd best remember that you'll be running for the rest of your life. Is that what you want? Is that the kind of man you want to be? You can't keep running forever, Otto. Because sooner or later, it's going to catch up to you. You will catch up to yourself!"

Lustrum didn't meet her gaze at first. When he did finally look her in the eyes, his face appeared more gaunt and haggard than she'd ever recalled it before. He was truly rotting inside, having sold his soul to Haglemann—a man who sucked the life out of everybody he encountered and didn't care what it cost them—without giving thought to the consequences he would reap.

"So what do you want me to do then, Maddie?"

"Fight back," she said, grabbing his hand. "I want you to fight back. Blansky told me some of those Russian goons are holed up at Haglemann's house. I want you to gather your men and the cops."

"The police work for Davis!"

"They work for *us*," Corsack said. "They no more want to deal with the Russians than we do."

"Who are these Russians you keep on about?"

"I don't know." Corsack shook her head and chewed at her lower lip. "Blansky said they were some kind of a criminal terror group that called themselves the Russian Business Network."

Lustrum nodded thoughtfully. "I've heard of them. If what I've heard is true, they're nasty customers. But I don't understand why Davis would get chummy with scum like that."

"Because Davis doesn't care about anything but himself and how much money he can make. Damn it, Otto, we, above all others, should understand how greed can blind us to the truth, force us to do things we wouldn't normally do. That's what Blansky helped me to see. And I think you see it, too."

"All right," Lustrum said, rising. "I'll go the cops and explain what's happening. But I can't promise what they'll do."

"Just convince them. I know you can."

"Well, you just go on believing, Maddie girl," Lustrum said, patting the side of her tear-stained face. He offered her a warm grin and added, "That's enough for me."

Unalaska

ALEXEI VIZHGAIL PREPARED to bring death to the American who had killed so many of his men. Under normal circumstances, he might have preferred to shoot the man from a great distance, rather than risk a fight hand-to-hand, but in this case he would make an exception. There was a lot more to being a soldier than possessing a superior skill and intellect in tactics. He'd known this from the time he was old enough to start understanding the dealings of his organization.

While most of Vizhgail's friends had shown an interest in acquiring the skills to perform cyber-based attacks against their enemies or use technology to enrich themselves and their cause, Vizhgail had focused his attention on the more practical aspects. He viewed himself as a soldier and bound to a duty. The regular Russian army had rejected him, as had the navy, on the grounds of class. His family was within the upper ranks of the government, and the boot-lickers didn't care to risk something happening to him that would anger his family.

The Network had brought him what he most desired: to fight for a cause in which he believed and, yes, if necessary, die for that cause. But that wasn't his plan this day. What he intended to do now in this very moment was to kill the devil who had destroyed his plans and his men, and decimated the organization he loved most. He didn't care about saving his own life—Vizhgail had rid himself of the fear to die long ago.

The only thing he feared most was that he wouldn't be allowed to die with honor. Under *no* circumstances could he allow that to happen. So he waited quietly in an alcove for his lone enemy to arrive. The seconds seemed to tick by with agonizing slowness into minutes as large drops of sweat left lazy trails down the back of his neck and the small of his back. It was hot in all of the battle gear, so he'd shed most of it. He risked a glance at the luminous hands of his watch and guessed that his men had made the motor launch by now.

Vizhgail began to wonder if they were already making their way across the open water when he heard it. The slight shuffle of a foot against the floor. It was the only sound he heard, but it was enough. He knew the American had entered the building, and Vizhgail's body tensed. He steadied his breathing, thinking that the man would hear the thudding of his heart in his chest, even though he knew the thought was ridiculous.

Then a shadowy figure moved past the alcove, a weapon held high and at the ready. There was an odd shape to his head, and Vizhgail realized he was wearing a pair of night-vision goggles. Excellent. That would block his peripheral vision and give Vizhgail the upper hand.

He tensed his legs in preparation for attack.

CHAPTER SIXTEEN

Bolan heard the movement a second before he felt the muscled forearm snake its way around his neck. The attacker pressed the forearm against Bolan's windpipe and locked the hold with his other hand, settling the weight on the soles of his feet. It was executed perfectly, as perfectly as anybody would execute it who had been trained to do it a thousand times over. The problem was that it had obviously only been done in training with a willing opponent, and not implemented with success in a real-life scenario. Trainees who resisted such a hold were usually not fighting for their lives.

The Executioner was.

Bolan ripped off the NVDs and flung them away as he twisted his head to face the weak point of the rear-naked choke. He fired an elbow into his attacker's midsection and followed it by ramming the stock of his M4A1 on to the outside of the left leg just below the knee. The hold loosened, and Bolan sucked in a breath, trying not to gulp so he wouldn't pass out. The Executioner lost a little momentum in the delay, but it wasn't enough to give his opponent the upper hand. Bolan broke the hold and delivered an uppercut that only glanced off the man's face, missing the point of the jaw, but it was enough to put a little distance between them.

Bolan turned to face his enemy, sizing him up. They were relatively equal in height and weight. He couldn't tell how old the man was, but he surmised the guy had at least ten years on him. He was also fast and seemed fit; a prolonged fight wouldn't be the best strategy in that case. Bolan would need to put him down as quickly and effectively as possible. Unlike with Rov, this fight wasn't merely to prove brawn.

Survival was at stake.

Bolan delivered a front kick, going low for a knee, but the guy stepped into it and deflected with a heel block. He followed with a hammer-fist punch that connected on the soldier's cheek. It carried enough power to stagger Bolan and caused him to step back to maintain distance. The guy might not have been the most skilled when it came to grappling, but he wasn't exactly a novice in hand-to-hand, either. Bolan couldn't afford to underestimate this one on any count. What he had already learned was that this guy didn't followup when gaining the advantage, and he was stronger in the brawl than in ground or grappling techniques.

Bolan could use that.

The Executioner moved in close and fired a double-punch to the abdomen, a move that obviously took the guy off guard. So he wasn't used to close-in fighting, preferring to keep his enemies at arm's length. Bolan drove a palm strike into the side of his face as he inserted a leg between his opponent's two, and then used his hip to bump the guy off balance. As the man staggered and tipped sideways, Bolan fired a straight punch that caught the man on the jaw and knocked him flat to the ground.

The guy recovered with surprising swiftness. Bolan heard the rasp of a knife clearing its sheath as the guy recovered and came toward him. His eyes had begun to adjust, and he could see the outline of the knife's very large blade, a standard size for a combat weapon. The man swung toward Bolan's belly, and it whistled through the air as the soldier stepped just out of reach. The man swung again as the Executioner went for his own knife, and this time he caught the material of the black suit at midriff level. The sharp blade easily severed it, catching a bit of flesh in its passing.

Bolan ignored the burning in his gut as he brought a Ka-Bar combat knife into play. The enemy pressed his attack by attempting another slash followed by a jab, both of which Bolan evaded. The Executioner side-stepped the attempt and immediately slashed down and across, connecting with the inside fleshy part of his attacker's forearm. The maneuver caused the Russian to rethink his strategy, and he staggered backward, stumbling at the last moment over some unseen object. Bolan used the distraction to his advantage and charged the man, who turned to see his approach. He lost his balance again and only because he fell on to his back did Bolan's blade cease to find its mark.

The man scrambled to his feet, winded, and immediately began to slash violently at Bolan in an attempt to keep the Executioner moving. He wasn't having it. He could not allow the man, awkward as he might be, to dictate the direction of the fight, or it would be over as swiftly as it had begun with Bolan's blood spilled into the dust. Bolan waited patiently for an opening, and eventually he got it. As the man made a particularly close slash toward Bolan's side, the Executioner twisted to the side and moved in so the two were facing in the same direction while standing nearly parallel. Bolan drove the knife into the man's right side just below the point of the bottom rib and shoved upward with all his force. As the guy stepped back, shock on his face and air escaping from his punctured lung with a gruesome wheeze, Bolan shoved him away.

The man's expression transformed from shock, pain and fear to one that bore only hatred and defiance. He managed to produce a guttural curse in Russian, about the only sound he could make, given his injuries, and staggered forward. Bolan drew his Beretta, quick-aimed his pistol and squeezed the trigger. A single 9 mm Parabellum round cracked through the bridge of the terrorist's nose and continued into his brain pan, scrambling gray matter under the considerable force of its path. The man's body stiffened a moment and then collapsed to the floor.

Bolan took a minute to catch his breath, his chest heaving with the strain of combat. He'd been pushing himself through every minute, and his job was still far from done.

He holstered his pistol and set about inspecting the knife wound. It wasn't serious, barely more than a deep scratch. He retrieved a small bandage from his medical pouch, did a quick sterilization of the area with a pad containing a mixture of alcohol and Betadine, then dressed it with sterile strips to keep it together.

The sound of footfalls demanded his attention.

Bolan stooped to retrieve his M4A1 and knelt, muzzle held high and ready, but the sudden play of a dozen or better flashlights signaled these weren't his enemies. Shaffernik had finally arrived with the cavalry. She approached, and as she got near he could tell she had Wexler and Philbin in tow.

"It's about time," Bolan said. He lowered his weapon and rose.

"Hold your fire!" she told her men. "He's a friendly. Fan out and find the others."

Her men did immediately as instructed while Shaffernik appraised Bolan with a practiced eye. He noticed her gaze drop to his abdomen.

"I'll live."

Wexler and Philbin did a quick inspection before Wexler said, "What the hell happened here, Blansky?"

"The RBN was using these abandoned buildings to hide the *Llewellyn*. You'll find that it's probably concealed within the docking facilities two structures to the south of us."

"You think there are still suspects present?" Shaffernik asked.

"No, I took out most of their force. A couple of them might be around here. I'm sure that I wounded one of them."

"Great, so they're hiding out like the animals they are," Shaffernik replied. "I'd better alert my men."

"Most likely anyone who was still left alive is gone. I'm betting this one—" Bolan gestured toward the deceased terrorist "—stayed behind to cover their escape."

"What makes you think that?" Philbin asked with a sneer.

"Because he ambushed me alone," Bolan said, unaffected by Philbin's attitude. "Obvious stall tactic."

Shaffernik nodded. "Yeah, that's right. For all their other activities they've operated in small groups."

"Which is exactly why I think... Wait up."

Grimaldi's voice called him again, and when Bolan replied, the pilot said, "We've got runners, Striker. Looks like four, maybe five personnel, headed out on a powerboat across Dutch Harbor. Looks like they're making their way for open sea. You want me to pick you up?"

"Negative," Bolan said. "Keep eyes on them, Eagle. See where they go, but try to stay out of observation range."

"Easy-peasy, Striker. Eagle One, out."

Bolan could just now make out Shaffernik's face in the darkness lit ever so slightly by the open doors at either end, the Alaskan sunlight now permitted to invade the shadows. "Have you got a trained pilot available?"

"As a matter of fact, yeah." Her eyes twinkled. "Me."

Yeah, this lady was sure impressive.

IT TOOK THEM ten minutes to reach the dock where Grimaldi had left the seaplane, and another ten for Shaffernik to familiarize herself with the controls. Shortly, they were airborne and headed toward the transponder signal with coordinates Grimaldi had entered into his flight instrumentation.

Shaffernik had left her men in charge of cleanup. Wexler and Philbin were ecstatic, since they'd be able to take credit for finding the *Llewellyn*. Bolan was happy, as well. That would go a long way to improving relations. Even Philbin had ultimately agreed to shake hands and made it clear there were no hard feelings.

Now the task would be to track the Russians to

wherever they planned to go next. Bolan was certain he knew where they were headed—the only place they could get help. Adak Island had been their safe haven to this point. There was little question Haglemann would help them out if they asked him. After all, he had a business relationship to maintain with the RBN. They were going to make him filthy rich, and he was going to rule over his financial empire with an iron fist.

Men like Davis Haglemann had always infuriated the Executioner. Many had begun their careers with a desire to improve the lives of others while improving their own situation, but then something took over. Greed and avarice and want for more than they could ever possibly use seemed to consume them, devouring their internal and natural moral compass from the inside out. It had been the same with the Hydra monster of the Mafia, the organization against which Bolan had launched his War Everlasting.

Men like Haglemann built their fortunes on murder, theft, extortion and the sweat of hardworking people just looking to make their way. Nobody wanted to admit they needed a hand, so they chose to look the other way for a few bucks. Even someone like Maddie Corsack, a woman who had paid the ultimate price losing her husband to military service, had succumbed to Haglemann's manipulation on some level. The fact she'd used the money for good was irrelevant, for she *had* taken it, and she'd allowed Haglemann to manipulate her with it.

Well, Bolan had a message to send to Davis Haglemann, and the time drew near to send it.

"Your friend's signal is coming through loud and clear," Shaffernik said.

From the passenger seat, Bolan nodded. He reached

out and tuned the radio to a dedicated frequency. "Striker to Eagle One."

"Go, Striker."

"We're getting your signal. Any thoughts about where the target's headed?"

"Don't hold me to it, but right about now I'd guess they were going toward some docks on the southwest side of the island."

Bolan looked in Shaffernik's direction. "Any ideas?"

She shook her head. "In a boat as small as he described, they won't get far. The neighboring islands are hundreds of miles in any direction."

"Meaning they'll need wings," Bolan said. "How are you fixed for fuel, Eagle One?"

"I'm going to be redline soon. Better head to the airport."

"We'll take over the observation and keep you posted. My guess is if they have an aircraft waiting somewhere, they'll attempt to make it back to Adak Island."

"Roger that," Grimaldi replied.

When they'd signed off, Shaffernik spoke. "What makes you think they'll go to Adak? You're talking nearly five hundred miles. Seems pretty impractical."

"They have allies there," Bolan said. "I was hoping they'd go to wherever they were holed up, take us to the head of the operation. But now, seeing they hardly have a plan, I'm thinking no such luck."

"So why do you think they'll go to Adak?"

"Ever heard of a man named Davis Haglemann?"

Shaffernik let out a snort. "Who hasn't? Big-time union boss, in charge of all the operations on Adak Island. That place would be abandoned by now if it wasn't for him."

"You're more right than you know," Bolan replied.

"You mean…"

"Yeah," Bolan said with a curt nod. "Haglemann's been in bed with the Russians. We don't know for how long, but I do know his top guy, Otto Lustrum, was employing a couple of RBN heavies."

"I know Otto personally," Shaffernik said. "He's always been a pretty straightforward guy. Typical longshoreman, a working man's working man, if you get me."

"I get you." Bolan shook his head. "The trouble is he let Haglemann suck him into thinking everything that glitters is gold. Haglemann got the good people of Adak Island used to his handouts. They took blood money, and they didn't even know it would prove to be their undoing."

"You saying the whole place is corrupt? That it can't be redeemed?"

"I don't worry about redemption," Bolan replied. "I'm not a therapist or psychoanalyst. I know only one course of action for men like Haglemann. The same one I just demonstrated back there on Unalaska."

"You live some kind of life, Mike Blansky," Shaffernik replied.

"Yeah," Bolan muttered. "Tell me about it."

ANATOLY BRUSCHEV WATCHED his friend Arlan die with a measure of helplessness and anger. As well, the American had wounded Kirillov, but then, for some strange reason, he'd allowed Bruschev to drag Kirillov to safety. At first, it hadn't made sense. Bruschev couldn't identify mercy since he'd never experienced it in his own life. Being raised on the cold, mean streets of the ghetto section in St. Petersburg had introduced Bruschev to the axiom that people were no damn good! But as Bruschev considered it, he now wondered if the guy had done this as a matter of pure tactics.

Of course! It made complete sense. By wounding Kirillov and letting Bruschev drag him to safety, the American had effectively eliminated two men from the battle. But now it didn't matter much to their cause. They were low on ammunition and supplies, Kirillov was unconscious, and there was probably just enough fuel to get them to Adak Island.

"We're fools," he grumbled.

"What did you say?" one of his comrades asked.

"I said we were *fools*! Fools to leave Alexei behind and fools to think Kirillov could survive such an insane trip. Even if we get him on to the plane and he survives the trip to Adak, I doubt we can find a qualified doctor to fix him. They're limited out there. Those people live like savages."

"It doesn't matter," Andrei Polakoff said.

Bruschev didn't like Polakoff; he never had. They had grown up in the same neighborhood. Polakoff had always been somewhat of a whiner. How such a gutless fool had ever managed to attain seniority in the Network was far beyond Bruschev's ability to comprehend. He'd been stymied when Alexei Vizhgail had left them with instructions and put Polakoff in charge of their expedition.

"Our job is to get these parts to Captain Paley's people aboard the *Belsky*. That is our number-one mission and takes priority over all other considerations. Let's not forget that."

Bruschev shut his mouth. He didn't wish to argue

with Polakoff, especially not in front of the other men who were juniors to him. He believed it best to set the standard through example and be obedient to superior officers. This was what Vlad Moscovich himself had taught Bruschev during the time they'd trained together at the secret academy set up by the Nasenko family. By setting the example, Bruschev was making a loud and clear statement: he wasn't above the rules, and he expected all of his peers and underlings to follow the same code.

"It's a code upon which I will rebuild the Network," Moscovich had once told him.

Bruschev had never forgotten that day, a day he knew would live with him for the rest of his life. Now, given their precarious situation, he couldn't help but wonder about his own longevity. This day he'd seen most of his friends and comrades fall to the fierce retribution of this American who fought like an army. Bruschev could remember only one other instance where such an individual had wrought this kind of havoc. He'd heard rumors whispered in the halls of the Nasenko-Godunov headquarters.

Bruschev had thought this man only a myth, but he'd seen that he was real. Yes, if there were anyone who could be the man who'd brought Yuri Godunov and his family to their knees, it would indeed be *that* man.

They reached their destination after what seemed like hours but had actually been just under one. It would be dark soon, and they opted not to leave until darkness had overshadowed the area. It was a risk, since much of the area was still a no-fly zone, save for traffic into and out of Anchorage and specific military missions, but they had no choice. If they waited, there was a good chance Kirillov would die before they even reached Adak Island.

"How long will it take us to reach the island?" one of the men asked.

"Three and one-half hours," Bruschev answered.

"He was talking to *me*," Polakoff said. He looked at the young man and said, "Three and one-half hours."

Bruschev bit back a stinging retort and instead went about helping to get Kirillov off the boat. The man had taken a turn and begun to experience a level of delirium. He'd let out a moan every time the boat maneuvered through rough water. Bruschev saw the wound had started seeping again, so he ordered his comrade to lay the body on the dock and quickly went about the task of redressing it with a fresh bandage tied as tightly as possible.

"Hurry up!" Polakoff said. "We're going to be spotted."

The sound of several boat motors on a fast approach lent gravity to Polakoff's words.

"It is much too late for that," Bruschev said, removing the Izhmash Bizon SMG slung across his back. "Our final stand will be made here."

CHAPTER SEVENTEEN

"I think we have a problem," Shaffernik said.

"I think you're right," Bolan agreed.

They were high above the action, but through the instruments they could make out the collection of watercraft bearing down on the position of the enemy boat. These weren't ordinary boats but patrol craft belonging to the US Coast Guard. There was also a much larger signature on it that could have only belonged to a cutter or perhaps even a US Navy cruiser.

"Someone reported them!" Shaffernik said.

"Your federal pals."

"Wexler and Philbin? But why would they?"

"I don't know," Bolan said. "But there's no way the Russians will allow themselves to be taken alive. And even if they do, they'll resist any interrogation."

"How do you know?"

"They have something to barter with," Bolan replied. "The *Llewellyn* has been found and secured, but there's still the missing crew. And as long as Vladimir Moscovich and his people are able to continue to act without interference, it's only good strategy for his pals down there to delay."

"Unless we can get to them first."

"Not going to happen," Bolan said. "I was hoping they would have led us to Moscovich, even if indirectly, but it doesn't look like that's going to happen."

"What do you want to do?"

"We should—"

"Attention, civilian aircraft, tail number N-C-C-5-Delta-2-1-7. Please respond."

Shaffernik looked at Bolan. "Should I answer?"

Before Bolan could reply, they heard, "Attention, civilian aircraft, tail number N-C-C-5-Delta-2-1-7. This is Captain August of the 477th Fighter Group, United States Air Force. You are in violation of a no-fly zone order. Your persons and aircraft are now subject to detainment and search. Please, put your aircraft down at the Unalaska Airport via the following coordinates."

The pilot repeated the instructions and advised them if they deviated from the flight path they would be shot down. That statement removed any question in Shaffernik's mind as to whether they should respond to the hail. Shaffernik confirmed her understanding and set the transponder for the most direct flight to the airport.

"Taxi to the terminal instructed by the tower. Once there, you will wait in the aircraft and prepare to receive military investigators."

"This is just great," Shaffernik said. "We not only lose the only lead you had to finding the terrorists, but now we got the military thinking we're the terrorists!"

"Story of my life," the Executioner replied.

Within twenty minutes Shaffernik had them on the ground, albeit the result of a very rough landing in the seaplane, a factor that demonstrated she was a bit rusty. To their surprise, the first ones to meet them weren't agents from the military but instead a local Unalaska police security unit escort with a single passenger: Jack Grimaldi.

"Good to see you, Sarge," Grimaldi said, pumping the hand of his friend enthusiastically. "Just sorry it's under these circumstances."

"It couldn't be helped," Bolan replied easily. He introduced Shaffernik, who shook hands with him.

Grimaldi pointed to the uniformed airport security officer who'd been driving. "Stan Kubicek, I'd like you to meet Mike Blansky. Stan's an old friend. We've known each other for years. Going all the way back when I worked for the Mo... Well, we go way back."

"Pleased," Kubicek said, shaking Bolan's hand. He tipped his hat toward Shaffernik. "Brenda, always a pleasure."

"Hi, Stan," she replied with a grin.

Kubicek looked at Bolan. "Jack here tells me you got some troubles in front of you."

"That's right."

"I'd say the best option for you right now is to get out of here. And before you turn me down, you should know the military called and advised they were sending someone to talk to you, and we were supposed to keep you here if you tried to leave."

Bolan considered this new bit of evidence. It had been his call to keep the mission quiet, and now it was coming back to bite him. The problem was that his plan *had* been the better of the two options. His choice to maintain only a loose alliance with his government had forced him to take the bad with the good. Part of that included their ability to deny his existence, and unless it was a really rough scrape, they wouldn't be there to bail him out. Maybe he could rely on Stony Man, but it would take time, and he wasn't carrying any credentials but the cover they'd assigned him.

"There's no story you can conjure that would amount to a hill of beans," Kubicek said in afterthought, as if reading Bolan's thoughts.

Bolan nodded and then turned to Grimaldi. "Is the jet ready to go?"

Grimaldi nodded. "Topped off with fuel and pre-flighted. We can take off on a moment's notice."

"Not at the moment," Bolan said. "In light of us finding the *Llewellyn*, the military has declared a new no-fly zone. Remember? They forced us to land."

"Possibly that's an issue for the little seaplane, but…" Grimaldi purposefully let his words drop off.

Bolan caught the reference. The Gulfstream C-35 belonged to Stony Man and had been outfitted with a significant electronics and sensors package. That package included countersurveillance and jamming capabilities that could effectively mask the plane from even the most advanced radar and detection instrumentation. Short of visual inspection, no one would know they had taken off. Bolan turned to Shaffernik. "I'm going to need your help again."

"Anything," she replied.

"I need you to hold off these investigators."

"How?"

"Stall them. You're in uniform and the deputy chief of the police force here in Unalaska. Tell them only you were onboard. They won't know the difference until they talk to Philbin or Wexler, and by that time we should be well on the way to Adak."

"I was hoping to go with you," Shaffernik protested.

"No can do." Bolan frowned. "Not this time. Besides, you're going to have your hands full here, and much of the success of mission depends on just how long you can stall the military investigators. They're going to have dozens of agents and security force personnel crawling through this area soon, and I can't afford those kinds of delays. The lives of at least ninety service personnel may rely on my being able to act quickly and without interference."

Shaffernik appeared to consider it for a moment and then nodded. She was smart, and she understood the situation. She wasn't the kind of glory hog who would allow personal feelings to stand in the way of saving lives. It was not only the mark of a true professional but of a great law enforcement officer. And Mack Bolan personally wished there were more like her.

"Okay, do what you've got to do. You're out there trying to save the world, least I can do is be charming and stall a few federal boys."

"You're top shelf, Brenda."

"Yeah, yeah," she said with a knowing wink. She pointed at him as he and Grimaldi turned to leave and added, "And don't forget this. You owe me *big*-time!"

Bolan pointed back at her on the run. "You got it!"

Grimaldi got tower clearance immediately, thanks to some quick thinking on Stan Kubicek's part, and in five minutes they were climbing into the twilight hues of open sky. Bolan decided the time was right to contact Stony Man and update them on the situation. He was also going to need to get Brognola to put in a good word with the Man, so they could get some maneuvering room. Since the military had interdicted the small RBN force that had escaped from Dutch Harbor, Bolan knew there was no chance of following them to locate the RBN's operation. That left Haglemann as his one, remaining lead.

And Mack Bolan had some unfinished business with that traitor.

Semisopochnoi Island

HOURS HAD PASSED and still no word from Alexei Vizhgail or his men.

Something in Benyamin Tokov's gut told him the man was dead, and they would not be receiving any of the technology Vizhgail had sent to salvage from the cutter. Moscovich wouldn't be happy when he got the news. Tokov's people had made every attempt to reach the man, but there had been no reply to their shortwave communications with Adak, or their satellite calls to Unalaska. They couldn't risk long transmissions, anyway, since the traffic would inevitably be seen, and when the source was traced it would land them in hot water.

While he would never have admitted it to anyone, Tokov hadn't bought much into Moscovich's plan to subvert military communications. Larger enemies with much greater resources had tried and failed miserably. And there was this tendency of Moscovich to want to work with Americans in order to achieve some lofty end. The Americans couldn't be trusted not to sell out their own mothers for a few extra bucks; that made such a tactic unsound to begin with. Tokov believed in a more direct approach.

It was one of the reasons their masters had instructed him to devise an alternate plan. Whatever else the heads of the Nasenko and Godunov families thought of Vladimir Moscovich, they knew he could be somewhat eccentric. Tokov had grown up with Moscovich, as he had with many of his comrades in the Network, and he trusted the man's intuition. Still, he was ultimately responsible for answering to the same powers that controlled the fate of his friend, and he'd done as he was told.

Ten hours remained until the *Belsky* arrived, and the captain of that vessel would expect them to be ready to board so they could make for international waters as quickly as possible. It was a lot of territory to cover. The United States would not dare fire on the submarine, even if they detected it, unless they perceived some sort of imminent threat. A Russian submarine that close to the water boundary but still outside the DMZ might be enough to raise the threat level, but it wouldn't cause a full-out mobilization.

But there was still time to deal with all of that. At the moment, they had more pressing concerns. The first was getting their equipment disassembled and ready to load. Whatever they couldn't afford to take aboard the submarine for reasons of space they would sink at sea on their way to the submarine. The other concern was their prisoners. Tokov had suggested killing them, but Vlad disagreed.

"Our fight isn't with the American military," he'd said. "It's with those in Washington who make decisions. The Americans here are just like us, following orders of those above them. We cannot fault them for that."

Tokov knew once Vlad had made up his mind, it would be very difficult to change, but of course, that hadn't stopped him when Tokov suggested they use the commander of the vessel as an example of what they *might* do if provoked. It would also sow mistrust among the American military personnel who survived if they revealed the traitor in their midst. That would disrupt American operations in other unique ways, a touch that Tokov had actually suggested at the last minute. Some of their team, including Alexei Vizhgail, had applauded him for the very idea. And it seemed to have worked.

Moscovich entered the cavern where the men were packing the last of the boxes. "How long until the *Belsky* is in range?"

"Less than twelve hours."

Moscovich nodded. "Any word from Alexei?"

"No," Tokov replied. "I'm convinced he's either been captured or dead. Knowing Alexei, he would have preferred to fight and resist until it was no longer feasible. My assumption is that he's no longer alive. And given how long it has been since his scheduled check-in, I don't think any of his team made it, either."

"I am sorry," Moscovich said with genuine sorrow in his voice. "I know he was your friend. He was mine, as well. But—"

"No disrespect, Vlad, but if you're going to tell me that he knew the risks, I would prefer you just shut up and don't say any more about it at all. We *all* know the risks. It lessens neither the blow nor the sacrifice."

Moscovich nodded. "I understand. Forgive me if I seemed insensitive. That was never my intent. I've been giving the American traitor some thought, this Gross."

"And?"

"I entertained the notion of killing him, but I don't think that will be necessary now. In light of what you've told me about Alexei, I think there might be a way to make him doubly useful to us."

"I don't see how," Tokov replied. "You said it yourself, Vlad. A man who would betray his own country, even his own shipmates, cannot be trusted. I think it would be wiser to put a bullet in his head."

"It would be if this idea had not come to me. But now I'm thinking there is a way we could use him to cover our escape. Throw a sort of bone to the Americans."

"I don't think I follow."

"Think about it. The Americans have no idea we've been working with Haglemann, at least not up until now. It makes no difference to our traitor if he gets out of here by plane or boat. He's just looking to claim his money, money that is easily retrievable since the account is actually set up under a false identity. If we send him out on the boat with the coordinates to Adak Island and give him Haglemann as his contact, imagine the uproar."

Tokov considered the proposal a moment. It sounded like a ridiculous nuisance, an extra detail for them to worry about, at first. But then as he gave it more thought, he realized the genius of it. It was about a hundred fifty miles by boat to Adak. Gross would have to locate Haglemann, explain his situation and then wait for a way off the island. Meanwhile, the American military would be storming the island. By the time it all got sorted out, they would be well on their way home aboard the *Belsky*. They could leave the Coast Guard crew behind, too, which would require a massive rescue effort and give them even more time to evade American patrols.

"It is nothing short of brilliant, I'll give you that," Tokov finally admitted. "But you'll have to send him now. It's going to take him at least three hours to get there, remember."

"More like four!"

"And what if he runs afoul of something or someone there?"

"Then his fate is his own," Moscovich replied. "It's not on our heads."

"So it is. Would you like me to take care of the details? My part here is finished for the moment."

"You can attend to it as you see fit. But there is another matter I wish to discuss, directly related to it. I will be going with him."

"What? What are you talking about? I thought you would be returning with us on the *Belsky*?"

"Under normal circumstances I would," Moscovich replied. "But this is my time. There will not be another opportunity, and I must see this through. We know the technology works and that it can be used against others. I've already put a plan in motion that will get me into America. A new set of credentials."

"When did you have time to prepare them?"

"They were prepared before we even left St. Petersburg. It was an arrangement I'd made with Bea Nasenko. If this was a success, and we've obviously now proved it, I was to move on to America and set up new operations there.That is my new mission, and it requires I go to America, not return to St. Petersburg."

"And you intend to do this alone?"

"Why not?" Moscovich put a hand on his friend's shoulder. "It's a burden I must bear alone. I swore this promise to Bea, and I will complete it. You know who she is to me, that she treated me like a son after I lost my parents. I can't deny her this. I know you would understand."

Tokov could hardly believe his ears. He'd known Vladimir Moscovich for a very long time, but he'd never known him to be the sensitive sort. He'd never demonstrated even a hint of sentimentality. He was honest and loyal to a fault, if not a bit overzealous about his methods, but Tokov couldn't argue with the results. Moscovich had planned this entire operation, and it had been a success, though a costly success. But what he now proposed seemed like lunacy and raised concerns with Tokov on how it would affect the outcome of his own mission.

"You realize that if you're captured by the Americans on Adak, or your attempt to get into the country is unsuccessful, if even *one* thing goes wrong, it will mean utter failure."

"I know this."

"Then why risk it? You have succeeded beyond the wildest aspirations of those back in St. Petersburg." Tokov grabbed his friend by the shoulders and shook him. "You are a *hero*."

"A hero?" Moscovich frowned. "If you want to know the absolute truth, my friend, it really doesn't matter a whole hell of a lot to me anymore. You talk of success and, yes, we have been successful, but we've paid a terrible cost. Terrible."

"I beg of you, Vlad. Don't risk it."

"I must. And I need your promise that you will not interfere."

"Vlad, I—"

"*Swear it*, Ben," Moscovich hissed.

"Okay," Tokov replied with a resigned sigh. "I swear it."

CHAPTER EIGHTEEN

Adak Island

The last thing Bolan and Grimaldi expected was an ambush. The soldier prepared to fight it out with the men who took them at gunpoint just outside Maddie Corsack's house, but a closer assessment revealed these weren't Russian terrorists. Bolan recognized them as employees of Otto Lustrum. Something had definitely gone sour in his absence, and Bolan decided it was better to err on the side of caution. If these were Lustrum's men and they hadn't killed him yet, Bolan couldn't believe they intended to now. No, something wasn't right here, and he put Grimaldi at ease while staying his own hand.

They intended to take Grimaldi, but Bolan warned them firmly that he was only the transportation, and if they tried to force them both, it wouldn't end well. The four gunmen argued among themselves a minute, realized the boss had said nothing about the pilot, and specifically recalled his instructions that if Bolan showed up alive they were bring him to Lustrum unharmed. Once it was agreed Grimaldi could go free, they piled into a sedan. Bolan remembered it as belonging to Lustrum's fleet of vehicles, and in the blink of an eye they had whisked him away and were headed into downtown Adak.

The traffic was a bit heavier now, and many more people were out, signaling the weekend had passed into a new workweek. Bolan felt weary and his bones ached. He wished he'd been able to talk to Corsack first, get his finger on the pulse of what was going on, but he knew it wasn't going to happen now that he'd agreed to go with Lustrum's men. Bolan looked at his watch. It had taken them three hours to reach the island, even by jet, and he figured by now Brenda Shaffernik had to be deeply engaged with the military investigators.

Bolan's conversation with Brognola had gone well, however. It seemed the Stony Man chief was thinking ahead and had already been in contact with the President. The Oval Office had agreed to lean on the Pentagon and make them ease up where it concerned the activities around Unalaska. He'd also agreed to start sending a military force toward Adak Island, something Bolan appreciated on a personal note. The big Fed had given him a bit of information about what the military team had been doing on Unalaska, as well.

The Executioner had been the one to prompt that last move by the President. After his encounter with some of the Russian gunners here, Bolan had theorized the RBN hadn't been headquartered on Adak but operated from a base on one of its many neighboring islands. Bolan knew the bureaucrats would think that idea had little substance, but he didn't give a damn. There were dozens of unpopulated islands spread throughout the Aleutians. Bolan read that one in particular, Semisopochnoi, had an active volcano that could erupt any time. Bolan doubted Lustrum had the answer, but Haglemann did, and Lustrum was the best way to the guy.

The vehicle pulled to the curb in front of a building that proudly displayed the emblem of the Adak police. Bolan pushed down the feeling of unease as he was escorted through the front door, down a long hallway and into a sparse office.

To Bolan's surprise, the department chief sat at his desk with Otto Lustrum directly across from him. The two men appeared to have been engaged in conversation for some time because there was a half-empty bottle of whiskey on the chief's desk, and both men were clutching tumblers half full of brown liquor.

"Come on in, Blansky," Lustrum said, waving at a chair near his. "Have a seat."

As Bolan did, Lustrum dismissed the two heavies.

The Executioner exchanged glances with the two men and tried to come up with a reason they were sitting here together. It didn't seem as if they would want to have much to do with each other, as they worked at cross purposes. In fact, theirs was likely a highly competitive relationship since Haglemann had put guns in the hands of the police but also equipped Lustrum and his band of mercenary laborers with weapons, as well. That Haglemann had been paying both of them was nearly laughable had it not been so serious in its effects on the lives of those working and living on the island.

"This is Chief Chakowa, but we just call him Bull." Lustrum said. His words had a small slur to them.

Bolan nodded at Chakowa, then turned his attention toward Lustrum. "I was surprised to find your men waiting for me."

"I needed to talk to you."

"You could have just asked."

"I thought you were dead." Lustrum took a pull from the glass, then slapped his head. "We're forgetting our manners, Bull. You want a drink?"

Bolan shook his head, and Lustrum repeated, "I thought you were dead. Fortunately, the coroner was able to tell Bull here pretty quickly that all the guys who were killed didn't match your physical characteristics. He was able to identify three of them immediately just by dental records."

"Not many on this island we don't have a full set of dental records for, you know," Chakowa added.

"Once we knew you weren't among the deceased, I figured you'd be back and just about figured out where you'd go when you came back."

"You figured right," was all Bolan replied.

Lustrum nodded drunkenly, although the Executioner could tell he wasn't that lit. "I did. So that makes me think you did the job yourself on my boys."

"They forced my hand," Bolan said. "I wasn't left with any choice. And if you're thinking about retribution, you should probably think again."

"We're not looking to bring you down, Blansky," Chakowa interjected. "Quite the opposite, in fact. We need your help."

"With what?"

"To take down Davis Haglemann. Once and for all."

"I take it, then, you know what he's been up to."

"We know some of it," Lustrum said. "Maddie told me everything she thought she knew. She told me you're not working with Haglemann's associates, that you're actually here to take the guy out. She said he's working with some Russian terrorist group. Is it true?"

Bolan sighed, wishful that he'd been able to keep that part of it quiet. Once they knew, the news would undoubtedly spread like wildfire, and that could incite any number of unpredictable responses. What Bolan didn't need while he was trying to put Haglemann out of business was an armed mob shooting at anything that looked like it might be a threat to them. That would only result in more disastrous consequences, especially in lieu of the fact the military was on its way.

But at this point in the game, Bolan would need allies, and he no longer saw any reason to keep it quiet. "It's true. Haglemann's allied himself with a group called the Russian Business Network."

Lustrum nodded. "I've heard of them. You, Bull?"

"Vague rumors," Chakowa replied. "Nothing more than that. But I don't see how they could profit from what happened here."

"That's because their efforts are a distant memory of events for most of you and the people here on Adak. A while back, a small military aircraft dropped a military inspection team here to get readings from some of the equipment they left behind."

Chakowa nodded. "Sure, it's a pretty regular thing. Military has some satellite communications and other equipment stowed on a few islands in the area to capture meteorological data, or some damn thing. I don't pretend to understand it all. They send a flight out quarterly with some personnel to collect those readings. And they pay us all a lease fee so we don't see any disadvantage."

"The plane carrying an inspection team went down in the Bering Sea forty-eight hours ago. Disappeared right off the radar, and all communications with it ceased. The military wasn't sure what happened, so they sent a US Coast Guard cutter called the *Llewellyn* to investigate. It disappeared, too, although we just recently located it at an abandoned docking facility in Dutch Harbor."

"I don't get it," Lustrum said. "What's that got to do with us?"

"The plane that went down was the same plane that came here three months ago."

"And that Coast Guard cutter, as I recall, stopped here to deliver some emergency supplies we requested for our medical facility," Chakowa said.

Bolan nodded. "I only recently came into that information, which is why I was able to trace the link here to Adak. Once I got inside the system, I realized Haglemann was the only one with the resources to pull it off."

"What about the hit on his club? Was that you, too?"

Bolan nodded.

"One of the men who died there was my friend, Blansky," Lustrum said. "And I knew all those guys. They had families. What's going to happen to them now?"

"Most all of us have families, Lustrum," Bolan replied quietly. It wouldn't do to alienate the guy or be confrontational. That wouldn't serve his purpose. "But they were working with enemies of this country, and they had done some bad things. You can't deny that much."

"They were just doing what I told them to do!" Lustrum rose, his face reddening. "It's my fault they're dead, and you had no right—!"

"Sit *down*, Otto!" Chakowa commanded.

Lustrum looked stunned at first, but he sat in a huff, anyway, some of the color in his face dissipating as he calmed.

Chakowa looked at Bolan. "Under ordinary circumstances I'd lock you up, Blansky. But in light of what you've told us and what Otto here told me, I don't suppose that's the right thing to do. Probably wouldn't help my career, either, since I sense you're probably one of the few people in all this who's on our side."

He threw a furious look at Lustrum before continuing. "I have to admit that Davis Haglemann had us all fooled. Frankly, I'm ashamed of myself for allowing this to go on as long as it has. I'm no criminal and I'm no traitor. And I'd like to run up there right now and beat the hell out of the guy."

"While I appreciate the sentiment, it's not a good idea," Bolan said.

"Why not?"

"I've been inside Haglemann's residence. I'm sure you have, too. The place has every modern security measure and countermeasure money can buy. I've seen it before, and believe me when I tell you that. You wouldn't get halfway to the front door before someone took you out."

"We could storm it."

"With what limited resources and weapons you have?" Bolan shook his head. "You've trusted your instincts about trusting *me*, and you should listen to them. I've done this kind of thing many times. I hit Haglemann's club, so you know what I'm capable of doing. Besides, this is going to turn into a game of capture the flag. I need the guy alive, so he can tell me where the Russians have set up their main base. He's the only one left who I think knows, and it's critical we get that information."

"So, what do you expect the rest of us to do?" Lustrum asked. "We can't just sit here and wring our hands!"

"I need you to keep your people under wraps," Bolan said. "Trust me, I know exactly how to deal with guys like Haglemann. But when word gets out about what he's been doing, you could well have a mob crying for his head. That wouldn't be good, especially since I don't think he'd hesitate to shoot innocent bystanders."

"Excuse me, Blansky, but you've only been among our folks a short time," Chakowa interjected. "You really think Haglemann's capable of something like that?"

Icy blue eyes pinned the cop with a hard stare as Bolan replied evenly, "If the current alliance he's forged with these Russian terrorists is any indication, you can bet on it. Men like Haglemann are motivated by one thing—greed. He's managed to buy off most of your citizens here on Adak, citizens who do the living and working and dying. Decent and honest people for the most part who aren't going to take kindly to some business mogul allying himself with thugs like those among the ranks of the Russian Business Network."

Bolan thought to say more but decided against it. He didn't have to preach to them—he could see they already knew the mistakes they'd made trusting Haglemann. No amount of talk or grandiose oratory would get better results than the dawning of a new ideal. It would be the job of Chakowa and Lustrum to con-

vince the others that Davis Haglemann was neither
their friend nor the beneficent business leader he'd tried
to make them think he was. Haglemann was just a two-
bit hood who happened to think everyone had his or
her price, and there was no one alive whose price he
couldn't meet.

Chakowa eyed Bolan with an expression of resolute
skepticism. "So a guy I've known for years, someone
who I trusted and thought was a friend, managed to
pull the wool over our eyes. Now you're asking us to
trust a total stranger."

"Betrayal doesn't lurk in every dark corner, Chief,"
Bolan replied. "I'm sure you understand that. And this
isn't about trusting, anyway. This is about keeping
Haglemann alive long enough to deal with the greater
threat. I let a source of information slip through my
fingers once. I won't allow it to happen again."

A long, uncomfortable silence followed as the Executioner let them think on that. He had just laid down
an ultimatum, and Chakowa was smart enough to understand it. Whether Lustrum did, at this point, wasn't
an issue. Sure, Lustrum had influence and he could
start real trouble, but Bolan figured Chakowa could
keep the guy in line. And something that Maddie Corsack had told Lustrum had obviously gotten to the man,
because his eyes were bloodshot and his expression
worn. That made two living large ladies Bolan had
encountered in just this one mission.

"Okay, Blansky," Chakowa finally said. "We'll do
this your way. But when you're done with Haglemann,
I want him in my jail cell. He's going to answer for
all of this."

"As the local law enforcement, it's only right you should detain him."

"I'm going to hold you to your word."

Bolan grinned. "It'll be my pleasure to keep it."

EVEN AS DAVIS HAGLEMANN hung up the phone and stared at it, a feeling of unease came over him.

Moscovich's call had been strange, to say the least. He was coming to Adak by boat, but he wasn't coming alone. He'd promised to be there in less than four hours. Haglemann couldn't understand how a guy like that could have the nerve to even set foot on Adak again. Part of him wanted to send a little personal welcoming committee for Moscovich. Hit them while they were still in the boat and let them sink to a watery grave in the Nazan Bay.

The more he considered that plan, though, the more he didn't like it.

Moscovich might have been little more than a thug and errand boy, but he had powerful friends in the Russian criminal underworld. They wouldn't stand for the outright murder of one their own. Then again, it was very dangerous out there on the open seas—anything could happen. But something in his gut told Haglemann that wouldn't wash. If Moscovich didn't make it safely to Adak, they would hold Haglemann responsible, anyway, and that could mean he'd have to leave this gig.

Not that it wasn't part of his plan to begin with.

Haglemann had never really wanted to enter into an agreement with Moscovich, but his actions had been driven by necessity. A lot of money had been riding on the deal, and once the Russians had demonstrated

their ability to manipulate the markets in his favor—
get him lucrative contracts and jobs on the side for the
local help and virtually an unlimited supply of guns
and dope he could smuggle for other entities—it had
been pretty much a no-brainer.

Of course, he'd been forced to spread around some
money to keep the locals happy, but that hadn't taken
much. Most of them were content to get their dividends
and had never looked closely at where the cash came
from, just as long as it came at regular intervals.

Haglemann had turned Adak into nothing short of
an Alaskan Mecca. They had taverns for the old-school
workers and nightclubs for the singles and younger
crowd. They had an airport, boats, carnivals twice a
year and a movie theater that played all the first-run
films. Haglemann had even managed to attract a number of high-end clothing retailers and department stores
to the area that sold goods at rock-bottom prices. Hell,
he'd even built the residents a full-featured gym that
included an indoor swimming pool and track that were
open year round.

Davis Haglemann's empire had once included a le-
gion of devout followers, but now it seemed as if all
of it was about to come unraveled. The Russians had
somehow been discovered by military authorities, Otto
Lustrum was acting belligerently, and even the recent
arrival of the mysterious Mike Blansky seemed fraught
with inconsistencies and warnings Haglemann felt it
would be unwise to ignore. He thought about simply
taking his fortune and leaving, letting the island succumb to whatever chaos might overtake it without his
wealth and influence to stay the course. He kept falling

back to the fear that if he did this, the Russians would surely hunt him down and destroy him.

Then again, what did he have to fear? Some men were just born leaders and builders. He was one of them. He answered to nobody, and he would do as he pleased. Yes, it was time to leave Adak and let come what may. He would do it tonight.

CHAPTER NINETEEN

The Executioner was prepared for war.

He'd donned a new skintight black suit, this one of lighter material. His feet were shod with custom-made combat boots that boasted thick, neoprene soles and lug heels containing a steel shank. Weapons of war dangled from the black suit, attached to a thin-profile load-bearing harness with no-snag fittings. Besides the twin combat medical pouches on his belt, ammunition holsters contained spare magazines for his Beretta 93-R and .44 Magnum Desert Eagle.

The Ka-Bar D2 combat knife was nestled in a leather sheath on his belt, and he'd selected six Diehl DM51 grenades and a piano-wire garrote with mahogany handles to take with him. His face was smeared with combat cosmetics, completing the picture of the death-dealing wraith he was.

Mack Bolan's war had never been as much about retribution as duty. Even in the early days when repaying the criminal underworld for the deaths of his father, mother and sister, and the almost intangible trauma imposed upon his sole-surviving brother, Johnny Gray, the Executioner had seen his war as something much larger than simple revenge. To seek revenge was stupid in its context. His war had always been one of striking at the heart of the monster, dealing justice to those who preyed upon the innocent.

It was as he wrote in his journal those first fateful days of his War Everlasting: "It looks like I have been fighting the wrong enemy. Why defend a front line eight thousand miles away when the *real* enemy is chewing up everything you love back home?"

And while Bolan's intentions were the best and his resolve unshakeable, he found on occasions there were a few people who didn't totally understand. One of those was a certain middle-aged, dark-haired woman who'd seen an awful lot of her own heartache in this life and simply wanted to move on with it. And she was stating her case in no uncertain terms.

"This is not a good idea," Corsack said. "In fact, this is a very bad idea."

"As you've already stated about a dozen times," Bolan replied, trying to mask his exasperation.

"And I'm going to keep stating it."

"Oh," Grimaldi said glibly. "I can't wait."

"You stay out of this, Jack," Corsack said. She fixed Bolan with a haughty mask of disapproval. "And you, mister, you're getting yourself into hot water. You should let the navy or army handle this. Maybe even Chief Chakowa."

"And as I've already explained, Chakowa has chosen to let me handle this," Bolan said, retrieving his FN-FNC carbine and checking the action. He paused to give her his attention. "The law here trusts me, Maggie. Why can't you?"

"Why? Because the law hasn't exactly been trustworthy in the distant past. And need I remind you that Lustrum hasn't, either? For everyone's safety it might be better if they just lock him up until it's over."

"Believe me, Chakowa actually threatened to do

that at one point," Bolan said. "But I think Lustrum will keep his word and stay out of it."

"Roger that," Grimaldi added. "Believe me, nobody wants to be around when the Sarge does his things and the fireworks start."

"Why do you keep calling him 'Sarge?'" Corsack asked offhandedly.

"Nickname."

"The point is this," Bolan said. "Haglemann's the key to finding the RBN's operation. By now, he's sure to know his reputation as a respectable businessman is over. He'll debate his next move, maybe initially he'll be defiant and refuse to run, but in the end he'll realize the jig's up, and he'll scram. Or at least he'll try. And that's when I'll take him."

"And you know all that from…?"

"Many years of experience," Bolan replied. "Like I told you before, I've been doing this for a very long time. I know how men like Haglemann think and how they act. They're small men who try to be mightier than they really are, and they love to walk over others to achieve whatever's their endgame. Only problem is, they will inevitably encounter someone who won't back down. That's usually about the time they show their true colors."

"Then I guess there's no talking you out of this," Corsack said.

"No, Why are you so worried about it, anyway? I would've thought you'd like to see Haglemann brought to justice."

"My reasons are my own," Corsack said. "And nobody else's business. I wish you all the best of luck,

Blansky. Just do me a favor and try to come out of this alive on the other end. Will you?"

With that, Corsack turned and left the kitchen. She went straight into her bedroom and closed the door quietly behind her.

Bolan and Grimaldi exchanged a moment of uncomfortable silence, each letting the other get lost in his own thoughts.

"Okay," Bolan said, whipping out the layout for Haglemann's house and spreading it on the coffee table. "Let's talk about the plan. I'll make the hit at 2300, just as we discussed. From that mark, I'll need twenty minutes to defeat any of the physical security at the hard site, get inside and find Haglemann."

Bolan pointed to a large, square rooftop marking. "This is the heliport I told you about. It's connected to the house with both an elevator and stairwell access. I'm likely going to have to cut the power to cover our escape, so you'll have to hit the rooftop while it's still lit. Once I go lights-out, it'll become much tougher to land."

"What about a spotlight? There's one on the police helicopter."

Bolan shook his head. "No dice. We can't be sure of the exact enemy numbers, and I don't want you doing anything that might risk getting you shot at. You'll have to come in dark. The last thing we can afford is one of them shooting you down before you even reach the target."

Grimaldi nodded. "Fair enough. I'll be there, and you can count on it."

"I know," Mack Bolan replied. "It's about the only thing I know I can count on."

JEFF GROSS HADN'T been keen on their plan to get him off Semisopochnoi Island via little more than a glorified powerboat, but he was even less enthused about having to make the five hour trip over cold, dark waters to Port Adak. He liked the idea of making the transit even less when he heard the leader of the Russians would be accompanying him. Gross had managed to conceal a pistol on his person just before all the trouble had gone down and they'd raided the *Llewellyn*, though, so that served as a small comfort for him.

Frankly, he wondered if this entire idea hadn't been bad from the start. He'd never really wanted to work with the Russians, but he'd been unable to resist the kind of money they offered him. Besides, he didn't figure he was selling out his whole country. Only a few of his shipmates, most of whom he never liked, anyway. It wasn't like this small band of cheap thugs could do much with one small Coast Guard cutter. They probably didn't even understand most of the technology they were trying to salvage. His understanding of the Russians were they enjoyed selling pornography and ripping off the credit cards of old ladies who had too much money, anyway. They weren't doing any real harm. The leader, who he knew only as Vlad, had even given his word they were going to let his shipmates go as soon as they'd finished.

Gross realized he was only trying to justify his actions to make the cake taste sweeter. The fact of the matter was he knew he was a treacherous prick. But that didn't matter. They'd been willing to meet his price, and soon he'd be on a beach in some nonextradition country sipping mai tais and enjoying the view. Who was he really hurting, after all?

Gross wasn't much for the trip to Adak. It was cold and dark, and his Russian companion didn't say more than ten words to him the entire trip. Gross had been instructed to sit in the back and keep his mouth shut, a ratty blanket his only way of keeping warm. They hadn't even bothered to give him a jacket. The fact that it was summer hardly mattered this far north. At night on the open water it was still as cold as a witch's tit. He'd tried to protest, but the other guy, who seemed to be some sort of a high-ranker in the organization, had told him to stop his bitching, or his one-way ticket to paradise would be of a different kind.

Gross had understood the warning, although he hadn't been very appreciative of it. Just because the Russians were paying him didn't mean they were entitled to treat him like a dog. He was still an American, and he knew more about their operations than he let on. They would start to be nicer to him or once he got to Adak he could find a way to make Vlad's life extremely miserable. He wasn't afraid of the guy in the least. He had his pistol and he had his pride, and he was willing to use the former if anyone tried to steal the latter.

Thankfully, after more than four grueling hours on the boat, Gross saw the dense outline of Adak Island ahead. He estimated they would reach the port in about forty-five minutes, and a quick check of his watch verified the guess. It was nearing ten o'clock when the boat reached the isolated dock along the southern part of the island, set off about a half mile from the main port in the mouth of Nazan Bay.

As Vlad pulled up to the dock, Gross rose and dutifully tossed the dock lines onto the nearby mooring post. He pulled with all his strength to bring them gently up to the dock without connecting the fiberglass hull against the wooden posts or scraping against any rocks. This area had obviously been chosen carefully, and Gross was actually glad for the opportunity to demonstrate his usefulness. He cast the ratty blanket aside and climbed the thick, rope ladder first until he reached the dock. He looked in all directions but didn't see a soul in sight, and he became ever more conscious of the weight of the pistol tucked in a special holster clipped to the small of his back, hidden beneath the loose wool sweater over his uniform shirt.

"Nobody to meet us?" he asked Vlad as the Russian climbed the rope ladder to stand beside him on the dock.

"They will be here," he replied in his rough English.

As if on cue, a pair of headlights in the distance winked on and off twice. Moscovich immediately withdrew a red-lensed flashlight and repeated the signal, but with two flashes, a pause, and then two more flashes. Gross heard the faint sound of the engine as it came to life, and within a minute a dark, late-model Hummer came into view. The two men walked the dock until they reached shore and climbed into the back at the direction of the passenger riding shotgun.

"Where's Haglemann?" Moscovich asked.

"He's waiting at the house," one of the men said.

And with that, they were off and running through the darkness.

Denver, Colorado

UNDER OTHER CIRCUMSTANCES, the blond-haired man who entered the small café directly across the street would have probably drawn a bit more attention had he not been dressed in a plain, gray suit with knotted tie loosened at the neck. But because he was attired just like any of the other businessmen who frequented the place for a late lunch, he didn't rate a second look.

Everything about the man, from the way he carried himself to his demeanor when ordering a tall glass of iced tea and a cheeseburger, exuded an air of command. In this case, only the waitress or short-order cook in the café might have known he was more than he appeared to be, since they were used to seeing his type visit often from the building across the street. That's because it was a building that housed a number of government types, including two entire floors dedicated to the Federal Bureau of Investigation.

But this guy was no Fed.

Not in any conventional sense. He hated monkey suits and he loathed bureaucratic red tape. Whether it was the CIA, NSA or DHS, it was much too much for this guy. Strange for a guy who'd come out of a major municipal police force. But then that had made him the perfect choice for the job of leading a team of some of the toughest urban commandos ever assembled. They were consummate warriors, soldiers of a cause just as was the man they called a friend and ally.

But today the blond man was alone and operating under very strict orders to play it all totally under the radar. The mission suited him, since he was pretty used to keeping his cards close to the vest, anyway. After all, the woman he'd been assigned to watch was anything but an average federal agent. Justina Marquez had been a New York City police detective in the Organized Crime Unit of the NYPD when she'd first encountered Mack Bolan. She'd thought he was just another dirt-bag criminal, but upon learning he was really in New York to bring down one of the most notorious Russian mobsters ever, she'd thrown all in and risked life, limb and career to help the Executioner complete her task. Now, four short years later, she was a decorated veteran of the FBI and a lead antiterrorist expert in her own right.

The blond man could admire the hell out of a lady like that. Such devotion to duty was rare, but especially among most of her kind. While there were many good police officers and agents in the FBI, there were only a few who would risk their careers to buck the system and do whatever it took to bring the enemy to its knees. Justina Marquez had proven she was one of them, and even had the bullet scar to prove it. She'd been wounded during her campaign with Mack Bolan to eliminate Yuri Godunov and his traitorous nephew, Stepan.

Barbara Price had been clear in her instructions. "We don't think the RBN has her targeted. In fact, we don't even think they know her identity. But seeing that we've confirmed they *are* operating within United States borders and this might be an act of revenge, we have to assume she could be in danger. Until Striker has confirmed the threat is neutralized, we think it's better we have someone with your particular talents handle this, rather than just entrust it to other members in Justice. Hal was fully confident you were our guy, and he picked you by name."

"I'll take care of it," the blond man had said. "No sweat."

And he'd meant every word of it. Brognola had

been right. This job was uniquely suited to his talents. To bring his compatriots into it would've been overkill. Besides, they were known to take separate assignments, too, whenever the need called for it. They couldn't all be everywhere at once. There were other considerations and other crises that needed handling, and sometimes it was good to work those alone. When they had to come together as a team, however, they became nothing short of an unbeatable force and one to be reckoned with by any enemies that came in their sights.

But none of that brute force would be needed. Today it was just a matter of watching the back of someone with a spirit much like his own. He could appreciate that, and he could damn well understand it. Mack Bolan was out there putting it all on the line to bring down the Russian Business Network. This gig was just one small way Carl "Ironman" Lyons could do his own part to help his longtime friend and ally. So, no, he didn't view this as any sort of duty beneath his abilities. Hell, just the opposite. He didn't mind it one bit.

CHAPTER TWENTY

Unalaska

Deputy Chief Brenda Shaffernik fumed as she sat in the cold, sterile temporary offices that Military Intelligence had set up.

They'd treated her like a criminal and detained her without submitting proof of any wrongdoing. At first, part of Shaffernik had regretted agreeing to help Blansky. But her resolve grew steely after she was met at the airfield, stripped of her equipment and put in handcuffs. It was bad enough when they took her to their headquarters for interrogation but even more disheartening when she requested an attorney and was refused.

As the lead investigator had told her, a guy named Rafferty, she'd been arrested under suspicion of collusion with the enemy and disobeying a no-fly zone order by the US military. Those were considered acts of terrorism, and as such, her current detainment was in the purview of the Department of Homeland Security, and she was in violation of the Patriot Act.

"The *only* thing you've got going for you right now," Rafferty had said upon her arrival at the facility, "is that you landed your plane immediately and followed instructions. That and the fact you didn't resist arrest."

Shaffernik couldn't help but wonder what the hell

had happened to Meltrieger. Why wasn't he raising hell with the military or the Pentagon or even the governor of Alaska? It had been her people and her intelligence that had allowed the military to uncover the location of the *Llewellyn*. Surely they understood that. And if they didn't, they had to have been in contact with Wexler and Philbin by now, who could have easily corroborated her story. No, there had to be a hell of a lot more to it than this. There was more than enough evidence to suggest no wrongdoing on her part. This was related to something else, entirely.

As Rafferty entered with a few other men and one woman in tow, Shaffernik got the feeling she was about to find out what that something else was. She hadn't been up against this kind of crowd since the panel interview she'd undergone when Meltrieger hired her. She'd been a lot more nervous then, however, probably because it was for a job she really wanted.

When they were seated, Rafferty opened the discussion. "Deputy Chief Shaffernik, I'm going to forego formal introductions for the sake of time. Suffice it to say there are a number of federal organizations represented by the people here. We have some questions, and we'd like some honest answers."

"I believe I asked for a lawyer."

"You'll get a lawyer in due time."

"I know my rights, Agent Rafferty," Shaffernik countered. "I don't have to say a word to you. *Any* of you. Not without counsel present."

"You're not actually under arrest," Rafferty replied.

"That wasn't my understanding," she said. "I've been a police officer for a long time. I'm pretty sure the law has no distinction between being detained but not actually being under arrest. That's a law enforcement tactic to skirt Miranda and a really old one. You ought to be ashamed for even trying that one on me."

"Look!" Rafferty said, slapping his hand on the table and causing several of the agents to jump in spite of themselves. "That kind of smart-ass attitude is exactly what's going to land you in a federal prison for the next thirty years if you don't cooperate."

"On what charge?"

"How does high treason sound?"

"You won't make that stick and you know it, Rafferty," Shaffernik said. She met the gazes of the other agents. "Don't you people see what's going on here? You've been fighting an unknown entity that is no longer unknown. These are Russian terrorists, part of a group called the Russian Business Network. They've been operating in this area for many months and completely undetected."

"Yes, that's the point. They've been operating on your island for months," one of the other agents with a crooked nose and a shock of red hair said. "*Undetected* by you or your personnel!"

Shaffernik shook her head. "Not true. They've only been on Unalaska for a couple of days. They were hiding the *Llewellyn* inside an abandoned docking facility off Dutch Harbor. Prior to that, they were operating out of Port Adak and possibly some other island in the western chain."

"Ridiculous!" Rafferty said with a snort.

"Wait a minute," the slight, soft-spoken female agent

said. "Let's not jump to any conclusions yet. I'd like to hear more of what Deputy Chief Shaffernik has to say."

The woman looked at Shaffernik and said, "Please. Go on."

Shaffernik turned to see all faces focused on her with anticipation—only Rafferty looked skeptical. The rest really were here to get information and do their jobs. By bringing them in, Rafferty had actually bought Shaffernik a reprieve whether he'd intended to or not. She planned to capitalize on that. If she could get community opinion on her side, then maybe it would buy them enough good will they'd pressure Rafferty into releasing her.

"As I've already mentioned, this all started when a group of gunmen armed with automatic weapons ambushed a federal agent named Mike Blansky. I arrested Blansky but subsequently had to release him when I discovered he was part of a government task force investigating the disappearance of flight 195B and the *Llewellyn*."

"Which agency did this Blansky purport to be with?" another agent asked.

"He didn't say," she said. "Or at least he intimated that he couldn't say."

"And you believed him?"

"Is this when he told you the Russians were involved?" the female agent asked.

She shook her head. "No, that information didn't come until later. He managed to infiltrate the local workforce here, which I can tell you is something not easily accomplished for an outsider. Somehow, though, he managed it, and he traced the problem to Adak Island. That's when it apparently all started to unravel.

Something he learned there led him to this entire plot being perpetrated by the RBN. That's also when he learned the *Llewellyn* had been brought to Unalaska somewhere."

"And how did he explain the Russians' ability to make an entire Coast Guard cutter disappear?" Rafferty inquired, seemingly quite interested now in what Shaffernik had to say.

"Apparently, they developed some sort of technology that can jam military communications. It can block radar, VTOL, even satellite and infrared. I'm no Luddite, but even I don't understand it fully. It creates essentially a blackout of sorts."

"For what purpose?"

"So they can steal military technology, near as we can tell. Blansky told us the men we encountered at Dutch Harbor had probably stripped some of the tech off the cutter. And it's probable they have members of the crew held hostage. But I imagine that's something you were able to figure out when you sent that navy SEAL team to attempt to capture those from the group who managed to escape."

"And how did you know about that?"

"Because we were the ones chasing them. Well... I mean I was chasing them in the plane while the rest of my people were mopping up after Blansky hit them."

"You mean what went down at Dutch Harbor wasn't your people?" Rafferty asked.

"No. We got there after the fact."

"So this Blansky did the job on them all by himself?"

"I suppose so," Shaffernik replied, even though she knew damn well it had been him.

"And how," interjected the red-haired agent, "did you manage to learn of the RBN's presence on the island?"

"They ambushed Blansky as soon as he came back from Port Adak," Shaffernik said. "He'd known they were operating there somewhere, but he *didn't* know they knew of his involvement."

"So you're saying that Blansky was not only going after them, but they knew about his involvement, too," Rafferty concluded.

"Right."

"And so why did your people go to Dutch Harbor?"

"Because he asked for my help," Shaffernik said. "We've already covered this ground, so I don't know why you're asking me the same questions again. We—"

The door blasted open, and in stepped Chief Dustin Meltrieger and the Unalaska Director of Public Safety, Commissioner McKeene. An aide had just rushed up behind them and was protesting the intrusion very vociferously when Meltrieger turned around and got right in the smaller man's face. His voice was low but loud enough that everyone in the room could hear.

"I don't care, you got that? Now step off me."

Something in the man's voice was enough for the uniformed aide to understand the implicit threat in Meltrieger's form. Now he turned his attention toward Rafferty. "Agent Rafferty, do you mind explaining to me just exactly what the hell you think you're doing?"

"Excuse me—?"

"There's no excuse for you, at the moment. When I told you I'd give you the full cooperation of my office, that was a promise. And I'm able to keep that promise because of the weight of the office of this man standing next to me. If you're not familiar, I'd like to introduce all of you to Commissioner Howard McKeene, the man in charge of all of public safety efforts here on Unalaska. Sir?"

McKeene bore a stern expression. "I just got off the phone with the governor, who just got off the phone with the President of the United States. Would you like to explain to us under exactly what authority you've acted in the detainment of a decorated deputy police chief? Not to mention your activities against an armed force on Unalaska territory that involved the use of military special operators to kill criminals who were being pursued by sworn law enforcement personnel?"

"Personnel who were, by the way, acting in coordination with military investigators?" Meltrieger added. "Deputy Chief Shaffernik, let's go. You're done here."

"Now wait just a minute—" Rafferty began.

"No more waiting," Meltrieger cut in. "You've seized and detained my deputy chief without cause, and you've denied her due process. If it hadn't been for her quick thinking and actions, you'd still be searching for the *Llewellyn*. Not to mention she was acting under *my* orders. So unless you've got the juice you think you have to detain the police chief and commissioner of Unalaska, you'd be best to let this alone and go chase down Mike Blansky's trail. And if you even think about trying to keep me from leaving, I'll slap the cuffs on you myself. You reading me?"

Nobody moved a muscle or attempted to stop Shaffernik as she rose without delay and preceded Meltrieger out of the room. Once they were away from there, she told her boss, "Thanks, Chief."

"You've got some explaining to do, Brenda. A hell

of a *lot* of explaining to do. So I wouldn't be thanking me just yet."

"Everything I said in there is the truth. But there's some additional information I wasn't able to give them that you should know."

"Not here," Meltrieger said with a shake of his head. "These walls have ears. Let's get the hell out of here, and then we can talk."

Stony Man Farm, Virginia

BARBARA PRICE ENTERED the War Room where Hal Brognola sat in contemplation. The Stony Man director had just returned from a briefing with the President. Price could tell from Brognola's expression that it hadn't gone well. She doubted very seriously that it had anything to do with Stony Man's efforts. The Man had some peculiarities, just like every one of his predecessors, but he'd always been consciously cooperative with the process Stony Man followed in its missions. Because they got results.

Price couldn't think of a better team. Kurtzman and his folks were top shelf when it came to the technology front. Able Team and Phoenix Force were two of the finest commando units in operation, crack combatants and good souls down to the last man. Each of them had paid a terrible price in the name of duty, and Price had come to not only love and admire them but she also just plain respected the hell out of them.

She couldn't have asked for a better leader than Hal Brognola, either. They had long shared a deep friendship and professional bond from practically the first day she'd come onboard. Brognola had handpicked her, and he'd had the cream of the crop from which to choose. Fortunately, she'd been savvy and wise enough to say yes when he came to call on her.

"Good morning, Hal."

"What time is it?"

Price looked at her watch. "Early. And I can tell you've been up all night."

"I caught a few winks on the way back from DC," Brognola replied.

"I didn't even know you were back."

The big Fed waved. "Sorry. Any coffee on?"

"Not yet," Price replied. "Feel free to make a pot, or you can wait until Mrs. Newton is up and about."

Brognola popped a couple of antacid tablets. "I'll make a pot shortly. What's the news?"

"The situation has reached critical mass," Price said. "I think it won't be long before Striker pours on the fireworks."

"That really doesn't come as a surprise to me. The word came in as my meeting was breaking up that they located the *Llewellyn*."

"Correct, but still no crew. And it just came to our attention that the local police force at Unalaska providing support to Striker got the hammer brought down on them by military intelligence, specifically NIS and a DHS task force."

"Damn bureaucratic red tape." Brognola shook his head. "I'm all for interagency cooperation, but sometimes you really can have too many irons in the fire. So, what do you recommend as our next move?"

"I'm not sure there's much more we can do. Striker neutralized the small expeditionary force on Unalaska that had been assigned to strip the *Llewellyn* of technology. Apparently, a few of them attempted to escape, and he was in pursuit with Unalaska authorities when they were ordered to put down at the airport for violating the no fly-zone. Coupled with a navy SEAL team operation against the surviving terrorists from the group hiding near Dutch Harbor, all of whom were killed in the battle, Striker lost his only potential lead to discovering where the RBN was operating."

"Uh-oh."

Price nodded. "Our boys somehow managed to dodge the bullet thanks to one—" she looked at the folder she'd been holding "—Deputy Chief Brenda Shaffernik. Apparently, she covered for Striker and Jack until they could get out of there. According to Kurtzman's tracking software, they proceeded by one of our jets straight to Adak Island. That's about the time we got a call from Striker confirming all of the information."

"So I'm betting he's gone back there to confront Haglemann."

"Correct. And we have good reason to be concerned because apparently the cat's out of the bag there about Haglemann and his little alliance with the Russians."

"And if the locals get to him before Striker…"

"It won't end well," Price finished. "Right."

"And Justina Marquez?"

"She's fine, and we just got word she's secure with no problems. Your idea of sending Ironman to keep an eye on her was a stroke of genius."

"I can't take all the credit," Brognola said. "It was Aaron who gave me the idea."

"Leave it to Bear."

"Yeah. At least not to make coffee."

Price laughed. "It'll put hair on your chest."

"It'll put hair on your *feet*," Brognola replied.

CHAPTER TWENTY-ONE

Adak Island

Mack Bolan watched with interest through a pair of field binoculars as the headlights of a Hummer swung into the drive at Davis Haglemann's estate.

He'd been evaluating the layout for nearly an hour, lying in the tall grass of a field that sat at an angle across the road that ran past the estate. Far in the distance behind the house and across Expedition Harbor were the high peaks of Mount Moffett covered with snow. While it was midsummer here, there was no denying the chill in the air. Bolan had been fortunate enough the field provided ample cover. There were a couple of guards he'd noticed roaming along a parapet of some kind that seemed to surround the helipad and parts of the house, but the majority of it was unpatrolled. Under the cover of nightfall, those guards were not able to see Bolan's specter-like form.

The soldier lowered the binoculars and checked his watch. He'd noted that it was almost time to begin his assault, and he didn't want to risk anything to chance. He'd be cutting it close at it was. The only thing that interested him now, however, was the arrival of new guests. Bolan couldn't imagine who might be coming to see Haglemann at this time. The word was out about the guy, and Chakowa had sworn to keep any and all as far from Haglemann as possible. That meant that whoever had arrived just now was either part of Haglemann's staff or additional security.

He had to wonder if these visitors were members of the RBN. Could it have really been that easy? Lustrum had sworn on his mother's grave that Rov and the man known as Zakoff had been the only two Russians foisted on him by Haglemann. Had there been others hiding somewhere else on the island? Bolan couldn't buy that and dismissed the notion immediately. There was still an unknown number from the RBN contingent active. Not to mention the fact he was convinced beyond all doubt that the crew of the *Llewellyn*, if alive, was being held prisoner wherever that contingent might be operating. It wouldn't be easy to hide eighty to ninety uniformed USCGC personnel without drawing significant attention.

Despite it all, Bolan wondered. Could it be Russian VIPs? If yes, then Fate had smiled on him, and he hoped the good fortune would continue. Until it was verified, though, Bolan would go with his plan and adjust it on the fly.

Time to move.

The Executioner set the binoculars aside and reached to the wool blanket near him. He lifted it to reveal the shadowy outline of another trusted ally: an MSG90A1 sniper rifle. Bolan had used the weapon for many years. It included a composite shoulder stock that was adjustable at length and height, and sported a Weaver rail system for sight mounting. Its greatest reputation remained its accuracy, a fact to which Bolan could attest. Capable of delivering a 7.62 mm NATO round at up to two-thirds of a mile in under a second, the MSG90A1 included a box magazine of ten rounds.

Bolan eased the weapon forward, closed his left eye and put his right one up to the telescopic sight. He peered past the illuminated reticle of the scope and tracked along the horizon until he found the first guard. The two were roving, so he'd have to take one and then wait until the other came into view. He could only hope he got them both before either could raise an alarm. If he didn't succeed in neutralizing the guards, the entire battle would be lost before it even got off the ground.

Bolan settled the sights on the first target, estimated the windage and calculated the distance of the bullet drop. He then took a deep breath, let it out, took a second and let out half. His timing was perfect as the roving sentry came into view, and just as his shoulder entered the outside of the scope, Bolan eased back the trigger. The bullet left the muzzle with barely a sound, thanks to the suppressor attached to it. A heartbeat later, he watched the man's head explode with the impact, and he dropped from sight.

Scratch one.

Bolan took a cleansing breath and let it go slowly, waiting for the second sentry to make his appearance. He could hear his heart thudding in his chest, and he tried to ignore it, putting all his focus and energy into being one with the rifle. The second sentry came into view, unaware that his comrade was down. Bolan squeezed the trigger once more. Like its predecessor, the round took the target in the head. He dropped like a stone.

Scratch two.

Bolan put the rifle aside, climbed to his feet and

sprinted toward the boundaries of the estate with satchel in hand. The satchel was packed with all the ordnance he could find within the miniature armory aboard the Gulfstream C-35. It had included ten one-pound sticks of C4 plastique, two five-pound sticks of the same, an ammonium nitrate cratering charge and a pair of M86 Pursuit Deterrent Munition antipersonnel mines attached to a special bandoleer.

He reached the large wall near a wrought-iron gate, then dipped his hand into the bag and pulled out a thin piece of cord lined with a loose plastic sheath painted olive drab. The cord was primarily designed to prime C4 explosives, but it doubled as a tool to cut through metal. The Executioner could have just used explosives to blow the door off its hinges, but that would have made entirely too much noise, forcing him to contend with more guards before he ever reached the house.

Bolan quickly and quietly primed the two hinges with the cord, stood with his back to the nearby wall and triggered the remote switch. There were a couple points where sparks flew, and then the gate dropped to the ground. The soldier caught it as it started to fall. He eased the gate out of the way, then inspected the area immediately behind it. That took some doing in the darkness, but Bolan eventually spotted what he'd been looking for, an electric eye positioned about halfway up the wall with a receiver at the other end.

He got on his hands and knees and crawled under the sensor, careful not to break the invisible laser beam that connected the two devices. Once on the other side, he rose and sprinted to a small copse. Bolan pulled a compact, portable night scope from his web belt and pointed it toward the front door. It looked just as it had the day he'd visited: guards and a houseman, although the guard complement had been doubled. He wondered if that was by design after nightfall or just due to the impending arrival of the visitors.

Whatever the case, the Executioner knew he'd have to deal with them first.

IT WASN'T EXACTLY what Jeff Gross had expected when they arrived at the estate, but he was nonetheless impressed by it. Obviously, Vlad had some influential friends to be invited to a spread like this on an island that Gross knew had a population of mostly poor people. It wasn't until Vlad introduced him to the master of the house, though, that Gross recognized the name of Davis Haglemann.

Haglemann shook his hand. "Welcome to my humble abode."

"Humble?" Gross snorted with disbelief. "This is a frigging palace compared to most of the huts on this island."

"Oh? You're familiar with Adak?"

Gross shrugged. "I've been here a time or two. Once on a tour while I was off duty."

"I see you're in the Coast Guard."

"I *was* in the Coast Guard," he said. "Now I'm a civilian."

"What he really means is he's AWOL," Moscovich said.

"I don't suppose you've got any civvies I could change into? Some place to clean up, maybe?" Gross inquired.

Haglemann nodded at one of his men who stepped up immediately and gestured for Gross to follow him. Once they were gone, Moscovich relaxed, and Haglemann took notice. He knew the Coast Guard man had helped the Russians in some way. He didn't know exactly the guy's involvement, but then he didn't really need to. He didn't give a damn.

"So," Haglemann began. "I notice your grand little plan didn't come off quite as you'd expected."

"It did not succeed in every area I would have liked," Moscovich replied. "But it wasn't entirely a failure. We've learned enough that I can continue with my plans."

"I think it's interesting that before you thought of me as little more than a buffoon. And now you've actually come crawling here for my help. Typical."

"I didn't come crawling in here," Moscovich replied. "I walked in under my own power."

"And what of your friend?"

"We had a deal," Moscovich said. "He did his part, and I'm holding up my end now."

"I get the feeling that *your* end somehow involves me, too."

Moscovich shrugged. "I did my part to get him this far. You've been well compensated. And since I surmise you'll be leaving soon, I don't see any reason why you can't take him with you."

"What the hell are you talking about?"

"Oh, come now, Haglemann." Moscovich snickered. "You aren't really going to try to convince me that it's in your best interests to stay around here. Frankly, I'm surprised you're still alive."

"Ah, I see. You're talking about the guy you sent to protect me," Haglemann said. "You actually think I owe you one now."

"What guy? I didn't send anybody to protect you.

Two of our men were here, and it got them killed. And your people, who promised to protect mine on Unalaska until we could get away with the tech from the Coast Guard ship, couldn't even do that much. What makes you think we'd send anyone else here to watch out for you?"

Haglemann's gut seemed to turn to stone, and by the expression on Moscovich's face, he could immediately tell he'd been duped. "You don't know a man named Blansky."

"I never heard of him."

"You didn't send him?"

"Like I said," Moscovich repeated, "I never heard of him."

"So that means—"

"It means that you let somebody inside. Why the hell didn't you contact me to verify?"

"I'd planned to but..."

"You stupid son of a bitch." Moscovich said something else in Russian and began to shake his head. "You screwed up this entire thing! I'd planned to pay you extra to help me get off this island and get into the United States. Now we're stuck here."

"Just shut the fuck up!" Haglemann could feel his face flush. "Just let me think about this a minute. We're not stuck here. I have a chopper. It's on the way, right now. It'll be here any minute. We can get out of here. You and me. I can arrange for a plane to take you anywhere you want."

"We can't leave here in a chopper!" Moscovich spit. "The nearest damn civilized airport is almost five hundred miles from here!"

"I have a jet. It's hidden on a neighboring island at

a secure air field. I put it there for emergencies. It has more than enough range to get us to the US. I'll take you there."

Moscovich nodded, and Haglemann thought the man was apparently giving it serious consideration. Then he abruptly reached inside his coat, produced a .32-caliber pistol, aimed it at the lone bodyguard standing nearby and shot the man in the face. The bullet traveled through the brain pan and exploded out the back, splattering the bookshelves with blood and gray matter. Haglemann felt the terror well in his throat in the form of a pool of bile. He'd known it might come to this, but he hadn't expected it would be so soon.

"Now wait just a goddamn minute!" Haglemann protested, raising his hands. "You've got nothing to fear from me! I'm not going to betray you. I never planned to betray you!"

"You're right, you're not," Moscovich said. "You see, this is trouble. You know entirely too much about our operation. You're a liability, and I can no longer afford it. The time has come to end our relationship. But I do appreciate the information you've provided regarding the jet. I think it will come in very handy. No?"

Haglemann started to open his mouth, but he knew it wouldn't do any good. Moscovich was convinced that his death was the only way out of their situation, and nothing Haglemann said would convince him otherwise. He waited for the moment of death, not stopping to wonder if he would hear the shot that killed him, but then fortunes changed. The heat and blast that came didn't emanate from Moscovich's pistol—it came from just outside the window of Haglemann's study, and it blew the glass out and send a whippet of flame into the room, igniting one of the curtains.

The distraction was enough to present an opportunity of escape, and fear propelled Haglemann. He sprinted from the room while Moscovich, who had been much closer to the window, recovered from the shock of the blast. Haglemann made the hallway and ordered the three men stationed there to cover his escape. He told the fourth, who'd just returned from showing Gross into a guest room on the second floor, to accompany him to the helipad.

His timing had been impeccable, and Haglemann congratulated himself on his timely escape. The fact that he hadn't had a thing to do with it didn't even occur to him as he ascended the stairs with his bodyguard in tow. He was headed for freedom. Yes, he'd cheated death once again.

It MAY HAVE seemed preposterous to go through the front door, but Bolan thrived on being unpredictable. The last thing the enemy would have expected was a frontal assault, and that's exactly what Mack Bolan was going to give them. Maybe these men were well trained, but they weren't prepared for the all-out kind of blitz Bolan had in mind.

The Executioner charged from the trees with his weapon held low and sprinted across the grounds in a crouch on an angled approach to the front door. When he got within thirty yards, he detached one of the DM51 grenades from his harness, yanked the pin and lobbed the bomb underhand so that it hit the pavement and skittered to a stop beneath the Hummer. The men guarding the front entrance to the house looked puzzled. One of them seemed to spot Bolan at the last second and pointed at him, raising his SMG.

Too little, too late.

The grenade blew beneath the Hummer with enough force to lift the vehicle a half-foot or so off the ground. Red-orange flame whooshed from the undercarriage to lick hungrily at two of the guards close enough to feel its wrath. Their polyester pants were immediately charred and flash-burned to their skin, producing screams of terror mixed with agony. At the same moment, flaming pieces of metal soared through the air, most of them missing the sentries on duty but a few leaving cuts and burns as they penetrated skin.

The concussion of the HE did enough damage to cost one man an upper limb, but the remainder somehow managed to avoid the deadly shrapnel. The noise and heat were other matters, entirely, and the explosion had done more than enough to distract them from the Executioner's approach. As usual, Bolan took advantage of that distraction to deliver a crushing blow to the survivors.

The first two he took down with a series of short bursts from his FN-FNC. Target Number One got a belly full of 5.56 mm rounds, churning his guts to mincemeat and driving him back until he came to a seated position on the sidewalk with his back to the wall. Number Two got pummeled with two rounds to the chest and a third that opened his throat. A stray round from another volley secured the job by smashing through his skull and brains. His body stiffened a moment and then the half-headed corpse collapsed.

One of the guards who had managed to evade blast and bullets took cover behind a massive potted fern and leveled his SMG at the approaching wraith-like form of Mack Bolan. He opened up on full-auto, another clue that he didn't have the training or experience of his opponent, and bullets sprayed wildly off target. One round just clipped Bolan's arm, a graze that didn't dissuade him from his course.

He'd known a hell of a lot worse, so Bolan ignored it. He raised his carbine and delivered a return blast on the run. The fern did nothing to stop the flurry of rounds. The gunner's body twitched and danced and knocked him out of his crouched position. His body hit the pavement, blood oozing from better than a half-dozen holes.

Only two guards were still on their feet and had gained some sense of their predicament. Unfortunately for them, Bolan was now on top of them, and they had no time to counteract his assault. Bolan had his own issue, having expended the remainder of his magazine on Fern Guy with no time to reload.

The Executioner continued in forward motion and planted a running front kick that drove the first of his two opponents into the wall. He switched the carbine to his left hand, drew the Beretta 93-R and in one, smooth motion snap-aimed and squeezed the trigger. The weapon spit a single 158-grain slug that hit the guy in the center of his chest.

Bolan wheeled to his right to see the other guard charge him with a bloodcurdling scream. He swung the FNC around as he sidestepped the charge and caught the point of the stock on the side of the man's head. The blow was glancing, however, because the man turned and charged again. The speed at which he'd recovered took Bolan a little by surprise, and before he knew it the man had his hands wrapped around Bolan's wrists. The pair was evenly matched regarding height and weight, so the soldier knew to spend any time grappling with the guy could force him to pay high dividends in time and energy.

He decided to let the man's energy do his work. The Executioner went limp and dropped on to his back in a judo circle throw. It was an old trick, but still worked on occasion. And while his enemy might have had strength and size in his favor, he didn't have much in the coordination department. The maneuver took the guy utterly unaware, and as Bolan fired the kick into his solar plexus and took him up and over, the air left the man's lungs with a forceful wheeze. The motion of the arc continued, and the man's body sailed over Bolan in a loop-de-loop that landed the back of the guy's skull on the pavement.

The fight was over before it had barely begun.

Bolan holstered the Beretta he'd still been holding, and then scrambled to his feet. He picked up and inspected the FNC, which he'd dropped to keep from getting his fingers broken or pinned beneath it. There were some scratches and a chip in the stock, but the action seemed fine. Bolan dropped the magazine from the well, added a fresh one and put the weapon in battery before slinging it across his back.

He then hurried to the front door, which was constructed of heavy oak, with reinforced hinges and wrought-iron handles. While it might have resisted a kick or battering ram, it would be no match for C4 plastique. The Executioner quickly wired it, set the explosives, found cover behind a massive stone flower bed and triggered the detonator. The blast not only took the door off its hinges, it blew the oak into splinters as if it were plywood.

Bolan waited a few seconds to ensure the enemy hadn't set up an ambush on the other side of the door, then he proceeded through the smoky hole with his .44 Magnum Desert Eagle in the lead.

CHAPTER TWENTY-TWO

Gross couldn't believe his luck. He'd barely managed to step out of his filthy, stinking uniform and headed toward the shower when he heard the blast. Cursing, he left the bathroom and rushed to the clothes the big bruiser who'd accompanied him had scrounged up. They weren't exactly top-of-the-line but they were serviceable. A pair of jeans, flannel shirt and black stocking cap. It had to be better than nothing, and Gross figured he could get something more appropriate for his new financial standing once he was safely away from this place.

He jumped into the clothes and got his boots on. The blast had been followed by some shooting, and Gross didn't know what to do. He had two options as he saw it. He could hide in the room and wait for a lull, then try to make a break for it, or he could find the house guards and get some direction. In any case, it didn't seem wise to hang the hell around this place. Something heavy was transpiring out there, and he didn't really care to stick around and see who came out the victor. It might not be someone on *his* side.

Gross jumped from the bed after lacing his boots, grabbed his pistol and headed to the door. He opened it and peered out just in time to see the guy who'd been with him come up the stairs and into view accompanying the main dude, Haglemann. He didn't know who this guy was, but he knew he had money, and he knew he had influence. Those were two very powerful things in combination, and it seemed only smart to follow him.

He looked down the hall, and when he saw nobody coming from the opposite direction, Gross stepped out of the room and followed his new ticket out of there.

MOSCOVICH SHOOK HIS head clear, trying to eliminate the cobwebs in the forefront of his mind. His eyes blurred as he tried to focus, and he noticed that there were a few cuts on his left hand. He turned his head slowly to the left and spotted the window that had blown out from the explosion. From the flames and the general direction, he guessed it was their Hummer that had blown up. Had someone thought to kill him and the American, Gross, or had this been an attempt on Haglemann's life?

Whatever the specifics, Moscovich knew things had officially gone bad for him. There would be no turning back from this now. He needed to escape, and he would probably have to affect some other way off Adak Island. The jet plane Haglemann had described was close, but how to get to it before he did would be next to impossible. The only way would be to commandeer whatever means he had for getting to that location. The chopper! Moscovich's mind began to clear as he overcame the initial shock of the explosion.

He would have to beat the guy to his helipad. He knew where it was—he'd studied the house very carefully on previous visits to secure alternate escape routes if it came to it. Unfortunately, it *had* come to it. They were under attack of some kind, or at least Haglemann was under attack, and Moscovich knew chances were good he'd get caught in the cross fire if he didn't act.

Moscovich rushed out of the study and headed for a back staircase he knew led to the third floor where he could gain rooftop access. Only one man would be leaving on that chopper, and it was going to be Vladimir Moscovich. No matter what the cost.

BOLAN STEPPED INTO the house with the FN-FNC carbine held tight and low, ready for any resistance. He met it— he responded. Two of the house guards stood side by side near the grand staircase and had pistols pointed in his direction. They were close, but the smoke and heat and light of the explosion had apparently stunned them, because their aim was off. Rounds from their pistols went high and wide, not coming even close to Bolan. He knelt, settled on his targets and squeezed the trigger, sweeping the muzzle in a rising, corkscrew pattern and cutting through the pair of guards with unerring accuracy. The high-velocity rounds punctured vital organs and ripped flesh from bone. The men danced under the impact of the rounds as Bolan cut them down.

Another man sprinted up the hallway, triggering his pistol on the run. These had obviously been bodyguards, because none of them carried arms of a paramilitary type. Typical for executive protection. They might have been trained with assault weapons, but they would not have access to them while on house duty. A guy like Haglemann probably hadn't seen a need for it, a stupid decision for a man in his line of business, dealing with terrorists.

Bolan leveled the muzzle of the FNC and squeezed the trigger. Only one round left the weapon before he sensed it had ceased recoiling. Jam! The soldier cursed and tossed the useless weapon aside. He dropped to the floor, drawing his Beretta 93-R as he did. He rolled out of the line of fire just as the guard adjusted his aim and pulled the trigger three times. The rounds thwacked into the polished hardwood floors in a spot Bolan had occupied a heartbeat before.

The soldier was now on his back, neck arched and looking above and slightly behind him. The Beretta came into target acquisition. The guard had a flash-frozen look of surprise on his face as if stunned he'd missed an enemy he thought he had dead to rights. It was the last thought that went through his mind as Bolan squeezed the trigger. A single, 9 mm round blasted into the man's face and continued up into his brain with enough force to blow off the top of his skull. His head snapped back, and his body followed a moment later, collapsing to the hardwood floor.

Bolan leaped to his feet and shook his head, taking only a moment to catch his breath. He'd trusted his instincts about the FNC, and that wasn't something he should have done. He knew that any weapon subjected to that kind of damage might well malfunction, and he'd ignored his experience in a moment of expediency. Well, no point in beating himself up. That wouldn't accomplish anything, and it was a lesson learned.

As Bolan made his way to the stairs and cautiously climbed them, he was aware of the fact things had gone easier than planned. He was ahead of schedule by at least ten minutes, which meant he'd have to stall for time once he located Haglemann and got to the roof. Grimaldi had affirmed touchdown for 2320, which meant Bolan and Haglemann could have a nice little chat while waiting for extraction. The only thing that could throw a monkey wrench in the works would be if Haglemann's chopper somehow got airborne and arrived first. Bolan didn't see how the guy could call for his bird to be in the air that fast, even in the case of an emergency. His people probably hadn't been trained to respond in such a way.

The other thing to consider was the resistance, although Bolan was sure the men he'd just encountered were the last real line of defense for Haglemann. He doubted the union leader had any reinforcements. He wouldn't have expected anything like this—Bolan was confident he'd been acting with surprise on his side. Based on what had just transpired and how easily he'd penetrated Haglemann's defenses, it was obvious that the man hadn't been equipped or prepared to repel such an assault. Ultimately, only time would tell the tale of the victor.

And time was running out for the good guys.

Fairbanks, Alaska

DR. IVAN BORGSTROM watched the seismometers with interest as he sipped at his coffee. He'd been awakened to a buzzing cell phone, and on hearing the news, he'd climbed into his Jeep and driven as fast as he safely could to the AVO offices.

The Alaska Volcano Observatory was a joint program between the United States Geological Survey, Geophysical Institute of the University of Alaska Fairbanks and the State of Alaska's Division of Geological and Geophysical Surveys. The communal mission of the USGS, UAFGI and ADGGS was the monitoring and studying of all hazardous volcanoes in Alaska, and to predict and record eruptive activity.

Their mission was in full swing that morning.

As soon as Dr. Borgstrom arrived, he went straight to the main observatory lab and began to direct the operations. Staff was in a scramble as no one had ever encountered something quite like this before. Leaning over the technician's shoulder, Borgstrom peered at the varying screens with great anticipation.

A staff member rushed up to him and shoved a stack of printouts into his hand, pointing to a particular set of readings she'd highlighted.

"All the data you asked for on Semisopochnoi, Dr. Borgstrom," Dr. Leann Leyna said.

Born in Japan and raised in Hawaii, Leyna had never been a stranger to volcanoes. They'd fascinated her since childhood, and she'd lived in some of the most volcanic regions on the planet. It's one of the many reasons he'd hired the young grad student and guided her through her PhD. While she'd never really gotten used to the cold weather, she'd proven an invaluable resource and good friend. Borgstrom considered her much like one of his own daughters.

"The last confirmed EC had been noted on April 13, 1987," Leyna added. "You can see there it had a VEI of only two."

Under other circumstances that wouldn't have been any indication, but Semisopochnoi was a bit different. In June 2014, AVO had noted a significant increase in seismic activity on the island in the form of an earthquake swarm, and the continuation of the anomalous activity had prompted them to kick up the Aviation Color Code to Yellow, but it had not warranted any other action than the continuous monitoring. Flybys had continued for the area, at least until the recent shutdown of air traffic by the military for reasons that were as yet unknown.

AVO had sent some recent information as requested about any potential dangers posed to military personnel, particularly air force, navy and US Coast Guard that were on maneuvers in the area. That seemed strange, since Borgstrom typically received that data months in advance, even if it were a planned alert exercise. He wasn't technically supposed to have that information, but he had some friends in high places, and they kept him abreast of the basics more as a courtesy. Borgstrom could understand the need for security when it came to military operations, but he was responsible for the safety of everyone operating near volcanic regions. Was it too much to ask he be shown a little courtesy now and again?

This most recent information was disturbing at best and the activity and tension in the labs almost palpable. Sugarloaf Peak was a stratovolcano feature at an elevation of 856 meters. And that puppy was definitely rumbling. In some subterranean caves, thermal imaging revealed that practically overnight they had experienced increases of temperature by a couple hundred degrees.

"If I didn't know better," Borgstrom muttered, "I'd say this could be a full eruption with a VEI of… Oh, wow, maybe as high as five?"

VEI was a measure of the eruption explosiveness on a scale of zero to eight. The Mount St. Helens eruption in May 1980 had been rated a five, and the Pinatubo in the Philippines back in 1991 had rated at a six.

The latter had also been stratovolcano, just like Sugarloaf on Semisopochnoi, and the sudden activity after seemingly no real threat for hundreds of years of benign readings could indicate they'd missed something along the way.

Borgstrom advised he'd be in his office and went straight there. He verified the data three times, checking it against the history of the island, before finally picking up the phone and calling the special hotline they had installed. Because of his unique position as overseer of AVO, Borgstrom had direct access to certain highly placed personnel and had been invited to use the hotline if he ever thought something might threaten national defense in Alaska as it related to volcanoes. This call would mean he'd have to reveal his knowledge of such activities, but that could hardly be something to worry about right now. The lives of potentially thousands of service members could be at risk.

The line was picked up on the third ring, and Borgstrom was thankful it was monitored twenty-four hours a day, three-hundred sixty-five days a year.

"This is Dr. Borgstrom with the Alaska Volcano Observatory in Fairbanks. I need to speak with the Secretary of Defense on a Priority Alpha matter."

"Please, stand by, sir."

Borgstrom drummed his fingers nervously on his desk while he waited to be patched to the highest-ranking military official in the US government. He knew he might be overreacting, but it was better to cry wolf and have it not be true than do nothing and let potentially hundreds or thousands get killed. Not to mention the fact the information and data they collected was open to the public.

The Secretary of Defense's sleepy voice finally cut through the secure airwaves. "Dr. Borgstrom. This is unexpected. What can I do for you?"

"I'm sorry to wake you, Mr. Secretary, but I have some very disturbing information, and I thought it prudent to contact you."

"Quite all right. What's going on?"

"Sir, we…" Borgstrom's words caught in his throat, and he paused only a moment to wonder if he was about to commit career suicide. No, he couldn't think that way. He was a competent and respected scientist. They would have to listen to him.

"We have been monitoring for the past six hours an unusual amount of seismic activity on Semisopochnoi Island."

"Where?"

"Semisopochnoi. It's one of the island bodies in the Aleutians, Mr. Secretary."

"Oh, of course, of course," he replied. "Please, go on."

Borgstrom knew the pedantic blowhard didn't have the first clue where it was, but he ignored that fact. "This activity is significant because it started very suddenly, and we had no reason up to this point to be concerned. There were no indications that it could or even would erupt—"

"Hold up there," the secretary cut in, clearing his throat and still trying to come fully awake. "What are you talking about? Are you saying there's a volcano about to erupt in Alaska?"

"Yes, sir," Borgstrom replied. "I'm calling *you* because I have it on good authority there are currently significant military operations going on in that region."

"How did you know that? Oh, never mind. That's

unimportant right now. So you're calling because of concern for those personnel."

"Yes. Mr. Secretary, I can't emphasize enough the dangers of this development. I've triple-checked the data, and I predict the Volcanic Explosivity Index of this eruption at five, the same as Mount Pinatubo in the Philippines."

"Could you elaborate on those effects? I'm not familiar with that eruption."

"It produced the second largest eruption of the twentieth century, exceeded only by Novarupta, which also occurred in Alaska, incidentally. The results were cataclysmic and had atmospheric consequences around the world. More than ten billion tons of magma were ejected, and twenty million short tons of minerals and metals were deposited surface-side. At present, we've noted phreatic explosions on Sugarloaf, that's the designation of this stratovolcano on Semisopochnoi, which would indicate that magma is already heating groundwater. There are steam blasts already visible to satellite cameras. Normally such activity would be an indication of eruption in the very near future, but in this case I don't think we have that much time."

Borgstrom could hear the Secretary of Defense utter a number of blasphemies under his breath before asking, "How much time are we talking about?"

"If these readings are correct, and I have little doubt to think they aren't, we have less than twelve hours. If you have any personnel on that island, or anywhere near it, you need to evacuate them immediately."

"Dr. Borgstrom, you *have* to be sure about this. I have information that indicates our activities are presently confined to Dutch Harbor, so there shouldn't be any military personnel near there. But there are some pockets of civilian population we should concern ourselves with."

"We have equipment on Semisopochnoi, Mr. Secretary, and I assume the navy does, too. However, the island is unpopulated, as are those islands closest to it. But given the circumstances, I thought it prudent to contact you immediately."

"You did the exact right thing, Doctor," he replied. "I'll need to contact the Joint Chiefs and President and brief them immediately. I will also need you to forward any and all data you have to my offices, so we can begin to put together an action plan. I'll have someone call you within a half hour with details."

"Understood."

"Thank you, Dr. Borgstrom," the secretary said, and he hung up.

Borgstrom looked at the receiver a moment before hanging up himself. The man on the other end of the line had sounded strange, to be sure, but then he'd woken the poor guy up at home with some very disturbing news. Had roles been reversed, Borgstrom probably would've sounded strange, as well.

In any case, he'd done his best to go through the proper channels and notify them of the impending eruption of Sugarloaf. He wondered now what he should do next, but even as he pondered the thought, he knew the answer. He could turn over the updates to Leann. He needed to get into the chopper and get out to the area as quickly as possible, so he could witness the situation firsthand. But could he really afford to do that? The Secretary of Defense would be contacting him soon, or at least someone from his office, and

Borgstrom knew he should stay available in the event he'd have to brief the President.

Such a possibility was likely, perhaps even inevitable. He couldn't afford to leave that duty to an underling, no matter how good.

Damn. He'd have to send Leann! Not that he didn't trust her—she was the best in her field and as trustworthy a soul as they came. It would just mean he'd miss seeing the eruption, and that was something most every volcanic scientist lived for. It was exciting and at once terrifying to watch the Earth cough up her lifeblood while showing off her fierce terror and power all at the same time. It was almost like witnessing the birth of a human baby, but with so many more ramifications. Well, nothing could be done about it. His duty was here, his dedication to the safety and conservation of human life came first.

Ivan Borgstrom was just glad for one thing—no human life was presently on Semisopochnoi.

CHAPTER TWENTY-THREE

Semisopochnoi Island

Benyamin Tokov felt his skin might be boiled off his body. Temperatures inside the cavern seemed to have increased dramatically, and the walls were drenched with moisture.

He'd been sleeping in an antechamber, back to the wall, when the sudden sounds of rumbling and heavy vibrations yanked him from his dreams. The change of environment seemed to have come like the spring of a pole vaulter, and Tokov wondered if there had been a change in the volcanic activity. Tokov was no volcanologist or seismologist, but he knew something about volcanoes. The sudden rise in ambient temperature within the cavern seemed to be a pretty good indication of increased thermal energy emanating from the crevasses of magma running beneath them.

Tokov looked at his watch. They still had more than six hours before the *Belsky* would be within signaling range. It would be at least another hour before the launches arrived to take them off the island and another hour after that before they were safely aboard the Russian submarine and away from this place. Tokov couldn't wait, but he also had to admit that these new developments had him a little concerned.

Of course, no volcano had ever started rumbling to life and then suddenly erupted after only a few hours of activity. They had looked carefully at the data before choosing this island, and there were no indications that an eruption would occur. The previous year about this time there had apparently been some sort of gaseous escape and seismic activity, but there hadn't been any earthquakes. And this activity couldn't have even been deemed a seismic event of any significance. The walls of the cavern remained standing, and nobody had been injured.

While Semisop was definitely coming to life, they were still a long way off from seeing any sort of serious eruption. Tokov knew enough to understand that. Still, there was no longer any reason for them to stay below ground, and he was sick and tired of the heat. Tokov climbed to his feet, dusted himself down and headed to where his men were waiting to tell them it was time to head into open ground.

Better safe than sorry, Tokov thought.

Part of Commander Louis Ducati felt as if he might just expire right there, but he forced such thoughts from his mind. He could not, no, he *would* not abandon his crew that easily. He would not die, and he would not succumb to his need for rest. There would be plenty of time to rest after they were rescued, and Ducati knew they would be rescued. He could feel it in his gut. Their people were coming for them, and they would be there soon.

He hoped it was sooner rather than later, though, when they felt the rumblings beneath their feet and a gust of heated air washed over them less than two minutes later. It felt as if they'd walked through a sauna, and it was damn hot. Not hot enough to burn anyone but definitely enough to make them all feel as if they'd been burnt. The worse part was there was no escape from it. They couldn't go anywhere.

Ducati had finally managed to get Rastogi to demand additional water for them or just shoot them. He wasn't willing to stand by and watch his crew die of thirst, although he knew that might just happen. Rastogi had tried to wake him when he witnessed the Russian leader leave the caverns with Gross, but he'd been too exhausted to wake up. Rastogi had told him after the fact, and Ducati could feel the anger swell in his chest.

That bastard! How anyone could betray their country was beyond his capacity to understand. What was it that drove men to such things? Ducati could understand a philosophical difference or even a religious objection, but from what he gathered, Gross's treachery had been solely about money. Greed. Was the proverbial allure of gold still so prevalent in society that a man might sell his morals and integrity down the river for it? That's what it amounted to, and Ducati wouldn't see it any other way.

Ducati looked around him at the suffering caused by that one heinous act. They couldn't just hang out here and wait for rescue. A prisoner's number one mission was to escape, and Ducati hadn't done anything to affect that. He'd wanted them to wait until this point for fear their captors might cut them down with the wicked-looking assault weapons they toted, but now he was convinced that could no longer be a consideration. Especially not when one of his people came to speak with him at Rastogi's behest.

"Sir," Rastogi began. When Ducati looked wearily in his direction, Rastogi pointed to one of his people. "This is Petty Officer Grant. He wants to talk to you about that rumble and heat blast we just felt."

Ducati nodded at his crew member. "What's up, Grant?"

The young man had a brush cut of red hair and large, green eyes. Ducati remembered him a bit and noted he was a good man. Trustworthy and did his job without complaint. He also recalled Grant's superior officers had given him good ratings in his last evaluation.

"Sir, we have to get out of here."

Ducati swallowed hard, his tongue feeling parched. "I understand, son. We'll be out of here soon. Somebody's coming for us."

"No, sir, I don't think you understand. You see, that seismic activity and the sudden increase in temperature? Those are aftereffects of phreatic eruptions."

"Say what? Slow down, man, start from the beginning."

"My father was seismic geologist," Grant said. "He lived and breathed it, sir. Believe me, he drilled that stuff into me. Phreatic eruptions are caused by active volcanoes where the magma level is rising. It heats the ground water and forms steam, eventually pushing that out through whatever vents might be available right in and around the caldera that's been formed. But after a while it starts to push to outlying pockets, and it eventually travels through the channels until it has some place to escape. The fact we got one like this just now, as far away from any active points, would indicate that eruption is imminent!"

Ducati couldn't believe his ears. He'd thought to

keep his people alive, but now he could see that waiting here and sparing them execution had been a very bad approach, indeed. If Grant was correct in what he was saying, and he'd just presented what Ducati thought to be an extremely convincing argument, the next wave of heat that came through here might be so intense it scalded them all to death. That was, of course, if a magma flow didn't just blast through and turn them all instantly to ash!

"What Grant says explains a number of things, sir," Rastogi said. "We just saw the rest of that Russian crew go past us, and they were beating feet out of here *fast*. They chucked some additional gallons of water inside the cages and then locked up and got the hell out of here. I think they know something's up, too."

Ducati nodded. It was all starting to make sense. Whether their enemies had known about a volcano or not, there was no denying the intent of their actions. They were leaving enough water to sustain the group for a day or two more. After that, they probably figured anything that happened would be fate, and it wasn't on their hands. Ducati didn't see it that way, but then he didn't have much to say about it. At least now that they were no longer under guard they could go to work on defeating the heavy chains and padlocks of the cages.

"Number One, get the section chiefs on board and let's start coming up with an escape plan," Ducati told Rastogi. "We're getting the hell out of here."

Adak Island

BOLAN ADVANCED UP the first flight of stairs. Halfway up he stopped to drop one of the M86 PDMs on the stairs.

The pursuit deterrent munition featured a hand-grenade style release firing mechanism. It deployed three trip wires that would latch on to whatever objects it was aimed at. They were particularly useful in jungle terrain, the hell grounds in which Bolan had learned much of deadly craft, but were equally effective in a dark environment such as this. The PDM contained a liquid propellant that, when activated, launched the mine into the air approximately eight feet before exploding. Normally, Bolan would not have deployed such a hazard that could harm bystanders or subsequent law enforcement, but these babies contained a mechanism that destroyed them if undisturbed for four hours. John "Cowboy" Kissinger—resident weapon-smith and armorer for the Stony Man teams—had modified them so they self-destructed after thirty minutes.

The Executioner turned to continue up the steps when his earpiece buzzed. There would be only one reason Grimaldi would break radio silence in an operation. Something had changed drastically in the original plan.

"Go, Eagle One."

"Striker, we've got trouble. As I was prepping for takeoff in the chopper, I saw another one lift up out of here on a bearing for your direction. It's heading toward Haglemann's."

"I was afraid of that. Chakowa promised me he'd keep everyone away."

"Maybe so, but nobody apparently nobody talked to the tower boys. They heard it was for Haglemann, and they immediately cleared it. I think it got missed."

"No way you can catch him?"

"I'm firing up now but not likely," Grimaldi said.

"I couldn't beat him there, even if he took the scenic route."

"Understood. Just get here fast as you can," Bolan said. "I'm going to need you."

"Acknowledged. Eagle One, out!"

Bolan grit his teeth in frustration. His one opportunity to catch Haglemann had started to slip through his fingers. He continued his charge up the stairs with a new resolve.

GROSS MANAGED TO get as far as the third floor when the bodyguard with Haglemann noticed he was following them. Gross froze in his tracks. He'd been caught in the open, and there wasn't much he could do about that. The bodyguard pulled his pistol, clearly presuming that the man was a credible threat. Gross jumped into the small space a doorway afforded as a bullet exploded from the bodyguard's pistol. The round zinged past Gross's ear close enough for him to hear the whiz of its passing. He snap-aimed and fired back but his shot was wide, serving only to cause the bodyguard to duck and look for cover.

Gross waited until the guy fired again, missing him and chipping out a large chunk of the door frame, then popped out of the alcove and fired three successive rounds. That was four bullets already gone from his revolver. Of course, he had spare rounds but no speed loader, so reloading would take time. Gross tried the door as he was shooting, and the handle turned smoothly. He pushed through into the darkened room. It was an empty bedroom, similar to the one he'd changed in.

Gross waited as the bodyguard fired his weapon

in response, then leaned out from cover and fired two more rounds. He got behind the concealment of the doorway, knelt and emptied the cartridges from his revolver. His hand shook as he fought to load the weapon, cursing under his breath as he absentmindedly touched the barrel and burned his fingers. What the hell was this all about, anyway? Why was Haglemann's bodyguard shooting at him? Did he really think they had something to fear from him?

Gross finished loading his revolver, snapped the cylinder closed and turned it until it click-locked into place. He thumbed back the hammer and risked another glance into the hallway. It seemed deserted, but he couldn't be sure. Maybe they just wanted to make it look as if they had left. Gross considered his next move. If he tried to follow them, he might walk into an ambush. On the other hand, whoever had caused those explosions and the gunfire he'd heard while following Haglemann and his bodyguard was a force to be reckoned with. He couldn't go back. Something told him that Haglemann's way out was the *only* way out.

Gross stepped into the hallway after another moment and proceeded carefully down the hall.

He'd nearly reached the point where the bodyguard had disappeared when a new form seemed to appear from nowhere. Gross started to raise his pistol and then noticed it was Vlad. The Russian stopped short and started to raise his own weapon, but Gross lifted his hands and shouted his friendly intent. There seemed to be just a moment of hesitation in the Russian, and Gross thought maybe he'd made a fatal mistake, but then at the last moment Vlad lowered his pistol.

"You're lucky, no? You nearly got your head blown off," Moscovich said.

Gross grinned. "I knew you wouldn't shoot me."

"You trust me?"

"Sure," Gross said with a shrug. "Why not?"

"Then you are a damn fool! You shouldn't trust anyone, because they will eventually betray you. It's the nature of this business."

"Yeah, well, it looks like your pal Haglemann's trying to cut and run on us," Gross said. "His bodyguard nearly killed me."

"You see? You cannot trust him."

"I take it he must have a way out of here."

Moscovich nodded. "He has a helicopter on the way. I plan to be on it."

"So do I," Gross said. "Then once we get somewhere semi-civilized and that doesn't have an extradition treaty with the United States, we can part company."

"I don't know if that would be wise," Moscovich said.

"Why not?"

"Because the continental United States is precisely where I plan to go."

Gross shook his head. "Well, no, thanks."

"We do not have time to argue here. We will miss our opportunity if we don't go now."

"And if we don't work together."

"Fine," Moscovich said. "But remember that I do not trust you, and we are not friends."

"We can stay together only as long as it's mutually beneficial," Gross said. "A temporary truce."

He stuck out his hand, but Moscovich ignored it and turned toward the door through which Haglemann and the bodyguard had disappeared.

He had just opened it when movement at the far end of the hallway caught his eye.

MACK BOLAN EMERGED on to the third-floor landing from the stairs and spotted two men opening a door he guessed led to the rooftop access and helipad. Neither of the men looked like Haglemann. In fact, he'd never seen either of them before. They were dressed in casual civilian clothes, not the suits of the house security. Bolan wondered if they were the visitors who had arrived in the Hummer.

Not that it mattered much, since on seeing him they both pointed weapons in his direction and opened fire.

Bolan went prone and thumbed the selector switch to 3-round-burst mode. He triggered the first volley. The Beretta spit a trio of 9 mm zingers downrange designed more to keep his opponents off their game than to necessarily connect. The rounds burned the air just above their heads.They whipped open a door leading off the hallway and dashed through it as Bolan checked his aim and fired again, this time aiming center mass toward the door. All three rounds connected, but he couldn't tell if he'd hit either of the men.

He jumped to his feet and sprinted down the hall in pursuit of them. Whoever they were, they had fired at him indiscriminately and then fled. That made them enemies and persons of interest. The soldier couldn't help but wonder if they had been left there to stall him while Haglemann made his escape. But if they'd been willing to lay down their lives for Haglemann out of some bizarre sense of duty, they would have held their ground instead of running away. Were they accompanying Haglemann in his escape or had they killed the guy and were now planning to use his chopper to get out of there?

Grimaldi said someone had called for the chopper from the Adak airfield, so that meant whomever had phoned either had been Haglemann or used Haglemann's authority. In any case, Bolan's mission was still intact. He needed to find Haglemann and take him alive. All other options were off the table now. There would only be one chance, and he couldn't blow it. The lives of many service personnel hung in the balance.

Hang on, the Executioner thought. Hang on just a little longer.

CHAPTER TWENTY-FOUR

Davis Haglemann and his bodyguard emerged on the broad, open roof that had a steep slope on either side like a chateau style A-frame. It had been designed in response to the heavy precipitation of winter so snow would not pile up and collapse the roof. Despite the hefty roof load capacity and steel-beam support construction, the laws of nature were such that nothing could be left to chance. In that regard, Haglemann's house had stood as much as a fortress as an estate.

It saddened him that he had to abandon the place, as he and his bodyguard took the flagstone steps down to the parapet and through the sheltered walkway just beneath the roof that led to the helipad. The corridor was narrow and barely high enough to accompany a tall man, the ceiling being a mere six-foot-two. That design had also been purposeful; in the event roof collapse occurred, it would not cut off access to the helipad and prevent entry or escape.

Unfortunately for Haglemann's bodyguard, it also made protecting his master a nightmare. Haglemann didn't really care one way or another. His men were tools, just like all the other people he'd used. Whether it was common laborers or smarmy business partners, Davis Haglemann saw them merely as objects to manipulate to his will.

Yes, Haglemann would miss all of this, and yet he knew he could start over. He wasn't happy about losing the empire he'd built here on Adak and all of the money he'd made, but there would be more opportunities to carve out a new life for himself somewhere else. Maybe the next recipients of his largesse would show him a little more gratitude instead of abandoning him the moment times got a little tough.

So he'd done business with the Russians. So what? He'd never committed any of the horrible acts they had, never murdered anybody. In fact, he'd paid Chakowa and his one-man police force to protect the people here on Adak. He'd sheltered people from outside interference, given them everything they wanted. They'd tasted of all the modern conveniences because of his efforts, never wanted for a thing, really. In return, all he'd asked for was their loyalty and hard work. They'd turned against him for it. Good riddance to the bastards!

Haglemann and his bodyguard were nearly at the other end. The union boss could hear the blades of the approaching chopper. He'd timed it perfectly. There was no way they could reach him before he got off the ground—soon he would be home free and headed for his plane. He was thinking about where he might wish to go next. Someplace warm would be a nice change.

Bullets burned the air, ricocheting off the walls and generating sparks as they entered the drywall and struck steel supports. Haglemann ducked and pressed toward the door. It seemed so far away, and yet it was just a few feet. As he reached it, Haglemann heard his bodyguard cry out, and he stopped a moment, turning to see what had happened. The guy was now on the ground, screaming as blood poured from the side of his neck. Haglemann looked at the guy only a moment, then he knelt, reached out and grabbed the pistol he dropped. He hadn't really used a gun much in his time, but he knew how all the same, courtesy of lessons on the firing range he'd had built.

Haglemann snapped off two shots that didn't come close to hitting either Moscovich or Gross, but he got the satisfaction of watching them throw themselves to the floor in fear. He looked down at the sensation of something near his foot and spotted his bodyguard clawing at the toe of his left shoe. Haglemann let out a mutter of surprise, then pointed his pistol at the man and squeezed the trigger, the bullet entering the back of his bodyguard's skull.

A mercy kill was the way Haglemann looked at it.

He shot another two rounds to keep his two opponents at bay, then the trigger locked. He looked at the pistol and noted the slide was back. The pistol had run dry. He didn't want to risk getting shot looking for additional ammunition, so he instead threw the useless weapon aside, turned and ran as fast as he could down the corridor to the door leading on to the helipad. The sound of blades slapping the air drew very close. He was home free!

MOSCOVICH UTTERED CURSES beneath his breath as he watched Haglemann toss his gun aside and continue down the hallway. He'd just witnessed the man shoot his own bodyguard, which told the Russian everything he needed to know about the union boss. The guy couldn't be trusted. Moscovich thought a moment on the irony of it all, since he'd just told Gross the same damn thing. If he'd made any mistakes at all, it had been allying himself and his people with Americans. They were their own worst enemies.

Moscovich scrambled to his feet and raced along the corridor, bent on ensuring Haglemann wasn't allowed to leave without him. He'd make certain the man didn't leave at all. His instincts had once before led him to the conclusion that Davis Haglemann was too unstable and untrustworthy to live. The American wasn't much longer for this Earth if Moscovich had anything to say about it.

The Russian glanced behind him and saw that Gross was not in pursuit. The guy was too occupied fighting the man they had first spotted in the hallway. He looked like a commando, dressed as he was, various implements hanging from an equipment harness of some type. He had dark hair, and he was big and muscular, but that's really all Moscovich could perceive from that distance. Well, the stranger was Gross's problem now, and Moscovich couldn't worry about him. Gross would either survive the encounter or likely die, and Moscovich didn't really care which at this point.

He had a score to settle with another American.

WHEN BOLAN DESCENDED the narrow steps and cautiously entered the door of a long corridor, he encountered the two men he'd met moments before. The first one had somehow managed to gain a lead over the other and was headed down the narrow hall. The younger man had just climbed to his feet. When he saw the Executioner he lunged at him awkwardly.

Bolan sidestepped and delivered a knee to the man's gut that knocked the wind from him and sent him reeling against the hard wall on the opposite side of the corridor. The man sucked down several quick gulps of air, attempting to recover from Bolan's surprise counter. The soldier pressed his attack with a haymaker that landed on the left side of the guy's face. Rock-hard knuckles split the skin below the man's eye and drew blood. The blow staggered his opponent, but again it wasn't enough to knock him down.

The man turned desperately in various directions, obviously looking for his weapon. Bolan spotted the pistol lying on the floor just a heartbeat before his opponent, and he stepped forward and kicked it away. Unfortunately, the motion distracted him, and Bolan caught a hard blow to the jaw that rattled his teeth. The Executioner shook it off and delivered a one-two gut shot. More air exploded from the man's lungs, and his head came forward. He clapped his opponent's ears with enough force to shatter both eardrums, then landed a booted toe in a front kick he was sure crushed at least one testicle and possibly both. The guy emitted something of a cross between a shriek and a howl. Bolan used the distraction to fire a low side kick that took out the man's right knee, and finished the job with a knife-hand strike to the nerve at the neck and shoulder.

The man's eyes rolled up, and he slowly dipped forward until he collapsed face-first on the floor unconscious.

Bolan picked up the revolver, disengaged the cylinder and ejected the unspent rounds before tossing it far away and continuing in pursuit of the second man. He didn't know his identity, but a good guess would be Vladimir Moscovich. At least he could hope it was. To get Moscovich and Haglemann simultaneously would make his job easier.

The Executioner could only hope Fate smiled on him.

HAGLEMANN DUCKED AS the rotor wash whipped his clothing about in a violent frenzy. He waited at the fringe of the helipad, watching for the pilot's signal. He wished the bastard would hurry up—he didn't have time for this! Finally, when he got the signal, he sprinted toward the chopper as the pilot climbed from his seat and crawled into the fuselage to open the door. As it slid aside and Haglemann went to step inside, he felt a severe burn on his right cheek and something caused his head to snap to the side.

Haglemann saw a smear of black and red streak across his vision and the intensity of the pain in his head increased to such a point that it caused him to stagger. The union boss staggered backward utterly surprised, and suddenly his legs would no longer hold him. He collapsed, realizing as his body sank to the hard, cold concrete that he'd been shot. He could see Moscovich come into his view, but he couldn't move a muscle. He watched as the Russian looked at his body only a moment and smiled. Moscovich stuck his pistol in the pilot's face and gestured with it to indicate the pilot should return to the cockpit.

Haglemann observed with a rising sense of help-lessness as Moscovich climbed into the chopper and slid the door closed. A moment later, the aircraft was up and moving away at tremendous speed. Haglemann could hear several loud bangs, like thunderclaps, and then he saw a pair of boots come into his increasingly blurry sight. The blood was running freely now. Haglemann wanted to scream in agony as he felt sudden pressure on his face, but his voice seemed to be working less effectively than his arms or legs.

And Haglemann wondered if this day that had begun as the one where he could get a fresh start would wind up being the day he died.

WHEN MACK BOLAN emerged on to the helipad, he watched helplessly as the chopper lifted off and powered away. He thought about firing on the aircraft, hoping to bring it down, but quickly dismissed the idea. He had to consider the pilot, who might, after all, be just an innocent bystander in this crazy situation. Bolan had always considered how his actions might affect innocent people and did everything he could not to let any harm come to anyone. He wasn't about to change now.

Bolan holstered his pistol and rushed to where Haglemann lay on the helipad. A significant amount of blood was coming from the guy's head, but somehow he was still alive. His eyes were open, and he bore an expression of shock and stark terror. Bolan muttered an encouraging word to let the guy know he was going to live. It looked as though a bullet had gone through the guy's right cheek and taken off a considerable amount of flesh.

Bolan turned Haglemann's head to the side gently and used his teeth to rip off the plastic, perforated top of a combat dressing that had been tucked into one of the pouches on his harness belt. He applied the bulky dressing to the wound, pinching a wad between the inside and outside of what remained of Haglemann's cheek. He held the second one in place with his left hand, using the helipad concrete to keep the pressure, so he could free his right hand to get a bandage out. He applied the small compress and hastily wrapped the bandage to hold it in place.

The job took less than thirty seconds.

The Executioner now turned and drew the Desert Eagle, the muzzle of the big handgun traveling the entire perimeter of the helipad in search of threats. None came, and Bolan nodded with satisfaction. He'd accomplished his mission. Haglemann's security force had been neutralized, and he'd captured the guy alive. Haglemann might not be able to do much talking, but then Bolan didn't need him to. All he needed was the location of the RBN's main operational force.

Bolan keyed up his transmitter. "Striker to Eagle One."

"Eagle One, here."

"ETA?"

"Two minutes."

Bolan checked his watch: 2313 hours. The pilot had left early once he'd realized the timetable had been altered.

"Roger that. Mission accomplished, and I have my package. Alive but wounded. Also, a chopper got away with someone else. My guess is he's an RBN connection, but I won't know for sure until I can question current company."

"Understood and acknowledged. I'm coming in now."

True to his words, Grimaldi's approaching chopper blades were heard by Bolan even as he signed off. He wasn't sure where Haglemann's pilot would be headed with the mysterious passenger aboard, but he bet Haglemann knew. It would be critically important to keep this man alive, and Bolan wondered a moment at the very irony of that fact. Haglemann was a traitor and an enemy of America, and yet he was now the individual who possessed the information that could save the lives of nearly one hundred Coast Guard personnel.

As soon as the chopper touched down, Bolan pulled Haglemann to his feet and hoisted him into a fireman's carry. Once he and his charge were aboard, Bolan donned a headset and gave Grimaldi a thumbs-up. Before long they were in the air and headed to the medical station on the far side of the island. Grimaldi had already called ahead, and Chakowa had confirmed they would have the doctor and his staff standing by. Haglemann would need considerable care, possibly even a skilled plastic surgeon to repair the damage left by his would-be assassin's bullet. But the guy would survive.

The flight took less than ten minutes from takeoff to touchdown, and a ground ambulance waited for them on the tarmac. Once they had Hagelmann loaded into the ambulance, Bolan ordered everybody out. At first, the doctor protested. One stark look from the Executioner's penetrating blue eyes was enough to let everyone know argument wasn't an option. They piled out and left Bolan alone with Haglemann.

"I won't insult your intelligence," Bolan told the man. "You know I don't work for the Russians."

Haglemann nodded.

"The guy who shot you and took off in the chopper. Was it Vladimir Moscovich?"

For a long moment it seemed as if Haglemann wouldn't answer. He just looked at Bolan, and the weighty silence that followed seemed broken only by the steady, rhythmic beep of the EKG monitor. Vital fluids dripped from twin IV lines, one plugged into each arm, and the steady drone of the ambulance engine provided the underlying hum that seemed to sustain the moment.

Haglemann finally nodded again.

"Where's that chopper headed?" Bolan demanded.

When Haglemann didn't answer, the soldier said, "You need to talk to me, Haglemann. There are a lot of lives at stake. The game's over. You're going to prison for the rest of your life. The only thing that will keep you out of the nastiest, dirtiest, darkest hole you can imagine is your cooperation. So kill the stoic act and tell me what I want to know."

"Ka-ka-naga," Haglemann managed to say with some effort. "C-Cape Chunu."

Haglemann had to stop and take a rasping breath, his airway obviously partially compromised by the additional padding Bolan had put there. He still had some questions to answer, though, and the soldier had to press him for as much information as possible while the guy could still talk.

"Now just nod at this question," Bolan said. "Try to save your strength. The group Moscovich runs. They're part of the Russian Business Network?"

Haglemann nodded.

"Where are they operating, Haglemann? Do you

know where Moscovich's people are? Where he's holding the Coast Guard crew?"

Haglemann managed to speak the words, another bare whisper, before succumbing to unconsciousness with a will to no longer remain awake.

"Semisopochnoi."

CHAPTER TWENTY-FIVE

During the flight from Adak Island to the waiting plane on a nearby island, a location Haglemann's pilot specifically identified as Cape Chunu, it finally dawned on Vladimir Moscovich. The wraith-like and commanding presence of the dark-haired man he and Gross had encountered back at Haglemann's estate: the black attire; the dogged fighting ability and military-style destruction he'd brought against Haglemann's security forces.

All of it came back to him in moment, a flood awash with memories of the stories he'd been told by Bea Nasenko and others in their organization time after time, the stories of the mysterious man who had nearly brought a revolutionary dynasty to its knees. He had encountered the man, and he hadn't even realized it. Something in his gut told him to listen and pay attention, to sit up and take notice of what had been happening, and he had missed it entirely. He'd allowed himself to be blinded by his own genius, his plans and endless strategies, and all the other machinations he'd conjured. The very revenge he'd sought, the recompense against the Americans for what had happened just a few years back, had completely obliterated his true goals. He'd lost his first and greatest reason for doing what he'd sworn to do, and it had taken him completely unaware until this moment. A blinding, brutal moment when he realized the American who had destroyed their plans had been within his grasp!

It was him—it *had* to be him!

Moscovich would not accept any other theory. They had been confounded once more by the same man who had confounded them the first time, and Moscovich had no illusions about what would be the consequences of this. He would destroy them for certain. They had not gotten away with the tech salvaged off the Coast Guard cutter, and their plans to continue the operations in America would be countered by the intelligence gleaned from potential survivors.

The man in black knew about Moscovich now, and there wasn't anything he could do about that. Well, at least Benyamin and his men would get away. Within a few hours they would be safely aboard the *Belsky* and making best possible speed for the motherland. By this time three weeks from now, his friends would be safely nestled at headquarters in St. Petersburg.

Moscovich shook that from his thoughts. He would have to move forward with his plans. He *would* get inside mainland America undetected, with his forged documents and a bit of luck, and he would set up a new splinter cell. Somewhere there he would create a new revolution to rise up and destroy the Americans.

Moscovich turned his attention to the pilot. "This plane of Haglemann's. It is a jet?"

"Yeah," the pilot said, nodding quickly.

"Let me ask you another question. Do you consider yourself a hero?"

"A hero?"

"Yes, you know. A crusader, a brave man, a strong man."

"Look, man, I don't consider myself nothing big. I've got a wife and kids, and I'd like to see them alive again."

"You think I'm going to kill you?" Moscovich asked, unable to keep the sound of amusement out of his voice. When the man nodded quickly, Moscovich added with glee, "Absolutely not! Such a thing will not happen! The jet, what is its range?"

The pilot shrugged. "About twenty-six hundred nautical miles."

"And it is fully fueled?"

"Of course," the pilot replied with a bit of huff. "I take care of my birds, man. I expect them to get me from point A to point B alive, too, you know. I do the maintenance checks myself. Every week I've flown out here and kept that aircraft in perfect working condition. She'll fly, man. Trust me, she'll fly."

"And you can reach the mainland United States, then."

"Better believe it," the pilot replied. "I can get you anywhere along the West Coast you want. Anywhere. And it's a private plane with a US registration and standard, on-file flight plan."

"Then we won't have to go through customs?"

"No, *everybody* has to go through customs. But we aren't carrying anything illegal. And as long as you got your passport and other documentation in order, you won't have any trouble."

"And I can expect *you* will not give me any trouble."

"Look, dude, like I said. You want to go anywhere, I'll take you there."

"Why so cooperative?"

"I figure if I'm your pilot, you aren't going to kill me. Not unless you can fly." The man swallowed hard and looked at Moscovich out of the corner of his eye. "I mean…you *can't* fly. Right?"

"Let's just keep what I can or cannot do out of the conversation. You would not want to know it, I think. But I will tell you this much. I am a man whose word is his bond. If you cooperate and do exactly as you are told—" he waved the pistol for emphasis "—and you do not try anything stupid and fly me where I tell you to? You will come out of this alive."

Moscovich pulled a wad of American bills from his pocket. "And a little bit richer. Eh?"

"Sure, sure," the pilot replied. "Whatever you say, man. You're in charge. I won't give you *any* trouble."

"I thought you might see it my way," Moscovich replied.

As soon as they were up again in the chopper and headed for Kanaga Island, Bolan placed a secure call to Stony Man. He ran down the events of the past few hours and then gave them the probable location of the crew from the USCGC *Llewellyn*.

"Wait a minute," Price said. "Did you just say they're located on Semisopochnoi Island?"

"That's what Haglemann said," Bolan replied.

"Uh-oh, that's not good news. Not good news at all, Striker."

"What do you mean?"

"Hold on, I'll let Bear fill you in."

"Striker, you aren't going to like what I'm about to say, so brace yourself," Kurtzman said. "About forty-five minutes ago, we received an all-points alert issued by NASA and the SIGINT group to the Joint Chiefs. Apparently, a report came down from the Alaska Volcano Observatory that read, and I quote, 'intense seismic and volcanic activity has been observed and recorded by our team from the Sugarloaf Head, a stratovolcano feature type,' end quote."

"You're saying there's an active volcano on that island?"

"That's our understanding. According to the AVO's resident director and credited expert, Dr. Borgstrom, this thing went superhot super quick. He's claiming that a full eruption may occur in as little as twelve hours. And the news first broke six hours ago, which means—"

"We're running out of time," Bolan concluded.

The Executioner chewed on that thought a moment. He still had Moscovich to deal with, not to mention it would take them some time to get there. He didn't even know how much time, actually. Grimaldi would know, however, and when he looked expectantly at the pilot, the man held up two fingers and then twirled his index finger. Bolan got the message: approximately two hours by chopper to reach Semisopochnoi Island.

"Something in my gut says Haglemann's telling the truth," Bolan finally said. "Since only Moscovich is here, it means whatever remains of the RBN team is on that island with them. If the AVO hadn't been able to predict this eruption, none of the Russians surely would have."

"That was our feeling, as well," Price said. "We've forwarded the information to the navy, and they already have a battleship on the way. It happened to be on joint maneuvers in the Bering Sea."

"Can they get there in time?" Bolan asked.

"It's very possible," Kurtzman said. "It's the USS *Kodiak*, a fast-deployment destroyer that can do upwards of forty-six knots."

Bolan nodded to himself: about fifty-two miles per hour. "It makes sense. Anything faster is probably out of range and couldn't get much smaller since we're dealing with perhaps more than ninety evacuees."

"And that's not counting the RBN force that may be there," Kurtzman said.

"What else do you think you'll need?" Price asked.

"Haglemann's under medical care. He's being watched by Port Adak authorities. We need to get him out of there."

"We can send a team to pick him up," Price said. "I know DIA agents are very interested in talking with him. By the way, your friend Shaffernik is in the clear."

"Good. We're chasing Moscovich, and we're not far behind him. We lost only a few minutes, and this bird is faster than his. I think we can intercept him before he takes off."

"What then?" Price asked.

"I want to deal with this personally, Barb. It's important. I started this mission, and I'll see it through. I'm going to send a message to the RBN this time. Do you know if the *Kodiak* has helicopter landing capabilities?"

"I'm sure it does," Kurtzman replied. "Nearly every modern destroyer does."

"Good. Let them know we'll be landing with an Adak police chopper and get the captain's clearance. I'll also need to know their antisubmarine warfare capabilities, and if they don't have any, we might want to send air support with torpedoes."

"Submarines?" Price inquired. "You think the Russians might have a sub in the area?"

"I'd bet on it," Bolan replied. "There's no other way I can see of them getting on to and off Semisopochnoi without somebody noticing. They probably came in by submarine under cover of darkness and transported the manpower and equipment to the island via assault craft."

"But how did they get the entire crew to that island, then?"

"That's the part I don't know. Maybe Moscovich will be able to tell me. If he allows us to take him alive."

"I wouldn't count on that," Price said.

"I wouldn't, either."

Cape Chunu, Kanaga Island

BOLAN AND GRIMALDI agreed that landing the chopper on the island posed a significant risk. They didn't know how well armed Moscovich was, and they couldn't risk losing their one potential way off the island. Bolan intended to eliminate Vladimir Moscovich, but he was worried about the pilot. He couldn't just assume the man had willingly brought Moscovich here. The guy could have been just a pawn in all of this, and Bolan wished for a moment that he'd asked Haglemann.

The Executioner got into position and clipped his harness to the rescue winch. It would have been easier to do this with a full crew to assist, but that wasn't to be this time around. He just couldn't risk injury to bystanders, no matter how willing Chakowa and his two deputies might have been. This was up to Bolan. He wouldn't endanger the lives of anyone else to do a job that only he could do.

The soldier double-checked that the harness was secure, then swung into the air. He dangled precariously from the winch as Grimaldi fought to bring the chopper close to the rocky terrain. They had performed a single flyby of the cape and eventually spotted the metal Quonset-style building they surmised sheltered Haglemann's jet. It sat on the cape with a long, concrete pad that probably served as the runway. Oddly, they hadn't seen a chopper on the ground, and that puzzled Bolan. Had Moscovich known they would follow him? It was possible but unlikely—not unless they had advanced tracking equipment aboard Haglemann's chopper. The other possibility was it had been a complete diversionary tactic. Maybe Haglemann's pilot had been given different orders in the event something like this happened. Again, that would have depended on a whole lot of preplanning, and Bolan didn't think it feasible.

No, somehow Moscovich was playing a dangerous game of cat and mouse.

Bolan had ordered Grimaldi to drop him more than a hundred yards from the location of the makeshift hangar on the far side of an outcropping that would obscure his approach. When they came into a hovering position thirty some feet above the ground, Bolan dropped the belay line and released the carabiner brake. He made a smooth, perfectly timed descent to the ground that would prevent minimal exposure for the helicopter but not so fast that it would break both legs on touchdown. With a quick slap of the disconnects and a salute from Grimaldi, the chopper arced up and away from the scene.

Bolan drew his Beretta 93-R and began to cross the unsteady ground at an easy trot, diligent to watch the terrain ahead for any hazards. It wouldn't do to twist an ankle on approach. As he traveled, keeping a wary eye open for threats, Bolan considered alternatives that would explain a lack of activity at the hangar site. One might be Moscovich had ordered the pilot to ditch the chopper somewhere else and make their approach to the hangar on foot. That would make sense, since anyone performing a flyby would look for the chopper on or near the hangar. Again, though, it would have meant Moscovich thought someone might pursue them. That didn't make much sense under the circumstances. Yeah, he'd seen Bolan, but the soldier firmly believed Moscovich thought he'd killed Haglemann with that head shot. He hadn't bothered to put an extra bullet or two into him; he wouldn't have left the guy alive for fear the man would talk, which meant Moscovich believed Haglemann was dead.

The only thing that made sense was that the chopper had either gone down somewhere else, and they were approaching the hangar on foot, or they had landed and used a wheeled maintenance lift to get the bird inside the hangar. In either case, it was unlikely they'd had the time to take off. Bolan intended to see to it they didn't get that chance.

As he drew nearer, the soldier stopped to observe for any movement or activity. The place was eerily quiet, and his combat senses were alerting him to danger. Something just didn't feel right to him as he looked toward the area below. There hadn't been time to grab his equipment, so he was going into this with only his remaining grenades, the Beretta 93-R and the Desert Eagle as his battle weapons.

Bolan's eyes scanned across the windswept tarmac. He had to admit the place had been kept in good repair. The Quonset hut looked equally well maintained with all the windows intact. He finally reached for the field glasses tucked in his belt and put them to his eyes. He checked each of the four windows that lined the hangar building on this side of the small ridge, but he didn't see anything moving inside. He wondered for a minute if the place was deserted, but then he noticed the odd way the windows cast a black sheen in the prismatic hue effect of field glasses when he looked through them at a certain angle. They were tinted! It explained a lot, and Bolan cursed his bad luck as he stored the binoculars.

He left his cover and started down the rocky decline, careful to test his footing first so he didn't dislodge any rocks. He was midway down the slope when the crack of a gunshot rolled past about a moment after a bullet struck a boulder nearby. That had not been an ordinary shot. It had come from a rifle and at a pretty good distance, no less. Bolan scrambled to get cover even as another bullet burned the air just past his head, and another report rumbled through the air. He risked a glance from behind the large rock where he took shelter. He couldn't tell from where it originated but felt pretty certain he was dealing with an amateur. The sniper had not waited until Bolan was in the open. Not that it would matter. If he couldn't get to the hangar, he wouldn't be able to stop Moscovich from escaping. And he wondered if he had fallen into a trap.

VLADIMIR MOSCOVICH EJECTED the second round from the rifle, then drove the handle home to load a third cartridge. It had been nothing short of good fortune that Haglemann had a number of hunting rifles and shotguns aboard his jet. The pilot had pointed them out, advising that Haglemann often was invited to go hunting during his business trips. And while apparently the guy hadn't exactly risen to the level of being a consummate sportsman, he had been more than willing to participate if it secured his business interests and helped him forge new partners who could enrich him in some way.

What a slob. The poor bastard had been nothing but a user of everything and everyone around him. Well, he had paid with his life for that, and Moscovich had been the one whose pleasure it had been to end Haglemann's existence. Now, he had an opportunity to end the existence of the man who had destroyed everything the Nasenkos and Godunovs, along with many others inside the organization, had worked toward.

Moscovich fixed his eye to the scope and watched for movement. In his haste, he had unthinkingly fired at the American when he still had somewhere to take cover. Stupid. He couldn't believe he'd done something as amateur as that, and yet he also knew it wouldn't matter much. There was no way a lone man could survive out here for long. Moscovich wanted to kill him, certainly, but if that wasn't in the cards now, then at least he could stall long enough for them to escape.

The American poked his head out from behind the shelter of a large boulder, and Moscovich got his first close look at the American through the scope. Chiseled jaw, dark hair, a strong chin and nose and a look of intense determination. A formidable opponent, to be sure.

But a dead one, Moscovich thought as he eased back on the trigger.

CHAPTER TWENTY-SIX

Bolan risked another glance, looking for any sort of clue as to the sniper's location. The shooter had to be relatively close, probably nestled in the opposing rock face that ran off the back corner of the hangar. Based on the direction from which the first two bullets had come, Bolan was betting on the several summer pines standing close together. Their full, green branches would make for perfect concealment from the naked eye.

As Bolan ducked behind the boulder once more, another shot rang out. He heard the round zing past him just overhead and tried to ignore the fact that had he waited another millisecond it probably would have gone right through his skull. So the sniper now had his location—there would be no second chances. The smoky visualization of a plan came to his mind, and Bolan keyed up the transmitter.

"Striker to Eagle One."

"Go."

"I'm east of the hangar on the rock face leading to the tarmac. I'm pinned down by a sniper in a stand of trees to the northwest of my position. I need you to buzz him, see if you can flush him out."

"Roger that, I'm inbound."

Bolan yanked one of the two smokers from his belt; it was white. Unlike traditional M308-1 White Smoke grenades in use by special warfare units of the US Navy, these variants were the brainchild of John Kissinger. They not only produced more smoke but featured a round tube on the bottom that extended the burn rate.

Bolan waited until the last possible moment to yank the pin from the grenade and toss the bomb very gently to his left so the upwind draft would bring it toward his area of operation. As soon as the grenade popped off and the smoke thickened enough to obscure his movements, he could just make out Grimaldi buzzing the area above the trees. The Executioner left the shelter of the boulder and charged down the uneven ground as fast as he could. At one point, a rock shifted out from under him at a soft spot, and he tumbled, banging his knee on the sharp rock and tearing his black suit. Bolan leaped to his feet, biting past the pain and continuing down the slope.

The Executioner reached the bottom and charged across the open ground until he reached the exterior border of the Quonset hut. He knew from that position the sniper wouldn't be able to see him. Grimaldi radioed him a moment later to advise he'd flushed out the sniper, just as Bolan had hoped.

"He took a few shots at me with the rifle, but I don't think he hit me."

"Roger that," Bolan replied. "Get out of there and stand by for my signal."

"Copy and out," Grimaldi replied.

Bolan checked the action of his .44 Magnum Desert Eagle, then tried the door at the side. It was locked. He considered trying another approach through the main doors but dismissed the idea in the next instant. With the door locked and the sniper, who most certainly was

Moscovich, otherwise occupied, Bolan knew this entry point would be the last one the enemy expected. In fact, he was betting the pilot was alone inside the building. He leveled the pistol at the door lock, turned his eyes and squeezed the trigger. The big gun boomed in his fist and the 300-grain boat-tail slug punched through the lock like a sledgehammer through a block of ice, destroying the mechanism entirely and leaving a gaping hole in its passing.

The Executioner eased the door open and slipped inside.

He crouched and let his eyes become accustomed to the gloom. The sun had penetrated the horizon quickly, lighting the dawn with furious colors as it normally did this far in the northern hemisphere. A cold shaft of sunlight from the front hangar doors, which were cracked just a bit, streamed through the narrow opening. The hangar had no smell but that of chilled air and chemicals, mostly lubricants and solvents, and the metallic twinge of aircraft aluminum. To one corner Bolan spotted Haglemann's chopper.

At the center of the massive Quonset hut was a sleek plane, a Learjet make that Bolan bet cost Haglemann a pretty penny. Probably a fifteen to twenty million dollar aircraft sat there in the gloom, and Bolan couldn't help but wonder how much of the money that had bought it was blood money. What did it take for a man to betray his morals and his country in the name of a fast buck? The Executioner had never been able to understand greed as a guiding principle. And yet it never failed that some people in the world eventually allowed the spell of wealth to overcome them, and ultimately it was the love of money that also proved to be their downfall. From the lowliest, two-bit gangster to some of the most powerful empires, greed had acted as a cancer that consumed the souls of those men as much as they had consumed the souls of their fellow man.

Bolan eventually spotted movement in the cockpit of the plane, shadowy reflections of the pilot. The guy was probably doing his preflight check, unaware of any trouble sneaking up on him. That was fine with Bolan. He wanted to verify the pilot's level of involvement, anyway, and this was his chance. The Executioner approached from the tail section and ducked under the rear fuselage to find that the steps were down. He drew close and crouched. If he attempted to climb the steps with stealth, the pilot might detect the vibrations in the plane as he ascended. He would have to make fast entry and get the man covered.

Bolan took a deep breath and charged up the steps, swung to his right and sprinted up the aisle. He reached the cockpit in under three seconds. The pilot turned, and his eyes went wide as he looked down the gaping muzzle of the Desert Eagle.

"Wh-what the f—?"

"I'll ask the questions," Bolan cut in. "You'll give answers. Where's Moscovich?"

"Who?"

Bolan had his first answer, even if the pilot was unaware of it. "The guy with the Russian accent. The one who shot your boss and hijacked your plane. His name is Vladimir Moscovich. He's a cold, calculating terrorist who has killed American service personnel and destroyed military equipment with wanton disregard for human life. And I'm here to stop him. Understood?"

"Yeah," the man replied. "I get you."

"The only question that remains, then," Bolan continued coolly, "is whose side *you're* on."

"He forced me to fly him here," the pilot replied. "I mean, he had the gun on me. He offered me money, but he said he wouldn't kill me."

"What did he offer you money to do?"

"Just fly Mr. Haglemann's plane to the continental US. He didn't even tell me where he wanted to go. He just said that if I took him there he wouldn't kill me. That he'd let me go."

"And you believed him?"

"Yeah."

"Well, the last man who trusted him was your boss, Haglemann. He's now lying in a hospital with the better part of his face hanging in shreds from his head. I don't suppose you'd want to emulate him."

"No."

"I thought as much. Then you won't mind if I secure you in the back until this is over. Right?" Bolan waved the muzzle of the big pistol. "Get up."

The pilot obeyed, and Bolan backed out of the cramped space to give him room. As soon as the man had cleared the cockpit, the soldier grabbed him by his shirt collar and steered him into the rear cabin. He sat him in a rotating seat, ordered him to face the wall and secured his hands to the seat with thick plastic riot cuffs he had on hand.

The soldier turned and descended the steps just in time to see Moscovich enter the hangar through the small opening and lean his body weight into one of the doors to shove it back. He was tall but not muscular, really. He had almost a lanky build with wavy, dark hair that hung down to his nape. His nose and lips were thin, and his cheekbones were high enough he nearly looked part Asian. The Russian crime lord apparently hadn't seen Bolan yet, his eyes having failed to adjust immediately to the gloomy interior, but as he finished moving the door open and turned, he noticed the soldier standing there with the Desert Eagle pointed in his direction.

"Vladimir Moscovich, I assume?"

The Russian froze and looked directly at Bolan for a moment before glancing at the hunting rifle he'd brought back to the hangar.

"Don't even try it," Bolan said. "You're not that fast."

"I must commend you, American," Moscovich replied in heavily accented English. "I made a very bad mistake. I underestimated you, and that should never have happened."

"No, it shouldn't have," Bolan said.

"I must know one thing."

"Ask."

"Are you the one who killed Yuri Godunov and crushed our plans to dominate the West once and for all?"

Bolan smiled coldly. "Yeah, I am."

"I thought as much. The Nasenkos were my family. I have sworn to hunt you down and destroy you. Or at least to destroy those you care about as you destroyed my own people. I have heard of your exploits." Moscovich laughed then, before adding, "You are a legend."

"I wasn't trying to be a legend," Bolan said. "I was sending a message, one that apparently went unheeded."

"Oh, no," Moscovich said. "We received your message. We just decided to reply, in kind. And I would have to say that we've done so."

"Where is the crew of the Coast Guard ship?" Bolan asked.

Moscovich didn't flinch as he replied, "Dead. All of them."

"You're lying," Bolan replied. "We know about your operation on Semisopochnoi Island and that you left your people behind there. What were they planning to do? Were they going to meet a submarine? Perhaps the same one that brought you in?"

"I don't have anything to say to you."

"That's fine," Bolan said. "Davis Haglemann had plenty to say. Oh, I can see that surprises you. He survived. You didn't kill him. You got sloppy, Moscovich. And now I think it's time to let you in on a secret."

"And what is that, American?"

"That you have very good reason to fear me," Bolan said. "I destroyed one part of your organization, and when I'm done with you here, I'm going to spend my every waking moment destroying the rest. I'm going to end the reign of the Russian Business Network, and the terror perpetrated by people like Godunov and Nasenko."

"How dare you," Moscovich gritted, his face reddening and the veins in his neck bulging. "You are a scourge to all with whom you come into contact. You represent everything that is evil with your society. Your own *people* betrayed you. How else do you think we were able to do what we did? There are so many in your society who will do anything, say anything, for money. All we have done is simply acted on that. Our philosophy is the only sound philosophy that can bring equality to all.

"You think I care about money or prostitution? You think I care about stealing identities? Phah! It's all vanity, American. All of it! I've proved to you exactly what I've known all along. You haven't destroyed us. You can never destroy those like us. There are too many of us! You're outnumbered!"

Moscovich was raving like a lunatic now, a madman who had suddenly become consumed by his own delusions. Bolan actually couldn't help but feel just a moment of sadness for the Russian. The guy had allowed his arrogance to drive him, and it had succeeded in driving him all right. Straight over the edge of the sanity cliff.

"Do you hear me? You can't win!" Moscovich raged. *"It's not over!"* As the Russian scrambled to raise his rifle, Bolan had the last word.

"Yes, it is," the Executioner replied as he squeezed the trigger.

CHAPTER TWENTY-SEVEN

The bow of the USS *Kodiak* knifed through the waters of the Bering Sea, displacing hundreds of tons as it made best possible speed for Semisopochnoi Island.

Captain James Aronica peered through the binoculars at the approaching land mass and the massive cloud of smoke that had formed over the peak of Sugarloaf. Bolan stood next to him on the bridge of the ship and watched with the naked eye, never dissuaded in his mission to rescue the crew members of the *Llewellyn*. Yet he couldn't stifle the hard, cold knot that had settled in his stomach. He could face countless enemies and win, yet he was helpless against the unmitigated power of nature.

Captain Aronica lowered the binoculars and shook his head. "It's going to be some kind of challenge seeing anything from the air. Even if our aircraft could safely penetrate that haze, I doubt it would be easy to find them."

"We'll have our work cut out for us, Captain," Bolan said.

Grimaldi had landed on the deck just an hour earlier, and Bolan had taken the opportunity to let the navy corpsmen patch him up before acquiring some additional weapons. He was ready to go in whatever it might take. A second ship was also on its way, and there were jets performing regular flybys of the area. All satellite feeds had been directed to her, and the joint command at Elmendorf-Richardson was on full alert.

A Russian submarine had been spotted heading toward American waters but had not yet entered from international waters. It appeared they may have seen the kind of military might converging on the area, and the sub captain had opted to fall back on the old adage that discretion was the better part of valor. One truth remained in all of it, however, and that was a small Russian U-boat was no match for two naval destroyers with ASW capabilities and an entire fleet of Air Force fighter jets that could deposit a load of torpedoes with pinpoint accuracy even underwater.

Aronica looked at Bolan. "So I understand you want to go it alone on this. Are you sure?"

Bolan nodded. "It's the best way. Don't worry. As soon as I find the *Llewellyn*'s crew, I'll call in for support. But I imagine the enemy contingent on that island needs to be dealt with first."

"And just exactly which of our enemies were crazy enough to *be* on that island when there's a volcano about to erupt?"

"Sorry," Bolan said. "I'm not at liberty to say. Just know that they aren't friendly, and they'll be well-armed. And they were good enough to make an entire Coast Guard cutter disappear for nearly forty-eight hours."

"Sounds like nasty customers," Aronica replied. "But you do know I have a security clearance that's probably as high as yours. I don't suppose that would buy me a little professional courtesy."

"If your chain-of-command wants to tell you," Bolan said, "that's not my affair. But I have my mission to protect, and I won't have any more dead or wounded service members on my conscience. Not today, Captain."

Bolan made it implicit in his tone this was really the end of the discussion. Aronica smartly chose not to pursue it. The Executioner felt bad giving the guy the brush-off, but he couldn't really afford to get into the details. For one, it wouldn't do his cover any good. Secondly, he couldn't risk any more lapses in security. His ability to operate independently for Stony Man might have been seen by many as a weakness, but for Bolan it was an added perk. He answered to no one in any official capacity, which meant he could work in conjunction with other agencies but not be weighted by bureaucracy. It suited him well.

Bolan quickly withdrew from the bridge and descended the steps to the deck. The police chopper had been taken by lift below decks and in its place the navy had substituted one of its two Sikorsky SH-60 Seahawks. It had been a mere stroke of good fortune the *Kodiak* was a DDG-51 class of destroyer because it was equipped with twin helicopter bays, whereas many of its predecessors and contemporaries only supported a helicopter landing deck without a storage capacity.

By the time Bolan arrived at the craft, Grimaldi was suited up and ready for action, performing a preflight check with his military copilot. Bolan smiled with a warm feeling of admiration. Stony Man had been coming through on all levels with their support, getting the Executioner whatever resources he needed. Despite his arms-length alliance with the government, he couldn't deny the symbiotic relationship that existed between them. There was little doubt he needed them as much as they needed him, and by working together a lot of lives would be saved this day.

Bolan wasn't about to rest on his laurels yet, however. He still had a lot of work to do, and he would be going up against an enemy force of unknown number. He also had no idea how well-equipped or well-armed his opponents. And what dangers did an all-out confrontation mean for the hostages? Would they kill them in the last moment? Bolan pushed the doubts and worries from his mind, choosing instead to focus on what lay ahead. He checked the action of the fresh M16A4 he'd brought from the destroyer armory that included an M203 grenade launcher.

It was time to bring the fight to the enemy and end their terror once and for all.

Semisopochnoi Island

COMMANDER LOUIS DUCATI knew they'd finally been liberated from their cages because a unified cheer had come up from every voice within their company. They had finally managed to obtain a chunk of rock big enough and strong enough to break the padlock from its massive chain. It hadn't been easy. The first few attempts had left about four of the crew members with scraped knuckles and volcanic dust rock as the only trophies to show for it. But when that chain finally rattled and the crew members cheered, Ducati knew they had gained their freedom.

Ducati couldn't be sure why, but he was no longer able to see. He wondered if the blindness was permanent, if he'd suffered some head injury or his wounds had been worse than the corpsman who treated him had first thought. Not that it mattered. They were going to get the hell out of there one way or another. He had his crew to worry about now—he could address his own burdens and worries at some other time. First duty was to his brave crew.

"Number One, get the teams organized. I want squads of no less than eight men. No more than two women per squad."

"Yes, sir."

"Also, set aside a detail of officers to look through the caverns and see if they can find any weapons. We need to get out of here, but I also don't wish to walk into some kind of potential ambush unarmed. Especially not if we could have capitalized on some sort of major blunder in their rush to get out of here."

"Aye-aye, sir."

"And intelligence. Collect any you find." Ducati paused and put his hand to his head, his temples beginning to throb. "We don't know if we'll need it later."

"We got it under control, sir," someone said. He couldn't see them, and he didn't recognize their voice. "We need to help you get out of here. Easy…"

Ducati felt his body being lifted off the ground, but then everything went dark.

MACK BOLAN BRACED his back against the wall, foot primed and leg charged for their assault. The SH-60 sped a true course directly toward the shore. Everywhere he could smell the hot-ash scents of a volcano that wasn't far from eruption, spewing its lava into the air. It was hot and unbelievably humid, and the air was thick with dust. The miasma of choking air was nothing short of stifling, and Bolan immediately began to sweat.

He steadied himself against the door, the harness attached and ready for his drop on to the island. Grimaldi brought the chopper as low as possible, keeping them out of the dense air above them, which was growing thicker by the hour. It wouldn't be long before the pilots were completely unable to see anything that was happening on the island. Immediately after they had taken off, Bolan had sent the signal for the amphibious assault boats to approach the target. Fifteen rafts in all, carrying special warfare personnel and combat medical corpsmen, pushed toward the shores of Semisopochnoi.

The Executioner's play was backed by the sharpest, toughest and most efficient military fighting force on Earth. The United States could in all of its righteous might unleash an unstoppable juggernaut of force if they were pushed too far. Bolan was proud of his countrymen this day. Damn proud, yeah, because they were fighting hard and living large. They were coming to save their fellow soldiers and ready to fight their enemies to the death, if that's what it took. And they were doing it in the name of duty and patriotism. It was those actions for which Mack Bolan admired them most. He was proud to call each and every last one of them his allies.

The chopper buzzed in to the shore, passed the beachhead, and came to a swift hover a dozen yards above the ground. Bolan took his line and pushed out, this time assisted by the helicopter crew. He dropped down the line and was about midway when he spotted the first of his targets. They were pushing in his direction, hiding behind whatever trees and boulders they could, shooting at him from those positions. It was hard to hear the reports but it seemed mostly they were using submachine guns.

Bolan flipped his M16A4 into action and swept the fighting field with sustained autofire as he descended. A plethora of 5.56 mm NATO rounds chopped the terrain and took branches off trees in some cases. The soldier hit the ground and detached the belay line, then rushed for the cover of a fallen tree limb. The heat was nearly unbearable, and it felt to Bolan as if he'd stepped straight into hell itself to do battle with its guardians. He checked his flank to make sure they didn't circle to overtake him, and then dropped a 40 mm high-explosive grenade into the M203. Bolan flipped the leaf sight into target acquisition, sighted on the nearest cluster of muzzle-flashes and squeezed the trigger. The M16A4 kicked Bolan's shoulder with the force of a 12-gauge shotgun. The grenade arced gracefully and landed on target, blowing three of the Russians who'd been shooting into the air. One was shredded to bits with metal shrapnel, and the other two were likely killed by the concussion more than the blast.

Bolan popped the 40 mm shell out, slammed a fresh one home and then broke cover and ran for better position. As he ran, one boot got tangled in a branch hidden by the sand-dirt ground and toppled him, but it proved to be a blessing in disguise. Machine-gun fire erupted from an emplacement farther up the incline, and the rounds buzzed over Bolan's head. He had escaped death but only barely.

The soldier rolled behind the cover of a thick stand of bushes, leveled his assault rifle and began to trigger short, controlled bursts at whatever enemy emplacements he could detect. The machine gun responded again, pelting the area around him with heavy fire but not quite coming close to him. Bolan knew it wouldn't remain that way if he stayed where he was.

Then the soldier detected a sudden *chug-chug-chug* sound and felt as if the ground around him had come alive. He looked up and realized Grimaldi had brought the chopper into position immediately above him, and the door gunner of the Sikorsky was returning fire with a .50-caliber machine gun mounted on the opposite side. The pilot was breaking every rule of modern air-to-ground combat, but he was doing so in order to protect the Executioner's position. Bolan couldn't very well blame the crazy ace pilot for that.

Bolan took the opportunity to scramble to his feet and move. The enemy had the high ground, and he needed to figure out some way of overcoming the terrible odds that presented for him. He continued along that path while Grimaldi buzzed the enemy emplacements and drew their attention. The soldier found a natural saddle, shallow as it was, that provided enough cover for him to ascend the slight ridge. As he climbed, he could see footprints and realized that it had been used previously, and very recently, at that. Bolan continued sprinting uphill until coming parallel with the enemy positions. He knelt and looked for the machine gun, eventually spotting it about forty yards and slightly left of his position.

Now he had the high ground.

Bolan aimed the M203, took a breath and let half

out before squeezing the trigger. The grenade launcher responded with another *plunk* sound, which was followed a heartbeat later with an explosion that engulfed the machine gun and its operator in a superheated gas ball. From that vantage point, Bolan could see that the pockets of resistance were faltering.

He lay in the ditch-like crevasse and began to snipe at the remaining RBN terrorists. He kept up the suppressive fire, taking only those targets that were viable when he could and trading out magazines twice.

Movement in his peripheral vision caused Bolan to draw his Desert Eagle and whirl, leveling the pistol at the approaching form. He eased off the trigger when he saw the man had short, clipped hair and wore a US Coast Guard uniform. He didn't have any insignia, but there was no mistaking the utilities. The man was crouched and running straight toward Bolan, but he threw himself to the ground and raised his hands when he saw the big pistol aimed at him.

"Whoa! Hold up, don't shoot!"

"Two seconds to identify yourself. Name and rank."

"Trask, Paul R. I'm an ensign aboard the USCGC *Llewellyn*."

Bolan holstered the pistol. "Well, keep your head down, Trask."

The man nodded and crawled to Bolan's position. He extended his hand, and Bolan quickly shook it before returning his attention to his enemies. Bolan triggered a few more rounds, then spoke to Trask while keeping his eyes on the enemy positions.

"Are your crewmates alive?"

"Roger that, sir."

"How many?"

"Last count was ninety-one, sir. Had a total of one-hundred-eight aboard, but that included the security force. Most of them didn't make it."

"Sorry," Bolan said. He triggered more rounds. "How did they get all of you here?"

"They had some sort of old tramp freighter that they used," he said. "We were brought into Dutch Harbor, and they transferred us to this point."

Bolan thought about that a moment. It made sense. It had probably been something Haglemann arranged, since there was a lot of shipping, and no real central authority would have been concerned with a lone freighter cruising around the area. At least not at that point. Only a few hours had passed since contact had been lost with the *Llewellyn*. A full alert hadn't been initialized by then.

"What about the freighter? What happened to it?"

"They sank it, I think. Once we off-loaded, we heard some explosions. That's all I really know."

"What about the rest of the people? Are they in a secure location?"

"Yeah. We'd just broken into small squads when we heard the fireworks start. Our commander, he…"

Bolan heard the hesitation. "What is it?"

"He's in a bad way, sir. He needs medevac, and he needs it now."

"Consider it done, Ensign," Bolan said, clapping a reassuring hand on the man's shoulder. The soldier keyed up his mic. "This is Point Guard One. Be advised, I'm calling the ball. Say again, I am calling the ball. Code-word Thunderclap. Repeat, Thunderclap!"

It was the signal he knew they'd been waiting for, the one that told them he'd beaten the enemy into submission, and they could bring in the cavalry to mop up. Above the noise and heat he could hear the approach of dozens of amphibious assault craft. He couldn't see much from that position, but he didn't doubt the resolve of those aboard the boats. The second Sikorsky had joined the action, and with Grimaldi they were pounding the enemy emplacements with heavy machine-gun fire, just in case a few enemy gunners had stayed behind. Bolan knew there was little more he could do at this point, and the remnants of RBN were beaten, exhausted and low on ammunition trying to hit something they couldn't see.

Bolan got to his feet and reached his hand down to help Trask up. They kept low, ensuring that a lurking enemy didn't try to take them down. Trask led Bolan up the incline until they reached the entrance to the cavern. Once inside, the Executioner was immediately blasted with a wall of heat that made a furnace seem downright tepid.

It didn't take them long to find Ducati, who was unconscious and being carried by four men. Another officer rushed to Bolan and saluted, which the Executioner returned subconsciously. If they wanted to think he was military, there was no reason to argue the point. It wouldn't have served any purpose.

"Name's Rastogi, sir. Acting first officer. You're a damn sight for sore eyes, I have to admit."

"Good to see you and your people alive," Bolan said. "Ensign Trask here gave me the information about your crew and its condition. I understand your captain's in serious condition?"

Rastogi nodded. "Commander Ducati, sir. He's a

good man but he's in very bad shape. Those bastards beat the hell out of him for no reason."

"They won't be any more problem to you," Bolan said. "To anyone. They've been dealt with. And help's on the way. It's over."

EPILOGUE

Denver, Colorado

As FBI Special Agent Justina Marquez put the key in the lock of her high-rise condominium, she sensed the presence of someone at the end of the hallway. She let her left hand drop and turned her body slightly as her right hand dipped into her coat and rested on the cold butt of the Glock 21 pistol nestled there. But then something stayed her hand, something about the outline of that form in the shadows. It wasn't the outline so much as the presence. A deep, heavy, commanding presence—a familiar essence in which she'd only come into contact a few times but had never forgotten.

"I know you're there," she said. "I can't believe it's really you."

The Executioner stepped from the shadows with a half smile. "It's me."

Marquez relaxed the grip on her pistol and turned to face him. She folded her arms and shook her head. "I almost killed you."

"Doubtful," Bolan replied.

"Care to come inside? I've got some wine."

"Inside, yes. I'll pass on the wine."

"Then, how about an ice-cold beer."

"That's more my speed."

"Come on," she said and gestured toward the door with her head.

Bolan followed Marquez through the front door and secured it behind him. She looked great, as usual. Dark hair and eyes, with a trim and shapely body. In the few years that had passed since Bolan had last seen her, the young FBI agent hadn't really changed all that much.

Still spunky and still beautiful, and yet still completely unattached. That was something the Executioner could understand. Marquez had become as devoted to the security of her nation as Bolan was. They were kindred spirits in that respect. It wasn't about anything romantic—they were from different worlds and content to live their lives separately.

Bolan had news that he thought he should deliver in person. He owed Marquez at least that much for the role she'd played in helping to bring Godunov and his thugs to justice.

Marquez poured a glass of wine and brought it into the spacious living area. Her decor was modern and stark. She noticed Bolan's appraisal and handed him his beer before kicking off her shoes and dropping on to the couch. She tucked her legs beneath her, and Bolan took a seat in a chair opposite.

"What do you think of my new place?" she asked. "You like it?"

"Some might think it's a little sparsely decorated. Too modern. But, yeah. I like it."

"It suits me and it's home." She raised her glass in a sort of toast, and Bolan reciprocated. "So, to what do I owe the pleasure of this visit?"

"What do you think?" Bolan asked with a grin.

"I'd say it's business. You never struck me as the kind of guy to pay a girl a social call."

"At least not to the type of the girl sitting across from me," Bolan quipped.

"All right. Spill."

"You've heard about the business in Alaska by now, I'm sure."

She nodded. "I got the official party line, but I could read through some of the bullshit in the field reports. I take it that was your handiwork?"

"Well, I can't take any responsibility for the volcano," Bolan said. "But, yeah, I'll admit to having a hand in it."

"Let me guess. The RBN was at it again."

Bolan was impressed. "How did you know?"

"I can't think of anything else that would bring you all the way from whatever hellhole you might have been spending your time in unless it had something to do with that. Do you need my help?"

"Not now," he said. "I could've used you up there, though."

"So what made you come here?"

"I worked with a lady cop up there. She was top shelf." Bolan took another drink of his beer and smiled. "She reminded me of you in a lot of ways."

"Really? I'm not sure how to take that," Marquez replied. She took a drink from her glass, but her eyes smiled at him over the rim.

"Their operation was headed by Vladimir Moscovich. You heard of him?"

"A bit here, a bit there. Nothing solid, although he's been flagged as an up-and-coming in the organization."

"You can consider him scratched. And a good num-

ber of the crew he was working with. My next stop is
St. Petersburg. I'm going to chop off the head of this
thing, if I can."

"Didn't you once tell me that these people were part
of a Hydra? That you cut off one head and a new one
just grows back? That what you really had on your
hands was, how did you put it, a 'war everlasting?'"

Bolan nodded. "Yeah. I said that once."

"And yet you don't give up. You don't quit, no matter how hard it gets. Why do you suppose that is?"

"*Everlasting* means just that. Without end. If I quit
now, the world's a less safe place. But if I stick it out,
maybe someone benefits. I see it as my duty."

"Some might call that a crusader complex."

"They'd be wrong."

"They would."

"And what do *you* call it?" Mack Bolan asked.

"Oh, me?" She smiled. "I call it heroism."

* * * * *

UPCOMING TITLES FROM

DON PENDLETON'S
THE EXECUTIONER®

KILL SQUAD
Available March 2016
Nine million dollars goes missing from a Vegas casino, and an accountant threatens to spill to the Feds. But with the mob on his back, the moneyman skips town. Bolan must race across the country to secure the fugitive before the guy's bosses shut him up—forever.

DEATH GAME
Available June 2016
Two American scientists are kidnapped just as North Korea makes a play for Cold War–era ballistic missiles. Determined to save the scientists and prevent a world war, Bolan learns he's not the only one with his sights set on retrieving the missiles…

TERRORIST DISPATCH
Available September 2016
Atrocities continue in the Ukraine and the adjoining Crimean Peninsula, annexed by Russia in March 2014. With no end in sight, a plan is hatched to force American involvement by sending Ukrainian militants to strike Washington, DC, killing civilians and seizing the Lincoln Memorial as protest against their homeland's threat from Russia. Can Bolan bring the war home to the plotters' doorstep?

COMBAT MACHINES
Available December 2016
What began in a Romanian orphanage twenty years earlier, when a man walked away with ten children and disappeared, leads Mack Bolan and a team of Interpol agents to fend off a group of "invisible" assassins carving their way across Europe…toward the USA.

DON PENDLETON'S
THE EXECUTIONER®

"An American patriot and Special Forces veteran determined to extinguish threats against both the United States and the innocents of the world."

The Executioner® is a series of short action-thrillers featuring Mack Bolan, a one-man protection force who does what legal elements cannot do in the face of grave threats to national and international security.

Available *every month* wherever Gold Eagle® books and ebooks are sold.

THE DON PENDLETON'S
EXECUTIONER.

Check out this sneak preview of
KILL SQUAD
by Don Pendleton!

"This is crazy," Sherman said.

His words were ignored as Bolan assessed their position. In the confines of the rail car, there was no chance they could conceal themselves. They were in the open, with armed men facing them. Once the shooters decided to push their way through, it would become a turkey shoot. If Bolan had been on his own, he might have considered resisting. But he had Sherman to consider, plus the burden of the other passengers. If he put up a fight, any retaliatory gunfire could overlap and cause injury to the innocent. That was something Bolan refused to allow.

He and Sherman were in line for the hostile fire. Bolan accepted that—with reservations where Sherman was concerned. The man was making an attempt to right wrongs, and he didn't deserve to become a victim himself.

The only way out was for Bolan and Sherman to remove themselves from the situation, which was easier to consider than to achieve. The soldier glanced at the window. The landscape slid by, an area of undulating terrain, wide and empty.

Another burst of autofire drove slugs against the connecting door. This time a couple of slugs broke through.

Bolan had already considered what he knew to be his

and Sherman's only option. He made his decision. He triggered a triburst through the connecting door to force the opposition back, even if it was only a brief distraction.

"Harry, let's go," he said. "Stay low and head for the other door."

"What…?"

"Do it, Harry, before those guys come our way."

Bolan fired off another triburst. Crouching, they made for the connecting door at the far end of the car. Bolan flung it open and hustled Sherman through. They paused on the swaying, open platform between the two cars, the rattle and rumble of the train loud in their ears.

The ground swept by, a spread of green below the slope that bordered the track.

Bolan glanced back through the connecting door and saw armed men moving into view. This time he held the Beretta in both hands and fired. Glass shattered. Bolan saw one man fall and the others pull aside. The delay would only last for seconds. He holstered the 93-R and zipped up his jacket.

"Have you ever jumped from a moving train?"

Don't miss
KILL SQUAD by Don Pendleton,
available March 2016 wherever
Gold Eagle® books and ebooks are sold.